THE
GUARDIAN

ALSO BY SARAH FINE

Adult Fiction

The Immortal Dealers Series

The Serpent

The Reliquary Series

Reliquary

Splinter

Mosaic

Mayhem and Magic (graphic novel)

Servants of Fate Series

Marked

Claimed

Fated

Young Adult Fiction

Guards of the Shadowlands Series

Sanctum

Fractured

Chaos

Captive: A Guard's Tale from Malachi's Perspective

Vigilante: A Guard's Tale from Ana's Perspective

Stories from the Shadowlands

Of Metal and Wishes Series

Of Metal and Wishes
Of Dreams and Rust
Of Shadows and Obsession:
A Short Story Prequel to Of Metal and Wishes

The Impostor Queen Series

The Impostor Queen
The Cursed Queen
The True Queen

Other Series

Scan (with Walter Jury)
Burn (with Walter Jury)
Beneath the Shine
Uncanny

THE
GUARDIAN

THE
IMMORTAL
DEALERS
SERIES

SARAH FINE

47N◆RTH

Text copyright © 2018 by Sarah Fine
All rights reserved.

Published by 47North, Seattle

www.apub.com

Amazon, the Amazon logo, and 47North are trademarks of Amazon.com, Inc., or its affiliates.

ISBN-13: 9781503904835
ISBN-10: 1503904830

Cover design and photography by Blake Morrow

Printed in the United States of America

THE
GUARDIAN

CHAPTER ONE

It was Christmas Eve, and Ernie was spending it magically disguised as a paunchy old mercenary with bad teeth. She gripped the steering wheel as her cards pulsed against her skin. This was the most complicated play she'd ever made, but she'd worked up to it. For other Immortal Dealers, especially the older ones, like Minh or Gabe, who knew their decks in and out and dealt the cards as easily as they breathed, this would be a snap. But Ernie had been playing with a full deck for only eight weeks, and this trick was seriously making her sweat.

The illusion had required several cards: Deceive, because obviously. Strength, because she'd be damned if she was taking any chances. Translate, because a North Carolina drawl would be as out of place as Sunday best at the swimming hole. Two different Wilds, because she'd learned in her self-imposed solitary training sessions that the combination was more stable. She had physically morphed using the Chameleon Wild and now knew what it felt like to be a dude—a little *too* dangly for her liking. An extra layer of illusion from the Mirage Wild, sort of like powder over foundation, set everything in place. Finally, she'd played Prolong, because she needed the whole damn thing to last until she made it past the checkpoint and delivered the goods.

The goods sniffled and wiped his nose on his sleeve. "How much longer?"

"Stop whining," she snapped. What he heard was deep and cranky Russian: *"Khvatit nyt!"* She actually felt bad for the kid as he flinched, but she wasn't herself tonight. She was the person who could get a scared Russian teenager back across the border to his army unit after he'd been imprisoned for a month at the hands of some seriously annoying Ukrainian rebels.

It wasn't the job the Forger had sent her here to do. That had resulted in the kid being kidnapped in the first place.

It had also escalated the war between Russia and Ukraine, which is what the Forger had obviously wanted. *This conflict is way too contained,* he had said. *Time for some far-reaching chaos.* Now the UN was involved, and the US was saber rattling, and Ernie was pretty sure it was her fault. Her first assignment as an Immortal Dealer. Her initiation into her new life. And a complete tutorial on why making a deal with the Forger was usually a mistake—the guy was ace at loopholes.

It had been a long two months.

She peered through the spotty windshield at the road stretching ahead of her. Fog clouded what lay ahead, though the faint glow within the haze grew sharper with every passing moment. Even if it wasn't the checkpoint yet, she supposed it worked as a metaphor. She could use a little light at the end of the tunnel right now.

"Is that it?" Sasha asked, his voice rising with hope and excitement.

"Maybe." *Mozhet byt.* It was, though. She could see it now, a roadblock, spotlights, and shadowy figures standing nearby. She glanced at Sasha, whose cheeks were covered in zits, whose Adam's apple stuck out a mile, whose uniform hung off his gangly body. His only mistake had been to get drunk and wander away from his unit, which had been stationed near Rogalik, a tiny town right by the border. With tensions between the countries already high thanks to the Forger's assignment—to spur Ukrainian leaders to push the Russians to give Crimea back—the chance to nab a vulnerable Russian soldier had been a little too tempting for some of the locals. They'd sold him to a rebel group.

She hadn't thought that fomenting demands for independence from Russia was a bad thing, but she'd never been into politics. Ever since those few fateful plays in a bar in Kiev, she'd been learning just how complicated things could get. She'd played Wisdom *and* Deceive on top of Translate to talk up a vice prime minister who had been adamantly opposed to defying the Russians, and that was all it had taken to plant a seed of passionate rebellion in his head. She'd felt all sly then, all sophisticated, with her deck and her power to change the world. Now she felt small—but determined. What mattered now was getting this kid back home to his family. Probably a totally insignificant thing in the wild, chaotic scheme of the universe, but she needed a little redemption. Yeah, she'd just been doing her boss's bidding, but right now her hands felt pretty damn dirty.

"Do you have your papers ready?" she asked Sasha, still speaking Russian.

He dug in the pocket of his uniform and pulled out a crumpled wad of identification papers, which he smoothed anxiously over one of his thighs. "Nice of them to let me have these back."

By "them," he meant the rebels who'd held him hostage for weeks. And by "nice," he meant that they'd shoved the papers at him at gunpoint after Ernie had played a few cards—Negotiate, Mercy, Aid—to make it happen. Ernie smiled. Sasha seemed like a sweet kid. Worth the effort. On her left forearm, Legs—or, rather, the tattoo of a gorgeous diamondback rattlesnake that was Legs's current manifestation—tingled with warmth. Maybe the serpent approved of what Ernie was doing.

Or maybe it was a warning.

Ernie squinted at the figures taking shape in the fog. Wide stances, guns tucked against shoulders. She couldn't see yet, but she was guessing their fingers were on the triggers. "No sudden moves—got it, boy? Don't do anything until they tell you to."

Ernie slowed the car, a pile of junk she'd bought off an old guy in a street market because she'd learned the hard way that trying to conjure an entire vehicle was mind-bendingly hard. She wasn't sure how Gabe regularly pulled his motorcycle out of thin air, but now that she'd tried it a few times herself, she'd developed a new admiration for his focus and skill. She winced and fidgeted in her seat. She didn't want to feel more admiration for Gabe. She didn't want to think about him at all.

It made his radio silence all the more painful.

Brushing off the distraction, Ernie sat up straighter, reminding herself that she was a freaking mercenary with thick, stubble-covered jowls, a pockmarked nose, bushy gray eyebrows, broad shoulders, and thick, gnarled fingers. She hoped. Sasha was squinting at her hands on the steering wheel as if they weren't quite what he expected to see. The tingling on Ernie's arm had become a sharp prickle. She pressed that arm against her middle, where she'd stowed the cards for the play in a special belt she'd had made, one that held them flush to her body. She'd learned that any disguise lasted longer when the cards were snug against her skin, a constant reminder to concentrate, a steady source of reassurance. The rest of the deck was in her pocket, at the ready, always.

It looked like she might need it soon.

"Why are they aiming at us?" Sasha asked, his voice cracking.

"I don't know." They were supposed to be expecting the delivery.

As Ernie pulled within twenty feet of the checkpoint, which was actually little more than a few orange plastic sawhorses across the road and a few generator-powered floodlights on either side, she slowed even more, until she could hear the sounds of the gravel popping underneath the tires, the whoosh of Sasha's nervous breathing, and the barked Russian commands coming from the other side of the barrier. Her Translate card allowed her to understand every word.

Don't fire until I give the order.

Make sure it's really him.

Ernie kept one hand on the steering wheel, but with her other, she drew the Diamondback deck.

"What have you got there?" asked Sasha, leaning forward to try to see. "If it's a gun, they will shoot us!"

"Shut up and let me focus." Now soldiers were jogging around the plastic barriers and surrounding the car. Her deck was pulsing hot against the palm of her left hand, and the cards that formed her disguise were making her sweat as they seared her stomach.

A soldier in a fur hat and a long winter coat banged on her window with the butt of his rifle. "Roll it down," he shouted.

Placing her deck hand back on the wheel, Ernie reached over with her other hand and cranked down the window, wishing she'd sprung for a slightly more modern ride. "I have Sasha Kuznetsov here, as promised."

The soldier tucked his rifle under his arm—with the barrel still pointed her way—and shone a flashlight in her eyes. "Give me your identification."

"I'm just a messenger," Ernie said as the passenger door was pulled open and Sasha was unceremoniously yanked out. She glanced to her right to see a group of four soldiers bundling him toward the other side of the barrier, back to Russia at last. "Now that you have your soldier, I'll be going."

"Get out of the car."

"I'm on Ukrainian territory," she said, her palm sweating against her cards as Legs prickled on her arm. One of the cards started to wiggle its way up from the rest, and she curled her fingers over it to keep the soldier from seeing. She'd wanted to keep everything normal for this gig, to do this exchange without having to pull moves that defied any laws of physics. Sometimes, though, Legs had ideas of her own. Beneath Ernie's fingertips, she could feel the card the spirit of her deck was suggesting she play. Warp. But she had no idea *what* she was supposed to warp, so she pressed on, hoping she could weasel her way out of this mess with words alone. "We agreed that the border guards on our side would take a little refreshment break so you guys could have your boy back without questions, but they'll return at any second. Let's not make trouble."

The soldier tilted his head and shoved the flashlight closer to her face. Then he yanked her door open. "Get. Out. Hands up."

Ernie exhaled slowly as she obeyed the order, keeping a tight grip on her cards. "You should really just let me go."

"What's wrong with you?" he asked, his voice rising in alarm as he stared at her. "What's happening to your face?" He lurched back, his movements sharp and panicky—and his finger on the trigger.

Oops. The stress was causing her illusion to slip. "Skin condition." She put her hands up with the Warp card face out, playing on pure faith in Legs.

The barrel of the soldier's gun abruptly bent into a *U* just as it went off—about a foot from his ear. He screamed and dropped the gun, staggering. "Shoot him!" he screeched, frantically jabbing his finger at Ernie as he scrambled back toward the barrier. "He's got a chemical weapon!" His comrades jerked their weapons up to their shoulders as the soldier continued shouting about melting faces.

Crap. Ernie fanned her deck in her left hand and caught the Shield card in her right just as the bullets started to fly. As the shots bounced off the clear, rubbery barrier that appeared between her and the danger, the soldiers began to call for the bazooka. Ernie dashed around the back of her car and squatted behind it as her shield gave out. The disguise had drained so much of her concentration that she didn't have much juice left. Closing her eyes as bullets shattered the car's windows and pinged off its metal carcass, she held her trembling palm open. "Legs, help me out before we get blown to hell."

The Escape card's slight weight felt reassuringly solid as it hit her skin. Her fingers closed around it as a voice shouted a command in Russian that was only too easy to understand.

Fire! The air filled with a sharp, explosive hiss.

Ernie gritted her teeth as the light and noise disappeared. She had only a second in the void to realize she hadn't properly envisioned where she was escaping *to* before her vision blazed with glittering Christmas lights reflected off a billion raindrops.

Gasping and wiping her face with her sleeve, she looked around. She was standing next to a busy thoroughfare, right under a blazing streetlamp. A red double-decker bus roared by, sending a torrent of muddy water splashing against her legs. Grimacing as the cold and wet seeped into her too-large boots, she stowed her cards and took a few steps away from the street, earning herself dirty looks from pedestrians who had to move out of the way to avoid her. She grabbed at the waist of her pants to keep them from falling down and leaned against a fence, trying to orient herself—not only to where she was but to *what* she was.

Her fingers probed her face. Back to normal, as far as she could tell. Still clutching her pants, she shifted her hips. Back to normal there, too, *thank god*. She shoved her hand under her baggy shirt and plucked the now cool cards away from her skin, joining them with the rest of the deck. She'd asked a lot of those cards, and they might be out of commission for a bit, until she and Legs had a chance to recharge.

"Which means I'm stuck with this," she whispered, wrinkling her nose at the smell of sweat and alcohol coming off her secondhand trench coat. She'd purchased the whole ensemble to fit her paunchy mercenary body, and now she was back to being a size six. She craved a shower and a snuggly pair of sweats, but she'd left her luggage behind in Kiev, which was . . . obviously not here.

Less than a block away, a sign pointed the way to Piccadilly. "I'm in London?"

"Merry Christmas," came a voice from behind her. She whipped around, nerves jangling. Minh, the Dealer of the Pot-Bellied Pig deck, was also leaning against the fence, dressed in leather pants and a silky shirt. The pouring rain fell all around him but not on him, thanks to his Shield card, she assumed. His black hair was spiky, and his brown eyes were amused as he looked her over. "Just a shot in the dark here, but I'm guessing you still have holiday shopping to do."

"How the hell did you find me?"

"I decided to check in on you a bit earlier, holiday cheer and all. To be honest, your concentration has been a little slack over the last few hours."

She sagged against the fence, shivering. "I've been working nonstop."

"And getting paid, I hope." He looked her over. "Please tell me this homeless chic is *not* your actual wardrobe."

"I was trying to clean up some messes I made." She sighed. "But there have been so many, all rippling out from one play I made."

"As always . . . except, wait. You've been trying to right every possible wrong caused by cards you've dealt?" His brows drew together in an expression of complete bemusement.

"Look, I made a play with a lot of ramifications! Caused a lot of chaos and a few international incidents. Exactly what the Forger wanted, I guess."

"Again, always. But it's not your job to go around trying to neaten things up." He shrugged. "Your bonus efforts most likely caused even more chaos, though, butterfly effect and all that. So you probably made him *extra* happy."

"Maybe that'll make him more inclined to keep his word, then." She raked her hand through her tangled, wet hair and tossed an envious look at Minh's invisible umbrella. Sure, it had probably been worth temporarily tapping out her Shield card to keep from being perforated by Russian bullets, but being dry now would have been awesome. "He promised to tell me what he knows about my dad once I did the job for him. But he never paid up."

"Is that *exactly* what Andy promised?"

She rolled her eyes. "No. He said he'd tell me about my dad after I 'earned my keep.'"

"And by now you've realized that he might define that differently than you do. A Forger thinks in decades, Ernie, not days."

Misery had formed a tight lump in her throat. "I just wanted to be able to tell my mom what happened to him." She scoffed. "That would have been a great Christmas gift, seeing as I can't afford anything else." Her Coin card had shorted out two weeks before, when she'd exhausted the payment the Forger had given her for the Ukraine assignment.

Minh patted her shoulder. "Come on. Let me buy you a drink."

"I should get home to my mom."

"You don't have to go empty-handed."

"What, are you and Bao going to take me shopping?" She laughed, imagining Minh's pot-bellied pig prancing down an aisle at Harrods.

Minh shook his head and drew his deck from his shirt pocket. "I'm going to give you the gift of employment. It's a job I was going to take myself, but it looks like you need a cash infusion more than I do at the moment."

"What is it?"

"You'll see." Minh drew his Transport card and smiled. "But let's have that drink first." Then he took Ernie's arm and pulled her into darkness.

CHAPTER TWO

Ernie ordered a Bombay Sapphire and a plate of olives, while Minh chose some sort of smoky cocktail along with hummus, spiced eggplant, roasted mushrooms, and toast. The place he'd transported her to, across town and a flight of steps down from the street, reminded her a little of the speakeasy back in Asheville where her whole odyssey had begun, with the exception of the accents. A piano and sax duo stood nearby, rolling out jazz that felt like a good massage and a stiff drink rolled up in one. She knew she should be headed home—she'd been looking forward to a few days off, training with her Spartan Race team, hanging out with her mom, catching up with her friend Dia—but being with Minh was a relief. She didn't have to pretend to be a normal person.

Ernie leaned her head on the high-backed leather couch they'd settled into. "How've you been?" she asked Minh as a waiter in a vest and wing tips brought them their drinks.

"I tried to help Alvarez get his cards back from Virginia for a while—she's still got two of them."

The mention of Virginia's name awakened a fury inside Ernie that had lain dormant inside her as she dealt with the crazy demands of the past months. "That evil hag and I still have some unfinished business. Do you think Alvarez will get his cards back from her in the end?"

"Considering that her Chicken deck has probably eaten the Emperor Tamarin cards by now, I'm thinking it's unlikely."

Ernie paused with her drink halfway to her mouth. "Did you just say '*eaten*'?"

Legs prickled sharply on her arm as Minh glanced at Ernie's wrist, where the diamondback's rattle was peeking out. "*Your* deck has eaten at least two other decks just in the last century," he said, "and who knows how many other stray cards. That's part of why it's so powerful."

Ernie rubbed her stinging arm, not sure whether Legs was taking offense or just getting a little restless. "I guess I thought that if one Dealer stole another's cards, that person would just have extra cards to play."

Minh shook his head. "It's a little more streamlined than that. The dominant deck absorbs the other, increasing its power. So when Virginia kept Alvarez's cards—she got Accelerate, as well as his Chameleon Wild, which sucks—the matching cards in her deck would just eat them after a while."

Ernie cringed. She wasn't sure how she felt discovering that her deck's power had come at the cost of other Dealers. "Does the other deck . . . feel it?"

"Yep. It sucks. And now, because Virginia's gone back to whatever bolt-hole she crawled out of, Alvarez is stuck. He either goes on, slowly aging, walking wounded . . . or he goes after another, weaker Dealer and tries to replace his cards by stealing theirs."

"He can't ask Andy for replacements?"

"You know how things work with our Forger—if Alvarez doesn't have a Mark to buy a favor without payback, Andy's going to demand a pound of flesh as payment. Possibly literally. Which means Alvarez is screwed—unless he screws someone else."

There were only two Marks left in existence, as far as they knew—and Gabe had hidden them. Would Alvarez go after Gabe to get to them? They might have been allies once, but alliances seemed to die quickly among Dealers. Ernie sipped her drink, trying to look calmer than she felt. The Dealer of the Chicken deck had wreaked havoc after pretending to be an ally, and they were all still feeling the consequences. "I need to go after Virginia. Someone's gotta teach her that you can't just steal from others."

Minh chuckled. "And you think you're going to be the one to do it? Virginia's *a lot* faster and stronger than she should be, which means Alvarez's cards can't be the only ones she's swiped. I got back the Healing card she stole from me, but it was much harder than I'd expected." He grimaced, maybe remembering how Virginia had literally eviscerated him in a vicious sneak attack as soon as Ernie had revealed her as a mole and a traitor. "She's not that old, I don't think. I only became aware of her around a hundred years ago—" He smiled and lifted his glass to a lady sitting at the bar nearby who gave him an odd look, then he casually slid his Conceal card from his pocket and whished it in the direction of the rest of the bar, muffling their voices.

"She's been a Dealer for over a hundred years, then," said Ernie. "That's not nothing."

He shrugged. "It's all relative. But she's got a decade or two on Alvarez, and I suppose she's getting up there with me and Gabe."

Ernie winced at the mention of Gabe and focused hard on Virginia instead. "We should definitely make her give Alvarez's cards back. And maybe we should take an extra few from her as a fine."

Minh leaned forward and squinted at her grimy coat. "Sorry—just looking for the sheriff's badge." He sagged back into his seat. "Those cards are Alvarez's problem, not yours. If he can't get them back after all the help we gave him, he doesn't deserve to have them in the first place."

"You sound like the Forger." Andy had straight up told Ernie that if she couldn't defeat Duncan, one of the most feared Dealers who'd ever existed, she didn't deserve to live. "Survival of the fittest. Is that really how the Dealers work?"

"Last time I checked, it wasn't a socialist operation."

Ernie rolled her eyes. "Helping an ally is hardly socialist."

"Then let me explain it this way: If the tables turned and it was your cards Virginia snatched? Alvarez would probably come after you to try to snag a few more, seeing as you'd shown yourself to be weak. Speaking of, watch your back. You're probably top of his list when it comes to a source of replacement cards. He'll be counting on your inexperience."

Ernie waved away the threat, remembering how, even with only twenty or so cards, Legs had helped Ernie hold her own against the Emperor Tamarin Dealer. "Turned tables or not, I'm me. And I'm *not* Alvarez."

"Which is why I'm drinking with you." Minh held up his glass, and Ernie tapped hers against it. "But the longer you're around, the more you'll understand why we all work alone."

"Then why did *you* help Alvarez?" Minh was the reason the guy had as much of his deck as he did.

"Being down one Dealer during that fight wasn't good. We were facing the Wolf Spider, the Hyena, the Komodo, and Duncan Carrig, our never-mourned and not-at-all-missed *former* Diamondback—who was, as I recall, trying to get ahold of the Marks so he could ambush the Forger and take the throne." He inclined his head toward Ernie. "We needed all the help we could get."

"Yeah, yeah. You were just being practical, right?" Ernie watched Minh as he savored a mouthful of his drink. "You want to sound all casual about right and wrong, but I know for a fact you try to err on the side of right whenever you can."

"The older I get, the more right and wrong seem to meld." His fingertips tapped against the rim of his glass. "I'm starting to think they're just the same thing from two different perspectives."

Ernie groaned. "That's such a cop-out."

"Don't be so naïve, dearie. Dealers work alone because we compete. For the best jobs, for the most cards. You never rest easy when you're around another Dealer, because there's always a chance you'll wake up missing a card, if not your whole deck. No one's clean or good here. Except maybe you, and even that will fade with time."

"You always seemed to be good, honestly."

"What *is* good, really, for a Dealer? Say I stop a terrorist attack, right here in London." He held up his hand when Ernie groaned. "Just go with it. What if my heroic intervention causes a tragedy somewhere else? What if someone I save turns out to be a mass murderer? What if the chain of events I break sets off a cluster of catastrophes somewhere else?"

Frustration caused a bloom of heat across Ernie's chest. "What's with the philosophical crap? If this is how you really feel, why did you help us defeat Duncan?"

"He crossed a line."

"Meaning there is one."

"Sure. One Virginia hasn't crossed."

Ernie coughed. *"Nazi."* She coughed again. Virginia had admitted, without shame, that she'd used her deck to help the Germans in World War II.

"You seem very focused on that."

"Seriously, dude?"

"Okay, fine. But she's not the murder-and-mayhem villain you seem to think she is, not like Duncan was, at least. She only pops up once every few decades. I think she's far fonder of dusty archives than the battlefield."

Ernie's brow furrowed. "What?"

"Virginia has an obsession with the Forger's toys. At least, if drunk Virginia is to be believed." He glanced at Ernie out of the corner of his eye. "We had a cold evening to kill in Santiago once upon a time. And if she wants to spend her entire existence on a wild-goose chase, all the better for the rest of us."

"The Forger's toys," Ernie murmured, remembering that Andy had called them that, too. "Like the Marks."

"And those barrier rune tiles."

"And the rune tile that made the animals attack their Dealers." Andy had admitted to making that one—he'd called it the "antagonist rune," and he hadn't seemed to care about the damage it could do. "Virginia was the only one who was in favor of me trying to use that rune tile to rescue Gabe from Duncan and his minions. She probably thought they would just take it from me and add it to their list of advantages."

"Shame on her for underestimating you. But she did take the barrier runes."

"So . . . the Forger's toys . . . that's the kind of stuff my dad was sending to my mom."

Minh nodded. "Redmond obviously knew where to look for them. I've known a few others who tried and failed."

"He was a historian. I never saw him without some old text in his hands." Ernie pushed away memories of her father, which were still painful after all these years. "This is exactly the kind of treasure hunt he would have loved." And suddenly, Ernie wondered whether his quest for relics had resulted in his disappearance. "Remember what Virginia said about my dad? How he stole from her? She said she did something to him that was worse than death."

Minh turned to her and met her gaze. "Ernie, if I knew what happened, I swear I would tell you. I met Redmond *once*, so yes, I know he was on the hunt for artifacts, too. Maybe the Forger's, maybe something else. But Virginia didn't admit to doing a thing to him until a few months ago, so I'm as much in the dark as you are."

Ernie desperately needed some light. "Did Andy create all of these toys we're talking about? Does he just huddle in a workshop in the center of the universe, making this stuff?"

Minh snorted. "Like some kind of evil Santa?"

"It just seems like there might be a lot of these toys out there. How long has Andy been the Forger, anyway?"

"About two hundred years."

Ernie sat up straight. "Wait—aren't you older than that?"

Minh ran a finger over his smooth, unwrinkled brow. "Amazing what a good skin regimen will do for you."

"You knew Andy when he was a Dealer? Which deck did he have?"

"He was the Lynx."

"You never mentioned this before."

"You never asked. Andrew is American. Or he was. And he'd been around for nearly a century when we crossed paths during the Revolutionary War."

"How did he become the Forger?"

Minh looked away from her gaze, his sardonic tone slipping away. "No clue, honestly. I knew Andy was power hungry—he tried to steal cards every time we were together, but at least he respected me each time I stopped him. He likes power—as long as it doesn't threaten his—and he despises weakness."

"Maybe that's why he seems so merciless."

Minh shrugged. "All I know is that one day he was the Lynx, and the next time I became aware of him, he was the Forger, and Phoebe was gone. She was the one who gave me my deck."

"What was she like?"

"I thought she was a god." He leaned back in his seat, staring at nothing. "She seemed so absorbed, as if her mind was floating through the universe even when she was standing right in front of you. Like Andy, she created artifacts, but I think they're of a different nature than his, which seem geared to sow chaos and conflict between the Dealers." He gave Ernie a sidelong glance. "Phoebe made the Marks. She told me they were out there when she made me a Dealer. Now that he's the Forger, Andy hates them. The idea of owing mere Dealers any kind of favor is repellant to him."

"That's more or less what he's said to me. I got the sense he'd be happy when they were used up."

"Phoebe was different. I think maybe she was inviting the contact."

It made Ernie think of stories from the Bible about how God had created man in part to have someone to worship him and interact with him. "I guess if you're living alone in the center of the universe, in charge of keeping the whole thing going, it's nice to get out sometimes, even if it's only to grant favors?"

"Eh. I think Andy just likes to cause trouble. He's pretty enamored of chaos."

"So he was a power-hungry Dealer—like Duncan. Maybe like Virginia. And he found a way to take the Forger throne or crown or magic wand or whatever from Phoebe. How the hell did he do it, though?"

"A Mark, for one. He must have used Phoebe's generosity against her. But I have no idea how he took her down. He might have tried to do it by force, or maybe deception, seeing as Phoebe was gentle but rather distant, maybe easy to ambush. But it's not like he shared his plan with me. We weren't exactly friends, and now I just steer clear of him."

"Doesn't he give you assignments?" Ernie asked.

"Every once in a while, just to make sure I know he's in charge, but mostly he leaves me alone."

"Is there any kind of historical record or archive that could tell us what kind of 'toys' Phoebe and Andy have made?"

"Unless you inherited your dad's formidable researching skills, that knowledge is most likely lost to the winds of time."

Ernie frowned. "I need to know what Virginia did to my dad, but I bet it involved one of those artifacts made by the Forgers. Maybe I can find her. Maybe Alvarez would help if I promised to try to get his cards back—or take some of hers to fill in the gaps? And if you came along, there'd be three of us, and we could—"

"I'm gonna need another drink." Minh tipped his head back and downed the rest of his cocktail in one gulp, then signaled the waiter for another.

17

"Come on, Minh. She did something terrible to my dad. Another *Dealer*. No one's seen him or his Dragonfly deck in almost twenty years. But she said she didn't kill him."

"Doesn't mean he's not dead." Minh accepted his refill from the waiter and leaned to whisper in his ear. The guy straightened, accepted a tip, and beamed at Minh as if he were a freaking rock star. "How about a little patience instead of a half-assed vigilante mission?" continued Minh after the waiter scurried away. "I'm sure Andy will tell you what happened someday."

"Yeah, but no doubt at the worst possible time." And if Minh wouldn't help her, then . . . "I don't suppose you've talked to Gabe recently?"

Minh's brows rose, instantly making Ernie regret her words. "Oh. This is interesting. I thought you guys were the new Trey and Tarlae, only white."

Although most Dealers played alone, Trey and Tarlae, the Raccoon Dealer and the Coconut Octopus Dealer, were a closely bonded couple. Ernie looked away. "Not exactly. I think he needed some space."

Two months ago, Gabe had promised they'd see each other soon—and had proceeded to drop out of her life completely.

"You haven't tried to contact him," Minh guessed.

Her cheeks burning, Ernie shook her head.

"Why not?"

"Space! I respect that!" What was she supposed to do—cling to him like a barnacle? If he didn't want to see her, she didn't want to see him, either. Not at all. Nope. She wasn't about to lay her heart on the table just for Gabe to toss it in the garbage. She wasn't about to go after him only to give him a chance to walk away.

Minh was quiet for a solid minute as Ernie squirmed. "Maybe you should reach out," he finally said.

"I'd love to hear about the job you mentioned," Ernie prompted, glancing at an ornate metal clock on the wall. She needed to get home for Christmas Eve, and chatting about Gabe was pointless. He knew where to find her if he wanted to, and he obviously didn't want to.

Minh considered her for a few more uncomfortable seconds, then said, "I just told the waiter to bring our middleman over."

"Middleman?"

"For the job." He rubbed his fingers together. "This one'll pay the rent for a few months." He glanced at her shabby coat. "Maybe a few years, in your case."

Ernie looked down at her soggy trench, suppressing a rush of eagerness at the idea of going home to her mom with enough cash to make a real difference in their lives. "I need to know what kind of job it is before I agree to it."

"You look like you expect me to cart you off to assassinate a nun or something. Which of course I would not do."

"Because you do have some ethics."

"No, because it would be unlikely to pay well." He gestured at himself. "Trust me, Ernie. I know how to make a living at this job. And I'm going to help you do the same." He winked. "If only to keep you from trying to act like the unofficial, unwanted sheriff of a town filled with outlaws who are *probably* as powerful and *definitely* nastier than you are."

Ernie started to grumble a reply as a man approached them, his hands clasped and his expression guarded. He looked to be in his forties, with a thick orange beard and a bald head, which he bowed as he stood a few paces away from Minh. "Sir," he said in a low voice. "Allow me to say how very honored I am to—"

"Oh, stop it," said Minh. "I'm the middleman to your middleman tonight." He elbowed Ernie. "My friend Ernie here has a big deck and some serious creativity, and I thought she might be an excellent and *ever* so slightly cheaper option for you."

The man raised his head, his orange brows high in surprise. "But I was told that you—"

"I had a higher bid for my services tonight," Minh snapped. "I'm given to understand that your boss has a rather urgent need, so I arranged for another consultant to take my place."

And that was probably why Minh had sought her out in the first place. Not to catch up but to keep some rich client happy. Ernie gave him the side-eye, but he was glaring steadily at the middleman, who Ernie realized was taking in her bedraggled appearance with a mixture of horror and amusement. "Ah, forgive me, sir," the middleman said in a posh accent. "Are you *quite* sure—"

Ernie sighed and reached into her pocket for the deck. She was exhausted, but Legs was tingling merrily on her arm, perhaps excited at the prospect of another mission. As the man babbled very Britishly about what was proper, how so much discretion was needed, how very sensitive and delicate the operation was, blah blah blah, she played her Nourishment, Pleasure, and Tool cards.

The middleman stopped midprotest as the trench coat and shabby, overlarge clothes disappeared, replaced by sleek black pants, a corset top beneath a moto jacket, and boots that actually fit her feet, along with a stylish belt, on which was holstered a rather impressive knife. "Um, I-I . . . That's very, *very* . . . ," he stammered as he stared at her. Ernie tried not to grin with pride as he finally found his words. "Miss, although I do not wish to offend you in any way, you cannot carry that kind of knife in London without attracting the attention of the authorities."

Ernie rolled her eyes and played her Conceal card, making the knife disappear. "Happy?"

Minh patted her knee. "I think we're good here." He stood up. "And I'm off." He poked her arm as she rose as well. "But do me a favor and check in with Gabe, okay?"

"I'm not sure if I can—" she began, but Minh vanished before she could finish. Ernie pressed her lips closed, then realized the middleman was still staring at her. She smiled at him. "I'm Ernie. Diamondback."

He offered his hand. "Chadwick. Er . . . nothing, I suppose." He gave her a sheepish smile. "But we shall all be most grateful if you can solve this highly distressing problem."

"I only have a few hours," she said as they shook.

"A few hours is all the job requires." He gestured toward the door.

Ernie adjusted her conjured jacket, wishing she could afford one that would last for more than a few hours before fading back to her previous baggy ensemble, and headed for the exit. As they tromped up the steps to the street, she could already hear the patter of raindrops and feel the slice of the winter breeze. Reaching into her pocket, she played her Shield card and smiled with relief as an umbrella appeared in her hand. No need for the fancy-schmancy, concentration-draining invisible kind, especially since she was already pretty tired and had no idea what she was about to be asked to do. She held the umbrella close over her head, trying to stay dry as Chadwick called a car. She could have offered to transport him, but she didn't feel like being that close to a stranger as the void pressed in against them. She also had no idea where they were going.

She eyed Chadwick's broad back as he hailed the cab. Heading off to parts unknown with a man she'd just met, even one introduced by a friend, would not be a smart move for a young woman in an unfamiliar city. But after being thrown into the deep end after she'd gotten her deck, Ernie had lost whatever fear she'd had. She could defend herself, and she could endure just about anything. That knowledge—and the unbelievably powerful deck in her pocket—was enough to keep her heart rate steady as she hopped into the back of a taxi with Chadwick, who brushed raindrops out of his beard and instructed the driver to take them to Vicarage Gardens, Kensington. "So who's your boss?" Ernie asked.

Chadwick gave the driver a hesitant look, but Ernie held up her Conceal card. "It's fine," she said. "He can't hear us."

"The Lord Speaker," Chadwick said, barely opening his mouth.

"What's a Lord Speaker?"

"As in *House* of Lords. Parliament. He is a man who would prefer his secrets not make the evening news. Lord Gore requires your assistance to suppress a scandal."

This didn't sound so bad. "One that's about to be made public?"

"Which is why it's time sensitive. He is being blackmailed, and the schemer has threatened imminent release of images and information that would bring great shame upon a prominent family."

So she'd need to find the blackmailer, destroy the information, and send the person off with a head full of jumbled memories. Ernie chuckled, already thinking of the plays. This wasn't so different than what she'd done in Ukraine, except the wages seemed likely to be better. Ernie imagined what she could do with a few thousand pounds. Maybe have an actual kitchen installed in her mom's shop instead of that sad little kitchenette. Maybe pay someone to deep clean the place, since her mom could barely manage to dust. Hell, Mara Terwilliger could barely manage to keep herself fed and clothed. Ernie sagged under the weight of her guilt. She'd been away too long, but the thought of coming back with heavy pockets eased the burden a little. "What kind of compensation are we talking?" she asked.

"I have been authorized to offer you three hundred fifty. Thousand."

Her heart leapt—*Forget a new kitchen, how about a whole new house?*—but she wasn't going to lose her head. "Is that the gross or the net? What do you get for commission? And you know that I can use my deck to determine if you're telling me the truth, right?" All she needed was her Discern card and a bit of concentration.

Chadwick nodded, his chin jutting forward a bit. "I have no reason to lie. My commission is ten percent off the top, and once the job is complete to my lord's satisfaction, the net shall be wired to any account you care to specify."

"Cool."

Chadwick grinned.

Ernie pulled out her Strike card and showed it to him. Helpfully, Legs made the symbol—a line with a triangle jutting to the right from its center—glow, painting Chadwick's brow with an eerie light. "But if you try to screw me over, Chadwick, I'm going to hang you by your beard from the London Bridge."

He stopped grinning and looked away, muttering something about how all Dealers were the same.

The taxi pulled up outside a block of ritzy-looking white town houses on a quiet road lined with stately, bare trees. Cars were parked on both sides of the residential street, and up ahead appeared to be a jumble of traffic. Chadwick cursed. "I don't believe it." He shoved the door open and got out of the car.

Ernie sighed and slid her Coin card—disguised as a credit card—to pay the driver, relieved that it actually worked this time and mentally adding the fare to Chadwick's very large tab. She got out and followed him, raising her conjured umbrella as the rain pelted down. "What's wrong?"

"Isn't it obvious?" He waved his hand toward the melee. "It must have already leaked!"

Her boots splashing in the puddles, Ernie trudged up the block toward the center of the action, a town house on the corner that was lit up with floodlights coming from the lighting rigs of two vans that had double-parked out front. A crowd of people milled about on the sidewalk, just outside iron gates that kept them out of the front garden. Two uniformed guards stood at the door to the house. A few neighbors could be seen peering between cracks in their curtains in houses across the street.

"Can you contain this?" Chadwick asked, rubbing his hand down his wet face, which had gone a shade paler. "I'll give you ten thousand out of my commission if you can."

"I don't know," she said as she got closer, taking in a female reporter earnestly speaking into a television camera. "But let me try." There might be a Dealer who had the power, focus, and know-how to pull knowledge from the heads of people sitting at home watching TV, but Ernie wasn't there yet. She pulled her cards and made the play she knew—Rend and Tool—with her focus on the television camera.

With a loud snap and bright spark, the camera burst into flame, and the camerawoman yelped and tossed it to the ground. Another slash of Ernie's cards, and the satellite dish and thick antenna both buckled and fell in pieces to the street. Chadwick let out a whoop of triumph, and Ernie smiled. People were shouting and shrieking, but no one was hurt, and she'd disabled the live feed. But several people in the crowd had their phones held aloft, recording or maybe even streaming. With a wince, Ernie aimed her focus at a guy standing nearest to her and played her cards again. They pulsed with warmth just like they always did, but nothing happened.

Had she run out of juice? It could happen if she played the same cards over and over, or if she used Augment cards like Amplify or Accelerate to intensify the impact of her Action cards, or even if she was tired or distracted. She'd thought she'd recharged over drinks, but maybe not?

A bright light made Ernie blink, and she squinted at the rain-slicked jumble of umbrellas in front of her to see the camera she'd just killed back on the shoulder of the camerawoman, as if nothing had happened. "Dear God," Chadwick muttered.

The satellite dish and antenna were putting themselves back together, too, and no one else seemed to see it. They were all focused on the two black police cars that had just pulled to the curb and disgorged several grim-looking police officers, who made a beeline for the house. When the iron gates opened to allow them entrance, several people in the crowd cheered.

Ernie drew her full deck and fanned her cards—she had a bigger problem now. She wasn't the only Dealer on the street. Nothing else could have caused all that equipment to magically repair itself. Heart hammering, she turned to Chadwick. "Sorry it didn't work out. Keep me in mind for the future."

While Chadwick gibbered in disbelief and the cops filed into the Lord Speaker's town house, Ernie disappeared her umbrella and stalked across the street, behind one of the vans. With a flick of her wrist, her Revelation card flew into the air, passing before her eyes but revealing nothing but a blur of gray. The Dealer was concealing himself. Or herself. Ernie scanned the street, raindrops sliding down her forehead and cheeks. Nothing unusual, except—

The sound gave it away. Above her head, she heard a familiar shriek, and a clack of branches told her the bird had taken flight. Ernie pulled her Light card and directed the beam at the sky. Through the silver flash of raindrops flew the kestrel, returning to her Dealer. Ernie's breath caught as she watched the bird arc downward and fly straight toward a tall figure on the opposite corner. He pulled up his sleeve and let his animal disappear into a swirl of ink on his skin, then turned up his collar and started to walk away.

For a moment, Ernie was paralyzed. It had been two months since she'd spoken to him. Two months since she'd seen him.

Two months since she'd kissed him. And two months since he'd said he needed time. Every night since, she'd pulled the blank card that had bonded them, the one with its hybrid creature and endless possibilities, and stared at it, wondering whether he felt her longing, wondering whether she could call him to her—and wondering whether he even wanted her to. Every day, she'd found herself hoping that he'd reach out just because *he* wanted to.

But those hopes had been met with silence. Until now, when he was walking away. Again.

She gritted her teeth and jogged after him. "Hey! You just cost me a few hundred *thousand* pounds!"

He kept walking as if he hadn't heard her. Irritation flowing through her, she whipped out two cards and played them before thinking about it—Capture and Friend. She'd done a version of this play once before, using her Ally card, when she had been trying to prove to Minh that she could deal but hadn't wanted to hurt someone who was on her side. And now all she wanted was the guy she'd been unable to get off her mind to talk to her, and if she had to fling a few ropes around him to do that, fine.

The ropes flew right through his body—*a mirage*—and wrapped around a tree. Before Ernie could make another play, a powerful arm slid around her waist and pulled her into darkness.

CHAPTER THREE

For a few seconds in the crushing obsidian void, Ernie struggled, but she was held fast against someone far stronger. She was afraid to play any cards for fear of losing them to the darkness as she was being transported, so she braced for impact and prepared to defend herself. The moment her feet hit solid ground, she twisted hard in her captor's grip and came up with her cards ready.

Gabe had his deck drawn but didn't make a play. He stood beneath the spindly branches of a birch, looking roguishly disheveled as ever, his long, dirty-blond hair pulled back in a haphazard ponytail, his jaw sporting a few days' worth of stubble, his jeans looking worn and his boots scuffed. "Figured you should be here for the holiday," he said mildly, his Irish accent sending a shiver of unbidden longing through her body, ticking her off even more. When he gestured at the windows of her mother's shop, Ernie realized he'd brought her back to Asheville.

"What the heck?" she snapped, reeling at the sight of her mother's home and antique business, a faint light glowing somewhere within. "Why, Gabe?"

"You would have regretted saving the reputation of a man about to be exposed as a child molester."

Fury blasted up Ernie's spine. "God*dammit*, Minh!" She didn't know whom she was angriest at—the Pot-Bellied Pig Dealer, herself,

Gabe, Chadwick, or the damn pedophile she'd been about to help—but it barely mattered, because only one of them made a convenient target. "It was none of your business!"

"None of yours, either."

"It was a job," she spat.

His expression softened. "I know you. No matter how rich the pay, you would have regretted helping anyone who'd hurt . . . *anyone*, I'm thinking, let alone a child. Minh should have found out what the client wanted before fobbing it off on you."

He was right. *Absolutely* right. But Ernie had left her rationality in Kensington. "Am I supposed to thank you for making that kind of decision for me?"

There was a flash of something in Gabe's shadowed blue eyes, but it was gone before Ernie could translate it. "You could have stayed and earned your commission if you were dedicated to the job," he said. "Instead, you chose to chase a mirage down the street."

Ernie clenched her fists and turned away with a growl of frustration. "Only because it was you."

"Which is a problem, love." He sighed. "You think there aren't a half dozen Dealers out there who know that about you?"

It felt like he'd punched her in the chest. How many times in the last few months had she wished for his advice and guidance? But having it now stung worse than a hive of yellow jackets. "Merry Christmas, Gabe. This is quite a gift."

"Didn't expect a whinge from you of all people."

"Screw you," she blurted out. "I'm doing fine on my own, okay? I don't need you big-brothering me. You suck at it anyway."

He chuckled. "I'll be on my way, then. Merry Christmas to you."

She whirled around. "*What?* Are you freaking kidding me?"

"I seem to be wrecking your holiday cheer."

"You're certainly wrecking something," she muttered. She wanted to turn her back and wish him a good life. She wanted to run to him and beg him to wrap his arms around her, like he had when they were in his haven just before their battle with Duncan, when he'd told her she'd better come out of it alive, when his hands had shaken and his desperation had been like rocket fuel for her heart. Now he stood there all calm and whatever-I'm-over-it, as if it had been twenty years instead of two months. She closed her eyes and let out a breath. "I just thought I'd hear from you before now, okay?"

"You could have summoned me anytime you wanted."

"You never gave me your number."

"That's just sad, love."

"You have yourself concealed all the time." She'd tried and failed to bring a vision of him to her Revelation card too many times for it to be healthy.

He came forward, tucking his cards inside the inner chest pocket of his jacket. "You of all Dealers, of all people, can reach me." He nodded toward her deck.

The blank white card slid up from the rest, making Ernie gasp. "Legs, you little traitor," she whispered.

"You connected us," said Gabe. "You carry a part of me with you all the time."

"You're acting like I stole something from you—but I saved our decks and our lives," she said slowly. "I did the best I could in that battle and in that moment." She remembered it so clearly, like it had happened in slow motion. He'd been bleeding out, at the mercy of his murderous brother, and she'd been a breath away from dying herself. "I didn't know exactly what would happen."

"You must have been thinking of using my power," he said. "You chose its form."

Ernie looked down at the card, its blank face, the hybrid winged snake on its back, and knew that was true. "The only way we could win was as a team, Gabe, and you'd already sacrificed yourself for me!"

"But that was my choice."

"You want me to apologize for rescuing you right back?"

He was only a few feet away now, tall and lean and unreachable, his face etched with the same weariness he'd worn for as long as she'd known him. "I never asked you to apologize," he said.

"And I didn't make you come to London tonight." This was so not the reunion she'd pictured.

"I did that for myself," he said quietly. "I wanted to see you."

The somber look on his face filled her with dread. "What's going on?"

He regarded her for a moment. "I'm thinking about giving up my deck."

"You . . . what?"

"It's been a long time, Ernie. And I'm tired. My deck is incomplete—"

"You're only missing one card!"

"I was tired long before the Forger took that Wild from me. I was hanging on to make sure Duncan couldn't destroy the world, but that's over now."

"You'll die," she whispered.

His arms rose from his sides. "For all this immortality, I'm still a man. And men aren't supposed to live forever. I should have died two centuries ago, and in the time I've lived since then, I've done too many things that I regret."

She closed the distance between them and shoved him, but as usual, it was like running up against a brick wall. "You're acting as if those are the *only* things you've done! We saved the world, Gabe. You've saved too many other people to count. I'd be dead if you hadn't protected me over and over again. So would my mom."

He smiled, sad and sweet. "You might have found your own way out of that jam. I think you can do just about anything if you set your mind to it."

"This is bullshit!"

"It's my choice."

"It's a sucky choice! It's not even rational!"

He took her by the shoulders. "When you get up past a hundred fifty, see how you feel."

"Minh's twice as old as you are, and he's fine!"

"Minh and I are *very* different." His voice was hard, like his grip, but then both softened. "You can't understand it right now."

Tears welled, and she bowed her head. "But I thought you . . . I thought you and I—"

"Look at me."

She did, and what she saw in his eyes made her ache.

"I'm not stupid enough to claim there's nothing between us," he said quietly. "I never expected you, never thought . . ." His fingertips brushed across her cheek and then fell away. "But if I let go of the Kestrel deck, it has to be about me. Not about us."

It felt as if she were caught in a crashing plane; the noise in her head was all screams and blaring alarms and broken cries to the Almighty. But it was easier to be mad than destroyed. She'd learned that ages ago, when her father had walked out of her life. The pain was still a massive scar on her heart, one that Gabe had just torn wide open. She clenched her jaw and wrenched the blank card from her deck.

"It was *always* about you, Gabe. You saved me to get to your brother. You went after *him* to get rid of your guilt. You don't want to be connected to me? Fine. You don't owe me a thing." She shoved the blank card into his jacket and backed away from him. "If you want to destroy yourself, I can't stop you, and you *know* that. And if you want to leave? Hey, I've been left before. So get the hell away from me so I can get on with my life."

She stalked toward her mother's shop. When she got to the door and looked back, he had disappeared. She turned around and slid down the side of the house, gasping, her face hot enough to use as a griddle. She tore up her sleeve and held her arm out, and Legs came slithering off. The diamondback rattler coiled herself in front of her Dealer and raised her head, her tongue flicking out.

"Can you believe the nerve of him?" snapped Ernie. "He ignores me for two months and then shows up just to tell me he's thinking of ending it all? What the heck?"

Legs watched her impassively. Ernie looked the reptile over in the glow of her mother's porch light, admiring her poise and the glint of gold and emerald off her scales. "How old are you, lady?" she asked. "You've probably been around a lot longer than Gabe, right? And *you* never complain."

Legs made a slow rustling sound with her rattle. Ernie had come to understand some of Legs's body language, but it was hard for them to share anything more complicated than that. Legs wasn't a normal snake. She had a killer mind for strategy, knew the cards so deeply she could coax miracles out of them, and had saved Ernie's butt more than a few times by either recommending plays or altering Ernie's to make them more potent or just straight-up smarter. "I'd be pretty lost without you. You know that, right?"

Legs met her gaze steadily. Ernie reached out and stroked Legs's body. "Thank you for protecting me tonight. I'll never take that for granted. Maybe someday I'll be good enough with the cards to pay you back."

Legs rattled. Maybe it was an admonishment—Ernie had dived in front of a knife to protect Legs, and Ernie had wondered more than once whether it had made the serpent more protective than other Dealers' animals. Or maybe that rattle was simply a *Yeah, I hope you'll be good enough someday, too.*

"I'm trying," Ernie whispered. She'd experimented with her cards, practiced and practiced, often with Legs coiled nearby, watching. But it would have been nice if another Dealer had taken the time to teach her. She'd hoped Gabe might do that for her.

She groaned and stood up. "I guess it's every Dealer for herself, right? I'm not even on his radar."

Legs rattled louder, though she didn't seem pissed off.

"Do you want to go hunt for a while? I'll be here all night."

Legs slithered down the steps and disappeared into the shadows, and suddenly Ernie wondered whether she'd just been hungry and bored. "I'm can't even hold a reptile's attention for more than a minute or two. I guess I never stood a chance with Gabe."

Ernie entered her mother's house feeling agitated, but when she saw the small, bare Christmas tree set up between the fireplace and the dusty glass cases that held Civil War artifacts, she let out a slow breath and summoned her patience. "Mom?"

Down the hall, back in the bedroom, Mara Terwilliger let out a sleepy, surprised cry. "Ernestine! I'll be right out."

Ernie looked at her phone. It was only about half past six in the evening, but the sun had set an hour ago, chased away by winter cold. Still, it was a little early for her mother to call it a day. "Are you feeling okay?" she called.

The bedroom door creaked open, and Ernie's mother came padding out in a ratty bathrobe and slippers, her gray curls in disarray and her horn-rimmed glasses crooked on her face. "I fell asleep reading a book." She smiled and held out her arms. Ernie accepted her mother's embrace, noting with a sniff and a pang of guilt that Mom hadn't been totally alone—she'd been keeping company with Mr. Jim Beam.

"I told you I'd be home tonight," Ernie said.

"I just lost track of time. I meant to order us some food!"

Ernie pulled out her deck. "I can handle dinner, as long as you don't mind vegetarian?" Like all the other Dealers Ernie had met, she hadn't quite been able to stomach meat since bonding so thoroughly with her animal.

"Sounds lovely," Mom replied, eyeing Ernie's deck with fascination. "You can do all that with those?"

"All that and more," Ernie murmured, pulling her Nourishment card and remembering a meal she'd once had with some friends at Plant, a local vegetarian restaurant: fried plantains with hot sauce, grilled beets, corn bread and greens with gravy, and a lemon chess pie. The food she'd envisioned appeared on the sideboard next to her mom's office, edging aside a cluster of tarnished brass candlesticks.

Her mother gasped at the sudden appearance of a feast, and Ernie rushed over to grab the antique candlesticks before they fell. "Can you get us some pl—" she began, but two plates and napkin-wrapped silverware appeared next to the steaming gravy boat. "Never mind. I guess Legs has us taken care of." She grinned as two bottles of Wedge Iron Rail IPA appeared as well.

"This is courtesy of the snake?" her mom asked weakly. "Oh my."

"Call her the diamondback, if you don't mind. It's more respectful."

"Oh *my*" was Mom's only reply as Ernie handed her a plate. "I guess you've become quite close."

"You could say that. She's out getting a dinner of her own right now. She likes to hunt." Ernie pulled up her sleeve to reveal her bare arm.

"Well, those woods are stuffed to bursting with voles and wood rats, so this is like a buffet for her. Not to mention the mice under the porch and in the cellar." She peered out the window toward the woods, a little smile on her face. "I could definitely get used to a friendly predator around the place."

"Listen, Mom, I know I haven't been around much in the last few months . . ." Ernie had popped in a few times to make sure her mom was doing okay, but her sole focus since being given her first assignment by the Forger had been to do it as well as possible—because he'd promised to give her information on her missing father once she'd earned her keep. And then she'd gotten caught up in trying to fix all the things she'd knocked askew, maybe because she'd just needed to feel in control of something. "But I'm sure Legs would be happy to meet you again if you're open to that. I know it was scary the first time."

Her mother let out a shrill laugh. "I'm sure it'll be fine."

Ernie rubbed her arm, glad Legs wasn't there to sense her mother's fear. "Let's eat." She loaded up a plate, grabbed her beer, and headed for the solarium. Her mother joined her a moment later. Ernie had used her cards to repair the glass door pane that Duncan had shattered when he'd broken in to kidnap Mom in the fall, but when Ernie flicked on the lights, she could see that it wasn't the only thing that had changed since she'd become a Dealer.

Pictures of Redmond Terwilliger were everywhere.

Framed photos of her father—at his college graduation; in front of a waterfall; picking peaches; hunched at a desk, poring over some antique book—sat on both side tables and the coffee table surrounding the settee. Her mother had hung their wedding photos in a cluster between the back windows, and on the wall behind the settee, she'd put up pictures of them together with Ernie when she was a baby. Ernie's heart beat unsteadily as she turned in place, looking at her father as she'd known him—bespectacled, long-haired, with a lean frame and a wry grin that said he never took himself too seriously. Memories flooded in . . . The sound of his voice, telling her to get her rain boots on so they could go fishing for smallies in the river. The way he would pull her into his lap when she complained that she was bored, how he would make up a wild story about some artifacts or history he'd been reading about, all for his little Weed, that ridiculous nickname he'd called her as she'd started to shoot up. The way he made her mom dance with him in front of the fire, in front of the Christmas tree, beneath the stars, beneath the sun, the way he'd drowned out her flustered protests by singing loudly, the way her mother would finally laugh and melt into his embrace while Ernie sang along.

Before she knew it, there were tears slipping down her cheeks. "Wow," she said hoarsely. "This is new."

Her mother had set her plate down and taken Ernie's from her, perhaps afraid that Ernie would drop it as she confronted this ghost from her past. She paused between bites of corn bread to say, "After I told you the truth of what happened when he left, I decided it was unfair to him, how I had handled it."

Ernie swiped the back of her hand across her face. "How you handled it . . ."

"I blamed him." She gave Ernie an apologetic look. "I told myself it would be better to be dead than to be left like that. I thought it might be better for you if he'd been around instead of me."

Ernie sat down next to her mother. "And now?"

Her mom looked around at all the pictures of the man who'd given his all to make sure his wife would be able to live a long and healthy—if not happy—life. "Now I realize I took *both* your parents from you. I didn't mean to, but I made you resent him. I was so wrapped up in my own pain that I couldn't pull myself together and give you what you deserved—a mother who could take care of you, and memories of a father who loved both of us more than himself."

"It's okay, Mom."

"Is it?" She gestured at a picture on the coffee table of Redmond Terwilliger sitting in a rocking chair, cooing at a round-cheeked, dark-haired baby. "The two of you were crazy about each other," her mom said, touching the photo. "And I made you hate him."

"I've never hated him." Although she'd tried to, because it had dulled the pain. "I just want to know what happened to him and where he is now."

"You think you could find him?" Mom looked at the lump in Ernie's pocket, where the cards were stashed. "Can you use *those* to contact him?"

"I've already tried. I wish it were that easy. When I ask the deck to show me where Dad is, there's nothing. The only thing I've ever gotten about him from the cards was the location of that artifact that was hidden under your bed."

"I was looking for that just the other day! Did you take it? I was afraid I'd lost yet another of the very few things Redmond had left me."

"I used it when I rescued you and Gabe from Duncan and his sidekicks. Any Dealer nearby had his animal jump off his arm and attack him."

"Can I have it back?"

It was Ernie's turn to be apologetic. "I guess it was single use. It turned to cinders after it had accomplished its mission."

"Oh." Her mother clutched her beer bottle with both hands, peering down at it. "It's just . . . I hate to lose a single piece of him." Her shoulders trembled.

Ernie scooted over to put her arm around her mom. "It saved our lives, Mom. I never would have been able to get you and Gabe out of there without it, and I would have been toast if those Dealers hadn't been so distracted." She thought back to that artifact, with its jagged antagonist rune, and wondered for the thousandth time how and where her father had found it. "I'm sure Dad would be happy to know it kept both of us from an untimely entrance into the hereafter."

"The animal tiles he sent me to use as a protective barrier are gone, too," Mom murmured. "When your friend Minh got me back here, I realized they were missing."

And Ernie knew who had them. Freaking Virginia. "I'm sorry, Mom. There was a lot going on, and I wasn't totally on top of it."

Mom patted Ernie's knee and sniffled. "You have nothing to apologize for."

"Do you have anything else from him?"

"No." She offered her daughter a watery smile. "But you never know, right? Any day, he might send another package. Those metal plates arrived only a few months ago. Checking the mailbox is the best and worst moment of my day."

Ernie closed her eyes. "And you don't have the Marks anymore, either. Although in that case, I'm glad. Too many dangerous people were after them."

"Marks—that's what those metal plates were called?"

Ernie nodded. "Gabe has them for safekeeping." She gritted her teeth as she thought about what he'd just told her, what he might be planning to do. "Of course, I'm not sure how reliable he is these days."

"Have you two had a falling-out?"

Ernie shrugged. Her anger at Gabe was dissipating quickly; worry and regret were creeping in to fill the void. "He's not in the greatest place right now, I guess. And I'm worried he might be about to make a huge, stupid mistake."

Mom leaned forward and picked up the picture of Redmond holding Ernie as a baby. "We fought, you know. Your father and I. When he told me he was leaving but that I'd be healed because of what he was doing, it didn't make a lick of sense, and I told him so." She stroked the image of his face, which had been captured in an expression of awed affection as he looked at baby Ernie. "I said terrible things. I told him it was all an excuse, that he was leaving me to die. I accused him of wanting to take the easy way out, of being selfish, of leaving me for some other woman, of not wanting to be a father. Even in my rage, I knew *that* one wasn't true, but I wanted to hurt him, Ernestine. I wanted him to feel the pain and panic I felt at the thought of losing him. I wanted to change his mind with the sheer cruelty of my words." She wiped her face on the collar of her robe. "I still remember the look on his face as he left for the last time—" Her voice broke, and she covered her mouth with her shaking hand, her eyes squeezed shut.

Ernie had a lump in her throat the size of Mount Mitchell. "Anger feels better than grief," she murmured. "I know how that goes."

"But more often, it *causes* grief. If I'd believed he loved me, if I'd believed what he was saying, I wouldn't have been living with all this regret for all these years." She looked over at Ernie. "It's eaten me alive," she whispered.

Ernie hugged her mother, doing her best not to tear up again. Her mother had been trying to resurrect her father through these pictures, as if that would repair what had been broken, but it wasn't enough. They couldn't feel whole until both of them knew where he'd gone and what had happened to him. Ernie knew he might be dead. It wasn't just what Virginia had told her. With Legs's help, Ernie had discovered that all those postcards she'd received from her father over the years, all filled with promises that he hoped to be home soon, seemed to have been sent over the course of only *one* year—and that the final one, a New Year's greeting in which he said he might have found a way to get back to them, was smeared with blood. It was hard to ignore the ominous there, but closure was closure.

"I'll find him," Ernie said, squeezing her mother's hand. "I don't know how long it'll take, but I promise you I'll find him."

"I believe you." Mom squeezed back. "But it sounds like you also might have some work to do with Gabe. Don't make the same mistakes I did, Ernestine. Don't push him away when he needs you most."

"I'm such an ass." Ernie tipped her head back to gulp down her beer. "I have to go to him, Mom. I'll be home by tomorrow morning, okay? I don't want to miss Christmas with you."

"I'll string the lights on the tree and keep the Christmas goose warm."

They both laughed. The shop didn't actually have an oven—just a hot pot and a microwave. "I'll take care of Christmas dinner," Ernie said. A pull against her skin told her that Legs wanted to come back to her. "Hang on a sec, okay?" She walked into the front parlor to find Legs coiled atop one of the display cases. Ernie held out her arm, and Legs twisted and shimmered, crossing the space to take form in swirling ink on Ernie's skin. Smiling at the new heaviness in her arm, making her feel more powerful and grounded at the same time, Ernie returned to the solarium.

"I'm headed out. You get some sleep and enjoy the food. Legs likes it when people appreciate her work."

"Will do." Mom leaned over and tickled Ernie's tattoo lightly. "Protect my daughter, please, Diamondback. A mother's gratitude is powerful. And merry Christmas."

Ernie smiled as her rattlesnake tattoo pulsed with warmth. "She heard you, Mom." She kissed her mom's forehead. "And I'll be back soon."

Ernie got out her cards, and Transport pulled itself from the rest, landing in Ernie's open palm with its card back—a diamondback rattle-snake devouring the world—glowing warm against her skin. It was time to go find Gabe.

CHAPTER FOUR

Ernie made a quick stop for a shower and a change of clothes back at her old apartment. She'd barely set foot in it since October and probably needed to get rid of it to avoid further drain on her modest finances, but it wasn't like she had time to go full KonMari and get her stuff into storage, either. Dressed in her favorite boots, jeans, a quilted jacket, and her fave Spartan Beast T-shirt—the one with the helmeted logo on the front and *CHALLENGE ACCEPTED* on the back—she pictured Gabe's haven and used her Transport card to whisk herself across the ocean. But when she emerged from the void, she was standing on a barren seaside cliff. No haven—or Gabe—in sight. The sky was a deep, inky black sprinkled with stars presided over by a pale crescent moon. Ernie inhaled the salty air as waves crashed far below her. "Where are you?" she murmured.

She shouldn't have given him the blank card. If it were still part of her deck, she could have played it. She was certain that it would have either carried her to him—or carried him back to her. But like an idiot, she'd forced him to take it, too eager to show him that he couldn't hurt her even as it felt as if her heart were breaking. Now she had to find him some other way.

Shivering in the fierce wind coming off the ocean bluffs, Ernie pulled her Friend-Lover and Revelation cards, hoping that this time would be different than all the others. Worry for Gabe sharpened her focus, and she already knew her will was strong—just not strong enough to overcome whatever concealment Gabe might be using to hide. Because as usual, he didn't appear in the moving images beneath the cards' symbols. All she saw was a gray fog. "Legs, help me out," Ernie whispered. "We have to find him."

A different card wriggled its way free of her deck and flipped itself onto her palm: Ally. And as she crossed that one with Revelation, the gray fog dissipated, revealing a couple lounging on a beach, the man rubbing lotion onto the woman's deep-brown skin. It was Trey, Dealer of the Raccoon deck, and his lover, Tarlae, Dealer of the Coconut Octopus deck. Most Dealers kept themselves concealed from being tracked, but Ernie thought they might have done what she had and allowed ally Dealers to find her if they wanted or needed to. Wary as she was, Tarlae probably wouldn't be in favor of such a move, but Trey, the far more open and friendly of the two, just might be.

Time to find out. Ernie crossed her Transport card with the Ally and Revelation cards and let herself be pulled into the suffocating vortex. She spent the few moments of her journey wondering how exactly it was possible to travel place to place. Magic, of course, but that didn't feel like a good enough explanation. The void felt at once infinite and as if it were only the size of her body.

Her pondering ended when her boots hit sand. Blinking in the piercing sunlight, Ernie shielded her eyes and looked around. She found Trey and Tarlae staring back, both of them with their cards out. But when Trey saw Ernie, his handsome face broke into a grin and he shoved himself off his beach towel to jog over to her. He brushed sand from his olive skin before pulling her in for a brief hug. "How are you, girl? What's up? Also, what the hell?"

"I would have led with that last question," Tarlae said, sitting up and adjusting her bikini top. Her sunglasses hid her eyes, but Ernie didn't need to see her glare to know the Coconut Octopus Dealer was already on guard.

"I'm sorry to bother you guys." Ernie looked around. "Where are we, by the way?"

"Fiji," said Trey. "Celebrating Christmas in style. We've got a picnic—want to join us?" He pulled two cards and added a third plate to a spread laid out on a blanket beneath a ruffled canopy nearby.

"I wouldn't want to impose," Ernie replied. "Have you guys seen Gabe lately?"

Trey and Tarlae exchanged looks. "Why?" asked Trey, stretching out the word.

"I'm worried about him." She paused, then decided full disclosure was best. "He said he's considering giving up his deck."

"What?" Trey's tone shifted to anger. "No. No. He can't do that—he owes me a favor!"

"Are you freaking serious right now?" shouted Ernie. "I tell you that he's thinking about ending his life, and all you're worried about is some stupid favor?"

Trey looked over his shoulder at Tarlae, who shook her head. "Come on, babe," Trey said to her. "She could help."

Tarlae's jaw clenched, and she looked away. Trey sighed. "Virginia took one of Tarlae's cards. I wanted Gabe to help me get it back."

"We can do it ourselves," snapped Tarlae, who was looking out over the ocean.

"If we could, maybe we would have done it by now." Trey's voice was calm, but Ernie could tell by his weary expression that they'd had this conversation before, maybe several times. "From what I've heard, Virginia got away with a few extra cards, and she still has a couple. Minh got his Healing card back. But she's still got two from Alvarez and the one from Tarlae."

"And I'm pretty sure she took the barrier runes." Ernie shook her head. "Have you guys actually faced off with her?"

"She's been undetectable for months," Tarlae replied. "Alvarez is losing his mind."

"You've talked to him? Is he weakened? Are you?"

"I feel it," said Tarlae. "It is a nagging ache, not a terrible pain, but I wake up every morning knowing Rika and I are not whole." She stroked the tattoo of the coconut octopus on her left forearm. The creature had lost two tentacles in their final battle with Duncan and the Dealers helping him, but she'd grown them back quickly. "We are resilient, though. We'll be *fine*."

"You're not going to be fine until you have a full deck!" Trey raked his hand through his thick, dark hair as his eyes shifted to Ernie. "I was actually thinking about coming to find you after the holiday. Gabe's been a hard man to pin down, but I thought you might be able to tell me where—"

"I've only seen him once." She tried to hide how much it hurt, but when Trey winced, she knew she'd failed. "I guess he's been going through some stuff."

"I don't understand. He seemed to truly care for her," Tarlae said as if Ernie weren't standing right there.

"He does, babe," Trey said quietly. "But if he's not sure whether he wants to stick around or not, I'm thinking it's probably hard for him to be around her."

Ernie hadn't thought of that. She wasn't sure whether it made her feel better or worse.

"If you weren't sure whether you wanted to go on living, you'd come to me, and I'd tell you that you were being an idiot," Tarlae said to Trey.

"I tried that," Ernie muttered. And then she'd shoved her blank card at him and walked away.

"He still has the Marks," Trey said. "I wonder if what's been going on with him has anything to do with that."

"What do you mean?" Ernie asked. The sun was beating down on her—she could feel her skin burning. She played her Shield card and pictured what she needed, and the card morphed into a colorful umbrella. "Would they make him feel depressed or something?"

"Only if he thinks about how he's the only Dealer who cannot use them." Tarlae rose from her blanket, looking lithe and dangerous. "We, on the other hand . . ."

"We respect the responsibility Gabe took on," said Trey. "And we need to help Ernie find him now."

"We haven't eaten lunch." Tarlae gestured at their picnic. "Is this really an emergency if Gabe doesn't even want to be found?"

Both of them turned to Ernie. "I have a bad feeling," she said, realizing that it was actually true. And it was more than her guilt over turning her back on him, more than the news he'd crushed her with. A deep, penetrating fear had run her through. "I think we need to find him as soon as possible."

"We can do that over lunch." Tarlae wrapped a piece of flowing cloth around her narrow waist, tied it in place, and stalked over to the canopy. She sat down cross-legged on the blanket and moved a few dishes out of the way before laying out a few of her cards. "Using Revelation to reveal location is one of the first things an inexperienced Dealer like you would do to find a person, Diamondback," she said as Trey and Ernie joined her. She popped a few grapes into her mouth and chewed before continuing. "But it will tell you little about an experienced Dealer who does not wish to be found."

Ernie shook her umbrella—which promptly shrank back into her Shield card and rejoined the deck—and looked over the cards that Tarlae had selected. "What's your strategy, then?"

"Gabe is an ally." Trey smiled as he watched his lover select and place cards on the blanket. He plopped down beside her and patted the spot next to him for Ernie, then grabbed a thick slice of bread and devoured it in three bites. "For you, Ernie, he's more than an ally,"

Trey continued as he slathered a second slice with olive spread. "For me, too, really. We're closer to friends, right? And in your case, maybe more lover." He pulled his Friend-Lover card, the one that embodied and entangled two relationships that were sometimes the same—and sometimes completely different.

Ernie felt the heat in her cheeks. What *was* Gabe to her? She had no idea right now, but maybe it didn't matter.

"—so maybe we can pool our power a little here," Trey was saying. He pointed to Tarlae's Wisdom card—the symbol was more complicated than some of the others and almost looked like two headless stick figures holding hands—and then to her Aid card, with its two overlapping ovals, with three dots on either side of the place they were joined. "We won't search directly for Gabe—we'll search for the best way to help him?" He glanced at Tarlae for confirmation.

"Exactly," she said, looking pleased that he had discerned her intent.

"Let's do it, then," Ernie said eagerly. "How exactly do we pool our power?"

"Tarlae and I do it all the time. We're not used to threesomes, but I think it could work." He winked at Ernie while Tarlae rolled her eyes. "Just layer your cards next to ours—a little overlap is good, but don't cover them up."

"Rika will not be eclipsed," Tarlae said with a nod to the octopus tattoo. "She is proud and will not help if she is not properly respected."

It sounded like Rika and Tarlae were a great match. Ernie pulled her Wisdom, Aid, and Friend-Lover cards out and carefully set them next to their counterparts from the other two decks, overlapping them only a fraction of an inch. "Now what?"

Tarlae held up another card, with three curved lines like parentheses and a series of dots within each curve.

"The Alchemy Wild?" Ernie asked. "I thought that was used to change one substance to another." She'd used it to turn water to gasoline once.

"That is the most concrete and obvious use for it," said Tarlae, not bothering to suppress another eye roll. "Used with a focused will, it purifies, perfects, and melds our combined cards." Tarlae laid her Alchemy card crossways over the top of the layered cards. "Creating a whole that is a brand new thing—one that is stronger than its parts."

"What about an Augment?" suggested Trey. "We could amplify the effect."

"Or sharpen its focus," Ernie said, pulling out the card that fit her purpose.

"A good idea," said Tarlae, granting Ernie a rare smile. "We want to know exactly how we can help, and sometimes that is a more nuanced thing."

"Good call." Trey pulled out his Sharpen Augment, just an arrow pointing upward, and laid it diagonally across the other cards, careful not to cover up any more of the Coconut Octopus deck.

Ernie followed suit and peered into the cards. "When will we know if it's working?"

"It's not like the Revelation card," said Tarlae. "It's not that easy. And you must focus." She was staring intently at her Wisdom card.

Ernie let out a slow breath. She might have practiced a lot with the cards over the last few months, but sitting still and concentrating were not her strong suits, which was probably why she'd been more successful with things that were "concrete and obvious." Clearly she had a lot to learn. "How long will this t—"

Trey shushed her. "Jeez, Ernie, give it a second. Just think of Gabe and ponder what he might need from you." He laid the tip of his index finger on his own Wisdom card and closed his eyes.

Ernie bit back more questions, knowing it was time to buckle down. Gabe might need them. Her fingers brushed her Wisdom card, and Legs answered with a tingling pulse. What did Gabe need from her? He hadn't seemed like he'd needed—or wanted—anything at all. At least, not from her. She'd had to shove that blank card at him to get him to take it. For all she knew, he'd tossed it in the garbage after she'd walked away.

It didn't matter, though, because that blank card wasn't the only thing that connected them, dang it. She'd had feelings for Gabe before the card had existed, and those feelings were what drove her now. Ernie pressed her fingertips into her Wisdom card and closed her eyes. Her thoughts were a whirl of questions and worries, but she focused on the sound of the waves crashing on the beach a few dozen yards away. The darkness behind her eyelids coalesced into a shadow on a light background, the shape of a person. Ernie's heart skipped. "I think I see something," she murmured. "Is that Gabe?"

"All I see is a knife," said Trey. "Weird. Am I supposed to help him off himself? That doesn't seem right."

"Definitely not right," Ernie said. Her eyes were clamped shut as she tried to keep her focus on the figure in her mind, as she tried to bring the person to the forefront.

"I see a cliff by the ocean," Tarlae said slowly. "Grassy hills. The sun is rising over them."

"Ireland," said Ernie. "It's early morning there. Gabe's haven is on a cliff like that. Do you see a structure? A stone cottage?"

"I see nothing but the cliff. There is a sort of boundary made of stones—"

"His haven is surrounded by old stone walls," Ernie said. "But I was there before I came here, and the haven was gone. Like it had never been there."

"Or like you couldn't see it," said Trey. "I mean, I'm sure he has concealments on it."

"But I am seeing this place in my mind's eye, so he hasn't concealed it," said Tarlae. "At least not completely." She gasped. "There is something not right there."

"What do you mean?" A sense of foreboding had seeped into Ernie's bones, making her shiver even in the tropical air.

"I can't figure it out," said Tarlae. "I saw a flash of something, like a scene from a different place, but it disappeared before I could make out what it was. Aren't the two of you seeing this?"

"No. Not at all." Ernie felt as if she were looking through a thick fog, straining to make out the lone figure walking toward her in this vision. The person was closer now, but all Ernie had was a vague outline and movement.

"Focus," said Tarlae.

Ernie gritted her teeth. "I'm *trying*." The figure was closer now, its face blurred. No, wait. The person was wearing a . . . bridal veil? "Oh, man," whispered Ernie. "This is getting weird."

"I'm still just looking at a knife. Kind of a dagger, actually," said Trey. "Pretty cool looking—runes on the blade. No symbols I recognize. Huh. I could probably conjure a weapon like that. But I'm not sure how it would help—"

The veiled figure stopped in front of Ernie and reached toward its face with long, oddly jointed fingers. "Oh my god." Ernie's heart picked up a panicked rhythm as the lacy veil fell. Her eyes flew open, and she jumped to her feet. "We have to go to that Irish cliff. Right now!"

"Didn't you say you were just there—and saw nothing?" Trey asked as he squinted in the sunlight.

Tarlae, who had kept her eyes open, waved her hand over her loose cards and let them rejoin her deck. "Ernie did not see all that was there to see," she said.

"Damn right I didn't." Ernie flicked her wrist, and her Wisdom, Aid, Friend-Lover, Sharpen, and Alchemy cards zipped back into her deck. "I don't know what's happening, but Trey, conjure that knife you saw."

"Right now?"

Ernie nodded. "I think Gabe might need it. Because the only thing I saw in my mind's eye just now was Virginia."

CHAPTER FIVE

Ernie, Trey, and Tarlae stepped out of the void and planted their feet in soft grass. Their decks were in their hands. The sun had risen over the hills and gave the dewy grass a crystalline sparkle, and the ocean waves had calmed, whispering against the bluffs below. It was postcard-perfect Irish coastline, a beautifully deceptive scene.

"You think he's been here all along?" asked Trey. He held a dagger in his right hand, its curved blade about a foot long and covered in black runes.

"Here and not here," said Tarlae. "That's the only way I can describe what I saw in my vision."

"You saw Gabe?" Ernie asked.

"I saw a flash of . . . something."

Ernie walked forward with her hands out, half expecting to bump into an invisible cottage. But she made it all the way across the space, to one of the squat stone walls that marked the property, without feeling a thing. She turned around to find Tarlae and Trey frowning. "How do we make whatever you saw in your vision appear here again?"

Tarlae looked down at her deck. "I—"

A deafening crack split the air as Ernie was hit by a gust of hurricane-force proportions. It blew her off her feet as a shrieking roar came from somewhere near where the cottage would be. The blast of fetid wind sent her rolling and skidding toward the cliff edge. Clawing for purchase with one arm, she screamed for Legs to help and pulled a card, which turned into an ice ax. She buried it in the soft earth and jerked to a halt, holding on for all she was worth and trying to figure out what the hell was happening. But just as she raised her head, the roaring went silent and the gust died.

"Did you see that?" shouted Trey, who was getting off Tarlae, whom he had apparently tried to shield against a stone wall on the opposite side of the property.

She got up, looking a little rumpled and a lot pissed. "I didn't see a thing, because you were playing Mr. Hero."

Trey seemed to be too freaked out to even make a joke. "I saw Gabe! And Virginia! They were in the ruins of the cottage, and there was a . . . a . . . I have no idea what that thing was."

Ernie let her ax turn back into her Tool card and slid it back into her deck. "What were they doing?"

"The thing . . . it was huge. I'd say it was an insect, but it was the size of an elephant. It was between Gabe and Virginia, and they had their cards out like they were dueling, and . . ." He shook his head and looked down at the knife he'd conjured. "Then they disappeared again."

Ernie turned to Tarlae. "In your vision—you said you saw a flash of something you couldn't make out. Did it sound like what he's describing?"

Tarlae waved a card and conjured herself a sweater to put over her bikini top. "It might have been. It happened so fast."

"No kidding," Ernie muttered. "What was that noise?"

"I think it was the *thing*," Trey replied.

"So Gabe and Virginia are facing off, and one of them might have conjured a mirage—seems like Virginia's MO—and . . . what would one of them do to make them disappear and reappear like that?"

"A quick Transport and Land or Sea or Air could take a Dealer or an enemy just about anywhere, but I don't know." Trey was watching the space where the wind and noise had come from, the space where Gabe's cottage usually was. "Why would the haven go with them?"

Ernie pointed at the dagger Trey had seen in his vision and then conjured. "That's the one piece that doesn't fit. Is that how we get them back and keep them here?"

"No idea." Trey walked over and picked it up. "But—"

With a shrieking roar and a blast of wind that blew Ernie onto her butt, the scene Trey had just described materialized in front of them. This time, Ernie rolled over by a stone wall and clung to it to keep from sliding backward toward the cliff's edge. Squinting through the billowing dust and flying debris, Ernie tried to understand what she was seeing. The cottage that had been Gabe's haven was in front of her, smashed to rubble. Gabe stood on one side of it, looking on the verge of surrender. His face was scratched up, and he was bleeding badly from a wound to his chest. Virginia, her snowy cloud of hair wild and tangled, her spindly fingers clutching her cards, was hiding behind a pile of rocks that had once been the fireplace. And a creature Ernie could only think of as a giant grasshopper was crouched in the cottage's ruins, roaring and slashing its barbed legs at Gabe.

As Ernie tried to find her feet and gather her wits, Trey bolted forward with his conjured dagger raised, running straight for the beast. It easily swatted him away with another ear-splitting roar-shriek, and he went flying over the cliff's edge, his cards fluttering in the air. Tarlae screamed and ran after her lover, dealing cards that pulled him and his deck back over the brink. Trey landed on the grass a few feet from the edge, the dagger nowhere to be seen. His cards landed in a pile around him.

Virginia laughed as she emerged from her hiding place and sent a hail of blades in Gabe's direction. "Your friends are here to help," she called to him, her voice carrying over the gale. "They didn't expect *my* friend."

The grasshopper monster snapped at Gabe, its mouth open to reveal rows of jagged teeth. It looked a little like Virginia when she was in her own monster form, which she often took to intimidate people when she was angry or dueling. Gabe played his Shield card, and the grasshopper's face collided with a police riot shield, which he then used to smack the thing in the head—but it grabbed the edge of the shield in its teeth and lifted it *and* Gabe up in the air. It shook its head violently while Ernie stood up and drew her cards. Death and Strike flew into her palm. She pulled them from the deck, imagining a giant spear impaling the creature.

"No you don't, Miss Snake," screeched Virginia as she sent ropes flying Ernie's way. Ernie threw her Shield card, and the ropes bounced off her clear barrier and fell to the ground. But at the same time, Gabe's riot shield disappeared and he went flying, landing hard on one of the stone walls. "Gabe knows how to end all of this," shouted Virginia. "All he has to do is give me the Marks."

As she spoke, Trey and Tarlae got to their feet, fanning their cards. Virginia cackled and waved three from her deck. Two glowing tiles floated from within the voluminous folds of her gauzy, lacy gown. With them levitating in front of her, Virginia shoved her palm toward the two Dealers. The tiles flew forward. On one was carved an octopus, and on the other was a raccoon. As they zoomed toward Trey and Tarlae, the two Dealers began to slide backward as if they'd been hit by an invisible freight train. Tarlae and Trey skidded toward the cliff's edge and tumbled over, and the two barrier rune tiles zipped back to Virginia's pockets.

The Chicken Dealer whirled on Ernie. "I don't have *your* barrier rune—"

"Because it doesn't exist anymore." It had been destroyed in a fight after Duncan had used it to keep Legs away from Ernie. "So you're out of luck."

Virginia gave her a treacly smile. "I doubt I need it to beat you."

"I guess we'll find out." Ernie said a quick prayer for Trey and Tarlae and ran for Gabe, who was struggling to lift himself off the wall. She aimed her Death-Strike play at the insectoid creature as she ran by, but the concentration she needed disappeared when she had to dive for safety as it charged forward, jaws open. Ernie felt the scrape of its teeth against her skin. A terrible stinging followed.

It was no mirage. That monster thing was real, though the space it had been standing in looked different than the surrounding terrain, hazier. Darker. Like its body was carving out its own space, separate from the Irish countryside where it had been conjured. Drawing on her years of Spartan training for obstacle course races, Ernie leapt over a stone wall, ready to keep running, but saw that the creature had returned to the rubble. It didn't seem able to stray too far from the scene of destruction. Ernie changed direction and raced over to Gabe, who groaned when she touched his back. "What is that thing?" she asked him as she pulled him up.

"No feckin' idea," he muttered as he leaned heavily against the stone wall. "But it's not from around here."

"How did she find you?" Ernie stood up and played Shield, Strength, and Prolong as Virginia sent debris from the demolished cottage flying in their direction. The rocks and roof tiles bounced off her clear shield, but Ernie wasn't sure how long it would last—the more a card was played, the weaker it became.

"She started tracking me after I came to see you earlier tonight," Gabe said, wiping blood from his mouth and wincing. "My guard was down as I came back to my haven. I didn't see her coming."

"And she brought that thing with her?"

Gabe shook his head. "She's got a weapon on her. Something . . . It's a rune tile, but I've blocked her every time she aims it my way. I'm not sure what it is, but it kept carrying us both to . . . somewhere else."

"Let's get out of here, then!" She showed him her Escape card.

"She's run me to ground, Ernie. My Conceal card's shot, and I've played Escape and Transport too many times for them to work. Shield's weak, and Strike is fading. And without my haven . . ."

"I can get you out. I'll come back for Trey and Tarlae."

"She can track me wherever I go. Your deck can't hide both of us, not when she's this strong."

"Then we have to figure out how to stop her."

"There's no *we*, love. *You* can go."

"I thought you knew me, *love*." She wanted to shake him, but he looked like he was in enough pain already. "I'm not walking away from you again." *Ever*, she wanted to add, but it didn't seem like the time.

He let out a ragged breath, pulled out his Healing card, and pressed it to his chest. "I'm too old for this."

"Shut up," Ernie snapped. "You're stronger than she is and smarter, too. The only difference between the two of you is a few extra cards." As she said this, her shield began to weaken, bowing inward as Virginia tossed more debris at them. It wouldn't hold much longer. She took Gabe's face in her hands and kissed him gently, savoring the fleeting touch of his mouth, his skin. "And you're not alone, Gabe. Just want you to know that." Her hands fell away, and she turned toward the danger once more.

If they couldn't flee, it was time to fight. She let the fading shield fall, played her Mercy and Ally cards to offer Gabe a few more moments of rest, and used her Weapon card to conjure the first thing that came to her mind: a fire extinguisher full of Raid. With Gabe shouting her name, Ernie jumped back over the stone wall and sprinted past the giant grasshopper with her weapon held high, sending a jet of noxious poison straight at it.

The thing responded with a shrieking bellow and charged at her. Ernie slammed the fire extinguisher into its mouth as it tried to bite her head off. It seemed to be trying to swallow the thing, so Ernie played her Warp card and made it grow jagged barbs, wedging itself deeper into the monster's gaping maw. The creature thrashed and stomped, nearly trampling Ernie as she staggered by, arms up, hoping—

A cage the size of a coffin appeared around Ernie and sent her straight to the ground, where she landed on her back with a bone-jarring crash. Her head slammed into iron, turning her world red and black. As she lay dazed, trying to sort out the terrible sounds coming at her from every direction, Virginia's face appeared above hers. She was leaning over Ernie's prison and smiling. "Time to go, little snakey," she whispered.

Ernie saw the flash of a glowing pink rune tile in Virginia's palm, and the sunny sky above her disappeared. It felt like she was being pressed flat by an enormous weight. She couldn't breathe. The only thing she could hear was a choked animal noise, but she wasn't sure whether it was coming from the monster or from her. She had no idea how long the crushing lasted, but when it lifted, allowing her to suck in a frantic breath, the sky was no longer sunny. It was also no longer blue. She blinked up at Virginia, who was still smiling, backlit by an eerie green.

"Welcome to hell," Virginia said. She waved a card, and Ernie's cage disappeared. But as soon as Ernie got up, she was encased in ropes from shoulder to feet. Her cards were pressed flat to her thigh. She couldn't play a single one, and Legs couldn't spring off her arm to protect her.

"I don't know what you're trying to accomplish, but I'm going to—"

"Oh, stop with the threats," said Virginia. She was breathing heavily and kept glancing around, almost as if she were afraid. "They're boring."

Ernie turned her head in time to see the grasshopper monster spit Ernie's barbed fire extinguisher creation onto the mossy ground, where it instantly disappeared. She braced for the thing to attack once more, knowing this time she was defenseless. But the monster didn't seem aware of her at all. Propelled by its enormous back legs, it leapt for a wooded copse a half mile away and disappeared into the murk.

"You really hurt my poor friend," Virginia said, smirking. "I should leave you tied up in case she wants an afternoon snack."

"I thought you said threats were boring."

The old woman guffawed. "You won't have such a smart mouth from now on." She stepped back and showed Ernie the rune tile she'd flashed at her earlier. "Do you know what this is?"

"I assume you're about to tell me."

"It's the best thing the Forger ever made."

"I was certain you thought the Marks were the best, considering all the trouble you're going through to get them."

"The Marks are rightfully mine," Virginia growled. She cast another wary glance around them before tilting her head and fixing Ernie with a shrewd look. "I don't have much time, but I think I'll use it to tell you a little story. Since we're here and all."

Ernie took in the scenery as she tried to move her hands and her cards, but the ropes tightened each time she shifted, keeping her pinned and making it hard to draw breath. She was standing right next to the destroyed cottage. The contours of the countryside were similar, but everything seemed . . . off. The smell in the air wasn't salt and ocean anymore but more of a swampy funk, and a quick glance out to sea revealed still brown waters. The sun above was enveloped in that green haze that tainted the sky. "And where is here, exactly?"

"When I first met Redmond," Virginia said, "I thought we'd be allies forever."

Ernie's focus on her surroundings dropped away at the mention of her father. "Allies?"

Virginia nodded as she inched closer. Her hair was still wild, like she'd licked an electrical socket. Her eyes were wild, too, but in a completely different way. "Redmond shared my interest in the Forger's runes. In *all* the Forger's toys. I thought Redmond and I would travel the world and find them together."

Ernie grimaced, thinking of her mother, abandoned and in despair. "And did you?"

Virginia's lip curled. "No, because as soon as I revealed to him the Marks I'd collected so painstakingly over the years, having ferreted out all the clues and defeated any Dealer who held the treasure before me . . . he stole them."

"And when was this?" Ernie's father hadn't been heard from in years, but he'd sent the Marks to Ernie's mother only a few months ago.

"Almost twenty years ago," Virginia answered. "He was a dirty thief. No duel, just sticky fingers. But have you ever looked at a Mark, snake eyes?"

Ernie had done more than that—she'd actually used one. It was how she'd gotten the blank card that had connected her deck to Gabe's. "It has a circle in the middle and a ring of circles around it. Lots of circles, basically."

"And each circle has a rune inside it."

Ernie's mother had recognized only one of them—the hieroglyph for "earth." "What do they mean?"

Virginia showed Ernie the rune tile. Wooden and about the size of her palm, the thing looked a little like the barrier tiles Ernie's father had also sent to her mother, though each one of those was carved with an animal. "Every rune symbolizes a place, and there are more than you'd think. More than any one Mark can hold."

"Okay . . ."

Virginia smirked. "By place, I mean a different *dimension*."

Ernie's mouth went dry. When she'd spoken to Andy, he'd mentioned different dimensions within the universe, but she'd been too focused on getting his help to ask whether he was being literal. She peered at her surroundings again, at the ruins of Gabe's cottage and the place where she and Virginia were standing, which seemed to be lit from above with dappled sunlight despite the drab green sky. Virginia followed the line of Ernie's gaze. "I've temporarily connected the two dimensions."

Terrible suspicions were taking shape in Ernie's head, but she wouldn't let Virginia see her fear. "Why?"

"I wanted to give Gabe a little demonstration of what I could do, to help him sort out his priorities. And then you got in the way."

"Is this the same thing you did to my father?" blurted Ernie.

Virginia smiled. "Redmond never saw it coming." Her delighted look soured. "I wish I'd known he'd had the Marks on him at the time." She stalked forward and shoved Ernie, who tumbled backward, out of the sunlit spot around the cottage. "But we both know who has them now, and I can't have you stepping in to help your boyfriend right when I've got him where I want him."

Ernie struggled against her bonds, her heart beating frantically. "This is pathetic," she snarled. "You can't duel with me, so you just tie me up and drop me in a whole different dimension? Where's your sense of honor?"

"I left my southern honor behind years ago, along with my mortality. And now I'll get in that damn bird's head, get the Marks, and be the belle of the ball. Thanks for playing along." Virginia moved close to the cottage, letting the out-of-place sunlight stream over her. "And enjoy your new world." She glanced at the woods. "Especially *her*."

"Wait," Ernie cried out, hating how weak she felt, how scared. "How am I supposed to get back?"

Virginia's grin was hideous. "Ask your father. Assuming you can find him."

And with that, Virginia held up the pink rune. The Chicken Dealer and Gabe's destroyed haven disappeared.

CHAPTER SIX

The ropes that had held Ernie in place vanished as soon as Virginia did. Ernie scrambled up from the cold, damp ground, clutching her deck to her chest as if it were a baby bird. "Are you okay?" she asked Legs, wrenching up her sleeve. "Legs?"

All she felt was a faint tingle, but suddenly it became so sharp and strong that Ernie gasped. It felt like her skin was about to split open. She knelt and held out her arm, offering Legs the chance to emerge.

Nothing happened—except that the pain was becoming unbearable. Ernie's heart was pattering so fast that it felt like she was about to have a coronary. Her eyes burned with tears, and her head was a messy tangle of thoughts. She shoved her deck in her pocket and looked down at her arm. The tattoo lay fixed on her skin as if it had been inked there at Red Rabbit Tattoo back in Asheville. Given the way it felt, she'd expected it to be red, swollen, and distorted, but instead, Legs simply looked . . . like a plain tattoo.

But by the feel of it, she was clearly struggling to pull herself off Ernie's arm—and it simply wasn't working. "Legs, if you can hear me, calm down. We're together, and we're going to figure this out." She gasped at a stab of pain right where Legs's rattle lay on her wrist. "Just . . . stay put for now, okay? I can't concentrate at all when you're fighting like this."

The pain dulled, just a bit. Ernie bowed her head and breathed. The cards pulsed a faint warmth against her thigh. "We're not helpless. We're going to be all right." She said it as much for herself as for Legs.

From deep in the woods, perhaps a mile away, came that shrieking roar. *Her*, Virginia had said. If that beast had been something the Chicken Dealer had conjured with her cards, it likely would have disappeared when Virginia had, just like the ropes. Which meant that the monster must be real.

This was probably its home dimension. And maybe it wasn't the only one of its kind.

Ernie scanned her surroundings, which bore a vague similarity to the Irish coast, with a few stark differences. Apart from the strange green tint to the sky and the swampy, flat look of the ocean, the contours of the terrain had changed. But she still stood in an area bounded by low stone walls, and the countryside was streaked with them. She trudged over to the place where the earth fell away to the water. What had happened to Trey and Tarlae? Had her allies been banished here, too? Virginia had sent the lovers tumbling over the sheer cliff face. Ernie hadn't seen whether they'd made it back up. She looked over the edge. Below her was a thick gray fog nestled against jagged rocks.

"Hello?" she called, feeling guilty about the ping of hope in her chest—she shouldn't wish that her allies were in Virginia's "hell" with her, but she couldn't help it.

The brown ocean whispered to her from a hundred feet below, but the other Dealers didn't answer. Ernie doubted they'd been transported to this dimension, now that she thought about it—the area Virginia had zapped from one realm to another seemed to be small, limited to Gabe's haven and a thin strip of land surrounding it. Gabe, Trey, and Tarlae must still be on Earth, or the normal version of Earth, at least. She hoped they were working together at this very moment to defeat Virginia and get that pink rune from her so that they could come get Ernie.

She wouldn't mind being rescued right about now.

The monster in the woods roared again. Ernie could hear the distant crack of branches, or maybe entire tree trunks, splintering and breaking. The tree tops shook. "I think we need to get moving," Ernie told Legs. "I don't want to have to fight that thing out in the open by this cliff."

She shuffled through her deck to pull her Transport card. Beneath the symbol, an angular *R* drawn with only straight lines, lay an image of the patch of Irish coast where Gabe's haven had been. It couldn't be that easy, could it? Ernie closed her eyes, centering her thoughts on what she needed. The card pulsed like a static shock, and a bolt of pain streaked from her tattoo right up her arm. Ernie yelped, and the creature in the woods let out a terrible roar. She looked down at her Transport card again, which continued to taunt her with the image of the place she needed to get back to.

"Of *course* it isn't that easy," Ernie muttered. Besides, she was distracted right now. Her cards couldn't do their best for her if she couldn't focus.

Legs prickled sharply on Ernie's arm, but it wasn't as reassuring as it usually was. She wanted Legs to be a physical presence now, and obviously something about this dimension was making it hard for her to emerge. Even though Ernie knew she wasn't alone, she was lonely. And, okay, scared. She remembered her father telling her when she was a kid that if she got lost in the woods, she should wait in one place for him to find her instead of blundering around and getting herself even more lost. Well. She was lost now, and she needed Gabe and the others to find her.

They'd never just give up and leave her here.

Right?

As she considered how Tarlae seemed interested only in protecting Trey and herself, she had to wonder. When she remembered Minh laughing at her for having a sense of right and wrong, for wanting to help Alvarez, the doubt crept in. And as she thought about Gabe, how tired he was, how distant, how ready to let go and give up . . .

She clenched her fist around her deck. "No." Then, as her voice broke and her eyes stung with tears, she whispered, *"No."* Giving in to despair right now would be pathetic.

But as the woods echoed with the sound of that insect monster's rage, Ernie figured her father's advice to stay put and wait for a rescue might not apply in this situation. She wouldn't stray far, but she needed to find shelter—or create some. Then she would see whether her cards offered any answers for getting back home.

It felt better to have a plan, even a vague one. Ernie scanned the countryside. To her right were the woods where the monster raged. In front of her, craggy peaks rose in the distance. But to her left, between the peaks and the sea . . . was that a road? Ernie stepped over the broken stone wall where she'd last seen Gabe, dragging her fingers over the rocks' rough, slightly slimy surface and thinking of her final moments with him. She'd wanted to take the time to tell him how she'd missed him, how she was sorry for being so thoughtless and mean when he'd confessed that he wasn't sure he wanted a future. At the very least, they were friends, and he deserved so much better from her than what she'd offered him. She wasn't sure what the right words might have been, but hopefully she'd have the chance to figure it out.

Though she could see a dim, pale green sun high in the sky, which seemed to indicate it was around noon, the day felt like it had been condemned to permanent twilight. She tromped through high grass until she reached a stone wall that ran perpendicular to the maybe-road, then hopped up on it. Her boots were already sodden with muck; everything here seemed to have a thin coating of slime, and the air was damp. Her hair was a heavy frizz hanging down her back, so she pulled the band off her wrist and yanked her mane into a ponytail before picking her way along the top of the wall toward her destination.

When she finally reached it, she hopped down from the wall. She had indeed reached a road, nothing more than a wide dirt path that wound along the coast and curved out of sight behind a hill up ahead. There were tire tracks and boot prints in the dirt, too, telling her that she and the monster grasshopper weren't the place's only inhabitants. She hoped that was a good thing. Maybe the locals could tell her what that thing was and whether there were more of them.

Maybe they could tell her how to find Redmond Terwilliger, Dealer of the Dragonfly deck. Ernie set out along the road, casting a wary glance behind her every once in a while. No one had seen the Dragonfly Dealer in years, Minh had told her. Well, if Virginia had used that pink rune to banish her father here, that made sense. Perhaps he wasn't dead—perhaps he'd been trapped in this dimension for the last two decades.

Trapped here, but not helpless. He'd managed to send Ernie's mom some of the relics he'd found—or stolen. Ernie's mom had received all those packages, and Ernie herself had received nineteen postcards, their postmarks blurred or absent—starting two years after he'd left their family. Maybe he'd sent them from here, and they'd made their way back somehow. His postcards always held promises that he'd be home soon, that he was trying to find his way back to Ernie.

It all made a lot more sense now. Ernie's throat got tight as she considered how her father must have felt when he found himself here. But he hadn't given up. He'd found a way to break the boundaries between this place and home. He'd found a way, and Ernie would, too. Maybe even with her father at her side. The thought of bringing him back to her mother sped Ernie's steps. A long shot, maybe, but she'd faced terrible odds before.

"You're in quite a pickle, aren't you?"

Ernie yelped and jumped to the side as the Forger appeared next to her. He was wearing rain boots and a long raincoat, and he'd braided his dark hipster beard and secured it with a jeweled bauble that looked grossly out of place in this drab environment. "Holy crap, Andy," she said by way of a greeting.

"You remember my name! That's a good sign. Although you only just got here, so . . ."

Ernie scowled at him. "What the hell are you talking about?"

"Virginia's getting nervy, isn't she?" he asked, clasping his hands behind his back as he kept pace with her.

"'Nervy' isn't quite the word I'd use," Ernie said as her heart regained something close to a normal rhythm. "But she's certainly dead set on getting the Marks. And you know why she wants them, right?"

He tugged at his beard bauble. "You know, I'm starting to think she was a mistake. I liked her focus, her drive. That's why I gave her a deck. She was bloodthirsty from the beginning. Matron of a great family that lost it all in the 'War of Northern Aggression.'" He chuckled merrily, seeming to enjoy his use of air quotes. "Disgraced and destitute, but man, was she determined. I loved it."

It sounded familiar. "Gabe became a Dealer to save his family," she murmured, her brow furrowing as she thought back to the night he'd told her of his first encounter with the Forger.

"Oh, Virginia was nothing like Gabe. He has a disappointing lack of bloodthirstiness—I guess his little brother hogged it all. I liked that about Duncan." He gave her a sidelong glance. "But in the end, the ol' Diamondback and I were a bit too similar." He jostled her with his elbow, making her cards flash with a painful heat against her thigh. "You're a nice, refreshingly obedient substitute."

Gritting her teeth, Ernie shot an elbow back, hard, and the Forger laughed. "Oh! Roar, little fluffball, roar," he said with a grin. "I love feisty women."

Ernie considered rewarding him with another elbow but then realized the guy had the power to help her get home. She offered him a tight smile instead. "Virginia gives 'feisty' a bad name," she said. "And I certainly understand why you might have a few regrets about handing her a deck, given what she's done with it—and what she wants to do."

"I should have predicted it. She was willing to do anything to restore her family's name, and I gave her the chance! Was she grateful? Hell, no. And now I think she's getting just a tad too big for her knickers." He turned to Ernie. "So you're going to handle her for me, aren't you?" He nodded, the motion slow and deliberate, as if he was prompting Ernie to nod, too.

She did, eagerly. To handle Virginia, she needed to be in the same dimension as her. "I can do that," she said.

He squeezed her shoulder, making her cards pulse with static, which lanced through Ernie's leg. "Perfect. Keep your eye on the sunrise, dear. That's what you have to do if you want to stop her."

"I'll be happy to keep my eye on whatever you want as soon as you get me back home."

He groaned and shook his head, all mock hurt. "I thought you knew me, Ernestine!"

She wanted to yank that stupid bauble right off his stupid beard. "Okay, then why are you here, talking to me, if you're not even going to help?"

"I wanted to let you thank me while you still could."

"While I still . . ." She stopped dead. "Wait. Did you make this happen just so I could find out what happened to my dad?"

"That's a little simplistic. But I did lay down all the pieces."

"Cool . . . thanks? Now can you tell me where he is?"

"For a supposedly strong, independent woman, you sure do expect a lot of hand-holding."

Ernie rolled her eyes. "Virginia stranded my dad and me here with a rune *you* made. Least you could do would be to help me find him."

"I made many runes to entertain my Immortal Dealers. But it doesn't sound like you appreciate my toys, even though one of them saved your hide."

Ernie shoved aside her whirling thoughts to get to the memory—the antagonist rune that had turned the animals against their Dealers. "It came at the expense of proud and powerful spirits who deserve better."

"Where's the admiration for my genius? Your dad was better about that. He used that Dragonfly deck to go on a proper treasure hunt."

One that got him stranded here, apparently. "Seems like you made runes to set Dealers against each other."

"Seems to be working according to plan."

"And while we're all fighting each other, we leave you alone?"

"Brilliant, yes? My predecessor never thought of that. Her creations are all meant to help." He said it in a sniveling voice, each word dripping with contempt. "But that's not what running the universe is about, am I right? The guy who came before her—now *that* guy knew how to create some chaos."

"How did she take him down, then?"

"Ugh. He just got tired of immortality and handed the throne to her. Thought she'd be a good caretaker. Can you believe that?"

"Yeah," Ernie said in a strained voice, thinking of Gabe.

"I've got no respect for that," Andy was saying. "I like a person who doesn't give up in a fight." He patted her on the shoulder, making her flinch. "Like you, Ernestine. You've got steel in your spine, even if you do whine a bit too much for my liking. So I'm here to offer you a deal." He smiled with apparent satisfaction when he saw Ernie's eyebrows rise with hope and interest. "If you make sure Virginia never enjoys the beautiful sunrise, I'll make the Kestrel a new Wild card to complete his deck. You'd like that, wouldn't you?"

"Virginia," Ernie said. "You want me to kill her?"

The Forger was watching her closely now, amusement brightening his gaze. "That's not what I said, but sure, if you want to, I wouldn't hold it against you."

67

"Why are you asking me and not, I don't know—someone who's more experienced *and* not trapped . . . here?" Where was she, exactly?

"Motivation for days!" he said, clapping his hands. "So break some eggs! Let's get this party started! Can't wait to see what happens!" He turned to her, and Ernie shivered as she watched his blue eyes bleed to black. Eyes were not supposed to do that. It wasn't normal. When he spoke again, his voice was eerily low, and each word vibrated along her bones. "*This* you will remember: Don't disappoint me, Ernestine. Virginia trapped you here. She trapped your father here. And she deserves to be punished. I allowed you to become an Immortal Dealer for a reason, and now you'll show me what you've really got." He leaned toward her, fixing her with his obsidian gaze. "Use everything you have, *including that magic deck in your pocket*, to keep her from ever laying eyes on the sunrise." He gave her a gorgeous smile soaked in menace. "Or I'll show you what chaos really means."

He vanished, leaving Ernie trembling in the middle of the road, trying to sort through what he'd just told her, trying to hold on to every word. It seemed to be good news, right? If there was no way home, he wouldn't have challenged her to take out Virginia. If there was no way to win, he wouldn't have issued the challenge—she hoped. He wanted her to make sure Virginia never saw another sunrise, or however he'd put it. And though Ernie didn't consider herself a killer, as she thought of what the Chicken Dealer had taken from her, she thought the old woman probably deserved to die. The new purpose—and the whisper of hope it brought—strengthened her as she resumed her hike.

When she rounded the massive hill, she let out a cry of relief. A village lay perhaps a mile ahead. The perfect place for her to try to get an understanding of how things worked here and for her to experiment a little with the deck of cards in her pocket. There had to be a way out of this dimension; she knew that now. She marched along, taking in the drab wilderness around her, now marked with some signs of human habitation. Or at least, she assumed so. A large metal box the size of a ranch house sat out in one of the fields. From the road, she could just make out the large padlock that connected the wide double doors.

From inside came a faint baa.

It was a barn. A padlocked metal barn. She saw several of them in the fields as she neared the village, but not a single animal was out for an afternoon of grazing. Ernie wondered whether that had anything to do with the grasshopper monster in the woods. As she reached the edge of the village, her suspicions became stronger. The buildings were also made of metal, all of them windowless, some of them mounted with wicked-looking rebar spikes. The structures were set on either side of the road, which had widened slightly. Ernie paused and listened. The place was eerily quiet.

She drew her cards. They felt like a talisman against any danger, as did her diamondback tattoo. Ernie focused on a memory of the serpent slithering off her arm on her mother's porch, almost like something out of a dream. As if in response, the tattoo flashed with pain, making Ernie grimace—but reminding her that she needed to concentrate. Grit crunched beneath her soles as she walked deeper into the little town. An acrid smell hung over the place, one that clung to the roof of her mouth, offering her the sharp tang of iron. The lights she'd seen were from lanterns, not electric bulbs. They'd been strung along the outside of the buildings.

Ernie paused as she came to a structure that had collapsed. Or been crushed. Within, she could see the ruins of a table and chairs. She turned in place, taking everything in. "Hello?" she called.

She was greeted by a distant cry, and she jogged toward the source of the noise. Past block after block of squat metal buildings, no windows, sturdy doors, all quiet. "Hello?" she shouted again.

"Here," came the faint, echoing reply. It sounded like a guy, but his voice was high and tremulous. "I'm down here!"

Ernie ran a few more blocks toward the sound of the man's voice, until the buildings opened up abruptly into a wide square. At its center was a round, fenced . . . pit? She slowed to a walk and looked around, trying to shake off a serious case of the creeps. The place seemed uninhabited, except for the desperate calls for help that were definitely coming from inside that pit. Ernie reached the waist-high wooden fence, the only thing that seemed to be made of wood in the whole village, and swung herself over.

She peered over the edge. At the bottom of the pit, about thirty feet down, sat a young man with shaggy, dark blond hair. He was cradling his left arm as if it was broken, and he was looking up at her with pleading in his eyes. "I swear, I'll never do it again. Please." His accent was a flat twang, almost midwestern, definitely not Irish. But he spoke English, and for that Ernie was grateful.

"What did you do, exactly?" she asked.

The young man blinked at her. "You're not from here."

"You're not kidding."

"Kidding?" He looked baffled. "Of course I'm not. I'm not even matched yet."

Whatever that meant. "Never mind. I'm wondering why you're in this pit." It seemed unlikely he'd just randomly fallen in, what with the fence and all.

"Happy to tell you if you pull me out. Have you a rope?"

"I've been around the block a time or two, dude. And I don't know the laws around here, so . . ." If he was some child molester or something, she wouldn't be ingratiating herself with the locals if she set him free.

"*Around* the block? Which block? Why would you do that at this time of day?"

"Ugh. Just tell me why you're down there."

"It was one extra bottle! That was all!"

"Of . . . ?"

He looked at her as if she were crazy. "*Water.* I don't wish for death." He bowed his head and chuckled. "Though I guess that's what I'm getting."

"You stole some water? That's it?"

"Just get me up if you can! Please! I don't want to die!"

Ernie drew her deck of cards. "Hang on." She felt a little strange, gazing at the familiar yet foreign symbols. She had a feeling she should know each of them by heart, but her thoughts were like sludge, and the meaning of each came to her a second later than she wanted it to. Finally, she pulled her Aid card, along with her Tool card, and pictured a sturdy rope ladder.

Nothing happened. Ernie peered at her cards. Had she gotten it wrong? Beneath the symbols lay faint, foggy images, and that didn't seem right.

"Get some rope or a ladder or something. Hurry!"

"Dude. Give me a second," Ernie snapped, sweat breaking out at her temples as she focused on the cards, trying to summon what she needed. "Legs?" she asked quietly. It seemed strange, talking to her tattoo, but she knew the diamondback was in there somewhere. "Can you help me?"

She heard the footsteps a fraction of a second before a hard shove sent her tumbling into empty space. Her cards flew from her hand. Her arms pinwheeled as she fell. She hit the side of the pit, which was slick and muddy, and slid the rest of the way down, landing in a sprawl at the bottom.

Aching and breathless from the impact, Ernie looked up. Standing at the edge of the pit, framed by the green sky, was a dark form whose face she couldn't see. "The penalty for helping a convict is sharing his fate," the person shouted in an obviously male voice.

"Well, I didn't know that," Ernie yelled back, pushing herself to her feet. "How about—"

The figure moved out of sight. Ernie cursed and turned to her water-stealing companion. Dressed in stained, old-fashioned-looking britches and a tunic of rough brown cloth, he was crouched at the opposite side of the pit, which was maybe twenty feet across.

And he was holding a handful of her cards, gazing down at them in horror. "I-I've heard about these. My uncle told me the stories. You're like *her*," he said in a shrill voice. With shaking hands, he tried to rip them up.

Ernie tackled him, brutal and hard. "Those. Are. *Mine*," she growled, her arms wrapped around his skinny frame, her fingers already clutching at her cards.

With strength born of panic, he twisted in her grip and elbowed her in the face. She grunted and rolled off him, then shoved herself to her feet and kicked him in the balls. He curled into the fetal position, groaning. Cursing under her breath, Ernie quickly gathered her cards. "I tried to help you, and the first thing you do is steal my cards and try to destroy them? Now I get why you're down here."

It wasn't a nice thing to say, but her whole body hurt, her cheek was throbbing, she was covered with mud, and the hope that had carried her over the miles to this village had been squashed under the weight of this dystopian reality. The insane old lady who'd stranded Ernie here had called it hell, and Ernie had just about decided she was right.

The guy's shoulders shook, and he was letting out sniffly little cries. "I thought—I thought—"

"I don't care what you thought. If you touch my cards again, you'll get more of the same. Don't mess with me today." She wiped a few of her cards on her pant leg, trying to clean them off a bit before looking around. The walls of the pit were oozy and wet. She touched the surface. Almost like clay, too slippery and forgiving to climb.

She needed that rope ladder now. On instinct, she opened her palm, expecting the right cards to pull themselves from the deck and land in her hand, but the deck was quiet and unresponsive. "What the hell is happening?" she whispered.

She glanced at her companion, who had scuttled over against the opposite wall and was watching her intently. Maybe her concentration was just shot. It had been a rough day by any standard. Or maybe she was doing it wrong? Every time she tried to remember how to play her cards, it felt like trying to grab a reflection on the water. "You stay where you are, all right? I'm busy."

The guy kept quiet, but his eyes were bright, and his focus was on her deck. "If anyone in town sees you with those, they'll kill you."

"Yeah? Then why'd you try to take them?"

"If I turned you in or destroyed the cards, they might have let me go."

"Wow, you're really giving me an incentive to help you out of this pit."

The thief leaned forward, his eyes glittering in the almost darkness. "If you know her, you can save us. You can tell her I'm not the enemy. *They* are."

"*Who?*"

His next words were cut off by a crashing sound, like someone banging a giant gong over and over. A horn joined the cacophony, adding sharp bleats of alarm. "Oh, gods," the thief cried, covering his head with his one good arm. "It's too late!"

"What is it?" shouted Ernie. "What—"

A shadow blotted out what little light there was. Ernie dove for the edge of the pit as something huge landed in the hole with them and let out a now-familiar roaring shriek. In the enclosed space, it made her ears ring, but she could still make out her companion's screams. Warm liquid splattered on Ernie's face as he fell silent.

The creature went quiet, too. The gong was still crashing and the horn was still blatting, but it didn't stop Ernie from hearing the sound of bones crunching.

The monster had its back to her. Ernie was right next to its barbed back legs. The bottom of the pit was just large enough to fit the creature, with a few feet to spare. Ernie shifted to the side, quietly as she could, to see the grasshopper chowing down. Her stomach turning, she clutched her cards, silently pleading. She needed to be somewhere else. Anywhere else. And the cards could take her there. She pulled the Transport card she'd tried to play when she first arrived and focused on the picture within, a grassy patch of coast overlooking a sapphire sea. It looked peaceful and lovely, especially when she felt so on edge, so desperate—that perfect little meadow was exactly where she wanted to be right then. It looked like something out of a dream.

The cards didn't answer her call. All of them were cool to the touch. But the tattoo—*Legs*—was right there on Ernie's arm, tingling in stinging pulses. It didn't change anything, though. The grasshopper creature moved to scoop up another mouthful of the doomed thief. Its leg brushed hers, and Ernie had to bite back a cry. She looked down to realize her pants were torn, revealing a stinging wound. She'd fought this creature before. She knew she had.

Why couldn't she remember it?

The monster grunted and turned its body first, then its head—and saw her. Its wide black eyes met hers, and its mouth opened, revealing rows of razor-sharp teeth edged with blood. For a moment there was nothing but tense silence between them, but then the thing let out a ferocious roar, sending slime billowing forth from its mouth. Ernie dove to the side to avoid getting hit. She looked around frantically. There was nothing in this pit she could use to defend herself. No sticks or rocks. No weapons.

And her cards were useless. For all she knew, she wasn't even immortal here. For all she knew, right now she was an ordinary person. Vulnerable. Killable.

Edible.

She backed herself up against the wall of the pit as the elephant-sized grasshopper swung its long body around to face her head-on. Muscles surging with adrenaline, Ernie widened her stance and shoved her cards in her pocket. She'd fight as long as she could.

The creature was staring at her now. Ernie had no idea what was on its mind, whether it recognized her, or whether it just saw her as a hunk of meat. For all she knew, this wasn't the same beast she'd faced before. The countryside might be infested with them, but all that mattered was the one about to eat her. She tried not to think about how it would feel when those teeth sank in. Selfishly, Ernie prayed that Legs would appear and grow huge, her fangs dripping with venom, her rattle warning of impending death. She swore she had a memory of it happening before. But if her diamondback wanted to fight, she'd be slithering off Ernie's arm right now. Instead, the tattoo was pulsing so frantically that it felt like Ernie's skin was about to split. Maybe Legs *couldn't* fight right now.

Which meant Ernie was on her own, and the creature was still watching her. What the hell. "Hi," she said to it. "The people in this village are nasty. Maybe you'd rather go eat one of them?"

Bloody slime dripped from the thing's mouth. Its lidless eyes regarded her coldly, which sort of reminded her of Legs.

Ernie blew out a shaky breath. "You're rather majestic," she said to it. "I mean, in a terrifying sort of way, but still."

It lurched toward her, and Ernie jerked back, her hands up to shield her face. "I'm sure you have a beautiful soul and are just very badly misunderstood," she babbled in a squeaky voice.

A tremor seemed to shake the thing from inside. Ernie felt the vibrations beneath her feet and clutched at the pit's walls. The creature made a grunting, choking noise. It swung its head from side to side, as if it were trying to shake something loose, and stomped its feet, leaving deep gouges in the mud. The choking noise grew louder, and the thing's body heaved, contorting.

"Hey!" shouted someone from above, another man, different from the one who'd shoved her into the pit.

The creature looked up and roared. Ernie craned her neck to see a broad-shouldered figure leaning over the side of the pit. "Hey, you great, bloody thing! I'll give you something to chew on!"

The monster had apparently heard enough. It reared back on its hind legs and leapt straight up, clearing the edge of the pit with yards to spare. The man at the top disappeared out of view, leaving Ernie to listen to the creature's earsplitting roar. She looked around, wincing as she saw what little remained of the thief.

The monster went silent again, and Ernie sagged against the walls of her prison. Was it eating that guy? Would it come back to finish her off as well?

A falling rope ladder smacked the rest of the questions right out of her head. Ernie staggered as a gruff voice from above said, "Climb up. She's gone."

Trembling from the terror of the last few minutes, Ernie obeyed.

CHAPTER SEVEN

As she climbed the rope ladder, Ernie thought about what the thief had told her. It sounded like people here had something against her cards. Keeping them hidden could be critical, especially since they didn't seem to be working properly—they couldn't protect her now, and she'd have to wait until she was on her own again to figure that out.

But that wasn't the only issue the thief had raised. He'd said Ernie was like "her." Another person with cards? Andy, the Forger, had called her an Immortal Dealer and reminded her that her father was one as well. The Dragonfly. Maybe the "her" the thief had mentioned knew him or what had happened to him. It might be a long shot, but Ernie was more determined than ever to find her father. So many things seemed foggy and uncertain right now, but the memories of her father were clear, deeply embedded in her mind, stitched into her very marrow.

If he was here, she could find him, and she could get them both . . . home. *Home.* Asheville. Where her mother was waiting. Yes. The thoughts steadied her upward pulls, her steps on the gently swinging ladder. It was hard work, but her muscles responded to the test, and she'd faced physical challenges like this in the past. It felt good and familiar, actually, as if her body were a machine, strong and steady even when her mind was a bit foggy. It took her only a minute or two to make it to the top, ready to meet her rescuer.

He was squatting near the fence, peering between the slats, his broad shoulders hunched. He didn't turn in her direction when she heaved herself over the edge. "Hey, thanks for the assist," she said. "I owe you one."

"One what? Are you hurt?" His voice was rough. Gravelly. Like a pack-a-day smoker. His accent wasn't Irish, either, as far as she could tell, but his vowels were rounder than the thief's.

"I'm fine, thanks to you."

"Then we should go. This is a bad place." He got to his feet, revealing that he was well over six feet tall, and turned toward her. He wore what looked like a ski mask made of rough fabric, holes cut only for the eyes, and a wide-brimmed hat pulled low so she could barely see them anyway. His hands were encased in leather gloves, and on his feet were heavily scuffed boots. He had a machete strapped to his back, its handle protruding just behind his left shoulder, and a strange-looking gun with a long, narrow barrel holstered to a thick belt around his waist.

Maybe he'd used those to drive the monster away, but she hadn't heard gunshots. He took a step toward her, and Ernie took a step back.

He put his hands up. "I'm hardly going to push you back in after I helped you up."

"Fair point." She looked around. "Where did the thing go?"

"Away, for now."

Ernie squinted through the haze, trying to see whether it had left tracks. "I think I'm going to head in the opposite direction of 'away,' if it's all the same to you."

"Opposites are never the same to me, but go any way you like. Although—you seem a mite *uninformed* as to the state of things. You'll be safer if you let me shelter you until sunrise."

Sunrise. She wasn't supposed to let Virginia lay eyes on the sunrise. And Virginia wasn't here—she was in another dimension. The one Ernie had come from. *Home.* For a second, she was caught in the churn of her own mind but then realized her rescuer was waiting for a reply. She scanned the windowless metal houses that rimmed the square. The last thing she wanted to do was get into a situation she couldn't escape from.

The stranger appeared to read the uncertainty in her gaze. "My shelter is not in this village."

She eyed him, considering. He'd just stopped her from being torn to pieces, and then he'd helped her escape the pit. But for all she knew, that was because he planned to sell her to the townspeople or eat her or something. He was right when he said she didn't know how things worked here. "How far is it?"

"Up in the hills. If you want to take your chances here, you may do that." He gestured down at the pit, then swung a long leg over the fence. "But I'm leaving before the mob comes out."

"Sounds like a plan."

He paused. "Because it *is* a plan."

"Never mind." Ernie climbed over the fence and walked next to him as he strode swiftly down the main road. The town was as quiet as it had been when she'd arrived, but there had to be plenty of people around . . . *somewhere*. "What's up with this place?"

He looked up at the sky.

"No," she clarified. "I meant, what's going on here? Is everyone hiding?"

"They're all scared, not that I blame them. But scared folk do scared things."

Ernie's stomach tightened as she caught sight of the first village inhabitant she'd seen outside of the thief and the dude who'd shoved her into the pit. A middle-aged woman in simple brown pants and a woven poncho stood next to the heavy metal door of one of the houses, holding a bucket of water in one hand and a gun in the other.

"Better get inside," she said, staring at a spot about two feet in front of Ernie and her new friend. "It might come back."

"Don't answer her," he said quietly.

"Seems rude," Ernie muttered.

"But it is not."

They passed by the woman without incident, but Ernie couldn't shake off the eerie stillness, the sense of doom that hung over the place. As they reached the edge of the village proper, her companion veered off the road onto a narrow footpath that led through an overgrown field of dry brown grass. He drew his machete as he walked.

"Afraid of an ambush?"

"It is wise to be ready."

Now Ernie badly wished she had a machete, too. Could she create one with the cards? She was almost certain she could . . . at one time. Now the deck was cold and silent in her pocket, and Legs was acting like a normal tattoo instead of the terrifyingly powerful animal spirit Ernie was sure she'd been before. She was an Immortal Dealer. The Diamondback. But right now she was feeling more vulnerable than she ever had. At least, she thought so.

They reached a dry creek bed, after which the trail opened up and wove between rocky outcroppings as it guided them uphill. The stench was less pungent here, and the ocean was a vast, dark shape off to her right, helping her stay oriented. The spot where she'd been when she arrived in this place was only a few miles away. She could probably get there in an hour or so if she ran. It was almost tempting to try, just to feel the comfort of hard exertion again. But it seemed safer to stay with her rescuer. Assuming he didn't plan to chop her up and turn her into jerky as soon as he got her back to his lair. "My name's Ernie, by the way," she said to him as her heart beat a little faster.

He didn't turn around. "Well met, Ernie-by-the-way."

"Just Ernie." After a solid minute of silence, she tried again. "Can I ask your name?"

"Yes."

She rolled her eyes. "What do you want me to call you?"

"Why must you call me something?"

"Seems friendlier."

"Are we friends?"

"No idea, bub," she said, irritation creeping into her voice. "Not sure how this works."

"I don't have friends anymore."

Not reassuring. "What happened to them?"

"Nothing good."

"Then maybe I should think twice before being your friend."

"You may think about it as often as you like, but it would not change reality." He sheathed the machete and turned off the path to trek up a slide of loose rock. "Careful here."

Ernie followed, bemused. He cared whether she tumbled down a hill, but not enough to tell her his name. "Where I come from, your friends aren't the only ones who know your name."

"I don't want my enemies to know my name."

"You have a lot of those?"

He laughed and swept his arm upward. "We're getting close. Top of the hill."

Ernie was panting now, less eager for the thrill of exertion. It had been a long day, and the path was like a steep flight of stairs now, marching toward the top. "Are you sure this hill isn't a mountain?"

"Does it matter what it's called?"

"You're not big on linguistic precision, are you?"

"Who has the time for such things?" His tone had warmed with amusement.

Ernie smiled. He had a sense of humor, which made him seem more human. "What's with the mask?"

"My face is with the mask. You ask very unusual questions."

Ernie snorted and tried to keep up. When he reached the top of the hill, he drew his machete again and began to hike along the rocky ridge that defined the peak. The land stretched out for miles on either side, though in the distance, another few villages could be seen, clusters of lights in the gloom. The one she'd just escaped was lit up brightly as the daylight faded, flames glinting off gray metal. It was almost sundown, and she'd been here for hours already.

She would be missed. A pair of blue eyes flashed in her memory. It quickened her breath, but it took several seconds for her to pull his name from the haze of hunger and thirst and exhaustion and fear. *Gabe.* Her steps stuttered to a halt as she thought about what had happened, but it was as if it had all taken place years ago, not earlier that day. He had been urging her to escape and leave him behind. Was that what she had done? Had she left him?

He wasn't the only one, either. "Oh, damn," Ernie whispered, a lump forming in her throat at the rush of memories. Her dad had abandoned them, and her mom had fallen apart. Ernie was the only thing holding her together, and now she was gone, too.

"Best keep moving, now," her rescuer called from several yards ahead, jerking Ernie from her thoughts.

She quickly swiped away tears as she reached a rocky hillock that jutted up from the peak of the ridge. Her mysterious companion picked his way between jagged rocks, disappearing quickly. Ernie jogged to catch up, her shoulders bumping on stone as she made her way through. Just as she lost sight of the ridge behind her, the close-set rocks opened up and became a small cave, lit by a few lanterns perched on outcroppings in the stone walls. There was a large wooden trunk at the back, and in front of it was a jumble of woven blankets. Dried animal carcasses hung from a rack that took up most of the wall to her left. "I wasn't so far off about the jerky," she muttered.

Her companion had to duck as he walked to the back of his hovel. He scooped up a blanket and tossed it at her. "Do you need to eat?"

She glanced at the dead animals. "I'm a vegetarian," she said quickly.

"Me too."

Her eyebrows rose. "I've noticed words and phrases don't have quite the same meaning in these here parts, but—"

"Those are for trading," he said with a jerk of his thumb toward the carcass wall. "And bait."

"Bait. For . . . ?"

"Yes." He opened the trunk and pulled out a large jar, obviously handblown, with thick glass sides. It was filled with orange and yellow chunks of *something* suspended in a yellowish-brown liquid. He set it down with a quiet chink on the stone floor of the space, then looked up at Ernie. "You going to stand all night?"

Ernie sat down on the blanket he'd chucked at her. "What's that?" she asked as he opened the jar and her nose filled with the unmistakable scent of vinegar. "It's pickled."

"Keeps it from going bad. Potatoes. Carrots. Turnips. Good enough."

"I guess so. You look pretty healthy. Except, I don't understand *how* you eat, seeing as you have no mouth hole in that fabulous getup."

"I'd prefer to sit down at the moment. As for the mask, it is best not to let the locals in Honeida get a good view, as they are so suspicious of outsiders. I stand out." He took off his hat and pulled the baggy mask off his head, revealing a strong jaw, keen brown eyes, close-cropped black curls, and very brown skin. He watched her as if he expected her to freak out or something.

"You realize that you're about six and a half feet tall, right? I hate to tell you, but the best costume in the world is not exactly going to help you blend."

His face split into a smile that made Ernie feel like she'd just won a prize at the county fair. "You underestimate me. I have some *very* good disguises."

Ernie laughed, relieved to be sitting here in this place, safe for the moment, with an actual human companion. "So—you're not a local?"

"Nah. But I've been here a long time."

"Any reason why you're hiding up here all alone?"

"It's a good defensible spot. Those stupids in the village, they cluster together in a group and wait for death to find them. She always does, too."

"Did they put that guy in the pit, knowing that thing would come and eat him?"

He rubbed at the stubble on his jaw with the backs of his fingers. "They try to keep her happy that way. Doesn't work. All superstition."

"*She* didn't seem like a superstition."

"I mean they're just trying to make up rules to help themselves feel more powerful. Rules for behaving, rules for eating, rules for water, rules for everything. You break a rule, you go in the pit, and you are her meal for the day."

"How is that even allowed?"

"Allowed by whom?"

"Aren't there laws?"

His dark eyes narrowed. "Where did you say you were from, Ernie?" He said her name like it tasted funny.

"The South," she said quickly.

He arched an eyebrow. "Oh? Me too. Aberida. You?"

"*Waaay* down south," she said, directing her attention to the pickle jar as her heart beat a little faster. "Tiny town. You wouldn't have heard of it."

"My hearing is excellent, and I listen well."

"I'm from Woodfin," she mumbled, leaning over the pickled vegetables. Her appetite had disappeared, but she needed to steer this conversation elsewhere. "Did you make these yourself?"

"Traded for them. Woodfin, you say?"

Ernie's head snapped up, and their eyes met. "Yeah?"

The lanterns cast long, eerie shadows across his face, and his expression gave nothing away as he considered her. "Not sure if I know the place," he finally said, looking away from her to rummage in his trunk. He came up holding a metal plate and a long, forked prong, which he stabbed into the vegetables. The carrots and potatoes and turnips slid off the prong and onto the plate with wet plops, and when he'd formed a little pile, he set it between them. "You may eat."

Ernie gingerly picked up a carrot and gave it an experimental bite, trying not to grimace at the pungent sting of vinegar. "That really clears the sinuses," she said. "So—you said you're from Aberida. How long have you been up here?" She assumed that if he was from the "South," then this was the "North," but really, she was flailing in the dark.

"Long time." His mouth was full of turnip. "Never meant to stay."

"Why did you?"

He ran his tongue over his teeth, reached back into his trunk, and pulled out a jug and a metal cup. "It is not an interesting story." He poured out a measure of clear liquid, sniffed at it, and took a healthy gulp before offering it to her.

Ernie accepted it and took a whiff, but it didn't give off much of a smell. Still, if he were trying to roofie her, he probably wouldn't have just downed half of it himself. "What is it?"

"It is good for cleaning weapons and for killing bugs in the stomach."

"Bugs?" With a suspicious glance at the pickle jar, she lifted the cup to her lips and took a healthy sip. The moment it rolled down her throat, her mouth filled with a harsh burn, ten times worse than the vinegar. She coughed, her cheeks burning. "Whoa," she said hoarsely, handing the cup back to him. "That's . . . distinctive."

"Good for killing bad dreams, too." He gulped down the rest of the cup, poured a little more, and set it next to the plate. "Where are you going from here?"

She took a few bites of pickled potato as she mulled it over. She had a vague feeling she was supposed to be somewhere, the place where she'd arrived in this dimension. But . . . "I'm actually looking for someone." She glanced up at her companion. A slice of light had fallen across his eyes, making it look as if he were wearing another mask. "He's from Woodfin, too."

Her companion paused as he reached for something on the plate, then he reversed course and went for the cup. "That is interesting."

"You said you might have heard of the place."

"I said I didn't know if I'd heard of the place."

"He came to this area a while back. Maybe you've run into him?"

He took a sip from the cup. "I do not run into people."

"His name's Redmond. Redmond Terwilliger."

He laughed, a rough, throaty rumble. "Funny name."

"Says the man who doesn't have one."

"Oh, I have one. It's just out of use."

"We could blow the dust off and give it a try, seeing as we're sharing dinner and a drink here. All friendly like—but not actually friends, of course."

He looked around. "Blowing will only cause the dust to coat our food and our throats, so I advise against it. And my name is Kotleho," he said with a small smile, which he covered by lifting the cup to his lips again. "You may call me Kot."

"Short and sweet."

"I am neither."

"So *have* you run into Redmond, by any chance? He's late thirties. He wears glasses. Long hair, though I guess he might have cut it." Wait. He wouldn't be late thirties anymore. He'd gone missing twenty years ago. "He may look older than that, though." Would he? Wasn't he an Immortal Dealer? Wasn't that what Andy had said? "Or younger." She cringed as Kot gave her a skeptical look. "I haven't seen him in a while."

"Why are you looking for him?" he asked.

"He's my father."

Kot bowed his head and considered the contents of his cup. "No," he said after a painfully long moment. "Never met anyone by that name."

Ernie slumped. She wasn't sure she believed him, but considering all the people who probably lived in this strange, desolate place, it *was* unlikely she'd run into one who'd known her dad. And for all she knew, Dad could be anywhere in this dimension now. He'd certainly had plenty of time to travel. "Do you have family around here?"

Kot shook his head. "Never had much family."

"If you don't have family, what's keeping you here? I mean, I agree with what you said earlier. This seems like a bad place."

"I can't leave until I catch her."

"Her? You mean the elephant-sized monster insect who rips people to shreds?" Though she knew it was unwise, Ernie took another mouthful of the grain alcohol to chase away the memories of what the beast had done to that thief in the pit. When she'd finished with the coughing and cleared her throat, she said, "Is there a way to kill her?"

"Nuria cannot be killed."

Ernie flinched at his sudden harsh tone. "Okay . . . you've *named* her?"

"No, she *has* a name." Kot had turned back to his trunk and was putting the jar of pickled vegetables away. Very slowly, like he needed the time. "I'll catch her someday," he said. "In the meantime, I do what I can to reduce the damage she does. And that is a big job."

"That's why you were in the village."

"Today was a bad day. I knew she would come if those stupids offered her a meal."

"A bad day . . ." Ernie had the sneaking suspicion that she had been part of why the monster's day was so bad. "Seems like she deserves a bunch of bad days, honestly."

Kot gave her a solemn look. "When Nuria has bad days, she makes the people of this land suffer. I doubt the town of Honeida was like this before she came here. Those who could leave have left. Those who couldn't . . . They wait for her to come and destroy them, and in the meantime, they destroy each other."

"What is she? They don't have bugs like that where I come from."

"She's not a *bug*."

"How do you even know she's a she?"

Kot scoffed. "It's fairly obvious, I would say."

Virginia had described the beast as female, too, so maybe they knew something about insect anatomy that Ernie didn't. "Why's this on you, though? Are you responsible for setting her loose or something?" Ernie's head was feeling a little swimmy. She reached down and put her hand over the lump of her deck in her pocket, needing to make sure the cards were still there. They'd been sickeningly cold.

"Nothing is on me except my clothing, and I didn't bring her here," Kot murmured. "She was here before I came to this place." He leaned back on his hands and gazed at the low ceiling of his hovel as if it were strewn with stars. "Someday, I'll get her. Someday, I'll make it all right." He heaved a sigh. "But not tonight." He sat up and put the jug away. Hunched over his open trunk with his back to her, he added, "Now you will go to sleep."

Ernie opened her mouth to ask more questions, but the words faded to black, along with everything else.

CHAPTER EIGHT

Ernie jerked awake in complete darkness and lay tense and still, listening to the loud snores coming from somewhere to her left.

Which meant she needed to head to the right. Away from Kot, who had probably roofied her after all. A jolt of panic sent her hand into her pocket. Her clothes were all on—muddy jacket, muddy jeans, muddy boots—and her cards were still there, safe and sound though cool to the touch. She sat up and put her hands out, groping for barriers or traps in the murk. Feeling nothing, she carefully crawled away from the slumbering man, toward the exit of the small cave. When her fingertips hit stone, she got up, sliding her palms along the rock and finding the place she could squeeze herself through. After a few minutes, she saw sickly green daylight above her, and a few minutes after that, she was standing atop the ridge, looking out on the valley, with the cave behind her.

She rubbed her face, knocking away the sleep. Had that drink been drugged? She chuckled. It probably didn't need to be, seeing as it had been the moonshiniest moonshine she'd ever laid mouth on. She hadn't had more than two sips, though. What the heck had happened?

She looked down at herself, running her hands down her body. Didn't seem like he'd done anything to her. He apparently hadn't even searched her pockets, or if he had, he hadn't thought her cards were worth taking. A relief, considering how the thief in town had attempted to rip them up. She pulled up her sleeve and looked down at Legs. Her arm pulsed, strong but less painful than it had been. It felt like the tattoo was calling to her somehow, but she wasn't sure what she was supposed to do with that knowledge.

A cool, swampy wind was blowing fiercely off the sea. It pulled her hair from its sloppy ponytail and whipped it around her head. Scowling, she put her hair up again as she surveyed the land and the sky. The sun was rising beyond the village of Honeida to her right, so that must be the east—unless the sun was also different in this dimension? Not that it mattered, since she could still use it to orient herself. The spot where she'd first arrived here was to the west, then, and the sea was to the north. A narrow trail led directly down the hill to the west, but at the base of the slope, between Ernie and her arrival spot, sprawled the woods where the monster Kot had called Nuria had been hiding out yesterday.

Where do I go now? Not back to Honeida. And she had no idea where to look for her father. Her gaze returned to the west, to the first place she remembered seeing green sky and brown sea. Instantly, her heart pounded at the memory. Virginia. Ropes binding her arms. A feeling of rage. And hope. And loss. She'd wanted to stay in that spot. She'd hoped someone would find her there. Someone who cared. Those blue eyes . . . Ernie growled with frustration as she tried to bring him to mind. Because it was a him, she was certain. If she returned to that place where she'd first been lost, would he be waiting?

And was there anywhere else to go, really? It wouldn't hurt to start there. But either she needed to go all the way around the woods, or she needed to get her damn cards to respond to her. Glancing behind her and then down at the wide swath of forested valley, Ernie headed along the ridge, with the wind gusting against her body as if it were trying to shove her right back to the cave. She badly needed to pee, so she did her business behind a boulder and scrambled across the grass, back to the path. Her stomach grumbled and her head ached. Her boots slid in the loose scree, sending her sliding a few feet with each step and coating her already filthy jeans with a thick layer of dust. She craved flat ground and a well-maintained trail. Running was so much easier when she didn't have to calculate every step or risk a broken ankle or a fatal tumble down a steep and rocky slope.

After fighting the wind for what felt like an hour but was probably half that, Ernie figured she was far enough from Kot's cave to find a safe spot and experiment with her deck. The ridge was lined with deep creases in the rock, and when she reached one deep and wide enough to keep her out of sight, she climbed into it and pulled out her cards again. Legs tingled on her arm. Ernie fanned her cards, which rippled with warmth. Her heart leapt—this felt right. And there! There was the card she needed . . . Transport. That's what it was. She slipped it from the deck.

It went cold as soon as she looked at its face. Ernie frowned at the vaguely familiar landscape beneath the symbol: bright sunshine, blue ocean, emerald grass. Was it showing her where she needed to go, or had it simply frozen when she'd been transported here? She shuffled through the other cards. Most of them seemed frozen as well, the images under each symbol either blurred or fixed in tableaux that struck chords within her mind but never a full symphony of memory. She struggled to remember the uses of some cards, but a brush of her fingertips over their symbols usually brought them back, like a whisper in her ear.

Tool—it showed a device that looked like a fire extinguisher, but with a skull and crossbones symbol on it. Wisdom showed an old woman wearing a bridal veil—Virginia. Chameleon revealed an old man in a grimy trench coat. He had a face deeply shadowed with stubble and a large paunch, and she had no idea who he was. Mirage and Deceive showed the same man, for some reason. But Friend-Lover— her breath caught. Beneath its skeleton key symbol was an image of a younger man with long dirty-blond hair and a rough-hewn face. She was sure she recognized *him*. He stared up at her with achingly deep blue eyes, as if he were about to reach up and stroke her face. But the image didn't move; it was like a photograph snapped during a moment of intense feeling. She stared without blinking. She knew him. She was connected to him.

But she couldn't remember his name, no matter how hard she tried. She pressed her fingers to the card and tried to bring him, all of him, to mind. The symbol tingled against her skin, but nothing else happened. She swallowed, wincing at the stale taste in her mouth. Did the cards just not work here, or was *she* the problem? She knew she was off-kilter, probably dehydrated and definitely tired, and needed to focus a little more. The cards had definitely emanated some warmth—the battery wasn't completely dead—so maybe it would all come together if she could get into the right state of mind.

She refocused on the Friend-Lover card and hoped she wasn't imagining the little trickles of heat running along its symbol. Her tattoo rippled with stinging prickles, and the card pulsed in Ernie's palm. For a moment, she felt the brush of a hand on her cheek, and her nose filled with a deep, masculine scent, earth and fire and whiskey. She shivered and grinned with relief. There he was, and his name began to take shape on her lips. "G—ugh!" An invisible force shoved her back so hard that her head conked against the rocks. The warmth and desire disappeared with a resounding echo inside her skull.

Ernie groaned and clutched the back of her head, breathing deep to try to recall the scent, to no avail. But when she opened her eyes again, she wasn't alone in her little hiding place. A grasshopper—a normal one, this time—had flitted onto one of the rocks. Bright green and the size of her pinky, it flicked its wings with a soft buzz.

"Hey," Ernie said to it. "Did you need a break from the wind? Me too."

She returned her attention to her cards. *Something* had just happened, and that was good. Deciding to try something a little less physically and emotionally demanding, Ernie pulled her Nourishment card.

Focusing on the symbol, similar to Transport except the symbol was a *P* instead of an *R*, Ernie imagined a fresh-baked loaf of sourdough and a crock of butter. Hardly health food, but these were dire circumstances. She could almost taste the tang of it on her tongue. She imagined the crunch of the crust and her teeth sinking through to the chewy softness beneath. She focused so hard that she felt like she was going to disappear into the card, like she could reach inside it and pull out the exact loaf she'd been picturing.

A soft weight plopped into her lap. She moved the cards, expecting to see bread, and yelped when she saw it was another grasshopper, nearly twice as big as the first. Brushing it off her leg, she scooted back against the edge of the rock crease—and realized that there were now at least a dozen grasshoppers of varying sizes in the crevice with her. They were perched on rocks nearby. All facing her.

A chill ran down Ernie's back. Holding her cards in her left hand, she awkwardly crawled out of the sheltered spot. The wind slammed into her, ripping the tie right out of her hair and sending it spiraling back along the ridge. Shielding her eyes from the swirling dust and grit, she trudged back to the trail.

The grasshoppers flitted onto the waving grass on either side of her. And now there were about a hundred of them. One flew onto her pant leg, and another landed on the back of the hand that held her cards. Its feet felt like needles on her skin, and she swatted it away just as a few others landed in her hair. Her arms waving, Ernie stumbled forward along the trail, swiping away grasshoppers as more of them appeared and leapt at her. She clutched her cards, wishing she could do something to make the damn bugs disappear.

The diamondback tattoo burned on her arm, sharp and sudden, and that only seemed to enflame the bugs—Ernie's pant legs were now covered with them, and at least one had found its way up her sock to crawl up her leg. When it reached the wound on her calf, her whole body awoke with pain. Ernie screamed and tore at her jeans, then drew her Escape card. It flashed hot in her hand but didn't whisk her away, and a heavy swarm of insects swirled around her, deafening her with the buzz of wings and panic. Covering her head with her arms, squealing as they crawled along her skin and into her ears, Ernie charged through the thick cloud, desperate for an out.

Instead, she found an edge—and stumbled right over it. With a shriek, she plummeted and hit soft earth, then rolled several yards before soft grass and mud killed the momentum.

Ernie shoved her cards in her pocket. Panting, she shot to her feet, amazed that she even could as she looked up at the outcropping from which she'd fallen, at least a hundred feet up the hill. She gasped.

Kot stood at the rocky edge, peering down at her. He held up a rope, then tossed one end down the slope. It landed about ten feet up from where she stood.

Ernie squinted at the ridge, looking for the plague of grasshoppers that had just been trying to devour her. Nothing. She couldn't have imagined that, though. A soft clicking told her that one or two were still trapped in her hair. After shooing them away with agitated yanks, she looked around. She was closer to the bottom of the hill—and the woods where Nuria had been—than she wanted to be. As much as she didn't trust him, she headed in Kot's direction. He held the rope steady as she used it to pull herself up. "Good morning," she said as casually as she could once she reached the ridge.

He dropped the rope in the grass and handed her the tie that had been ripped from her hair by the wind. "You left without breakfast." Once he'd given her a moment to restrain her hair, he offered her a small bundle of cloth, and inside it were a few pickled carrots and potatoes. She accepted it. If her cards wouldn't nourish her, she had to keep up her strength a different way.

Kot had his mask tucked beneath the shoulder strap of his machete. He wiped his fingers on it as he watched Ernie eat the carrots. "We should go back to the cave," he said as he scanned their surroundings. "Not safe out here now."

"Did you see those grasshoppers?"

He nodded. "Not good to be out in the open when they find you."

Ernie shivered. "No kidding. But I can't spend my time here hiding in a cave. I have to get down there." She pointed to the coastline. Her tattoo had hurt more there than anywhere else, and the cards had pulsed the strongest. She had a connection to that place, and she couldn't escape the feeling that *he* was waiting there for her. The man whose blue eyes made every cell in her body react. She swallowed a last bite of carrot and looked up at Kot. "I'm hoping to meet a friend in that spot."

Kot's eyebrows rose. "Your father, you mean?"

"No, a different friend. I'm friendly."

"Where was this friend when you were in the bait pit yesterday?"

Ernie sighed. "I don't know. But I think he would have been there if he could have." She had little to go on except that feeling, that and the image on her Friend-Lover card, the look on his face, the promise in his eyes. "I think he might be looking for me down there, so I should . . . just be there, you know?" She squinted into the distance, almost imagining she could see the place, even though it was miles away. Or maybe a whole dimension away.

"I'll go with you if you truly must go." Kot cast a wary glance toward the woods. "But we should move quickly and be back by dark." He set out along the ridge.

Ernie followed. "Why are you helping me?"

"I help others when I can," he said without looking back.

Together, they hiked down the north face of the hill. If the sea weren't such an ugly brown, it would have been a nice view, laid out vast and still beyond the rocky coast. "Why's the water that color?" she asked when they finally reached the bottom and trekked toward the gravel road.

"Tarnterra's factories. Spitting poison into the sea." Kot shook his head. "The sludge has been carried north, more each year." He waved his head toward the sky. "And the sky . . . all of it is ruined. It's the same everywhere."

"Everywhere is plagued by a giant grasshopper monster, too? Oh, and a bunch of normal grasshoppers who like to attack random people?"

His brow furrowed. "It is not usually random. And no, as I told you, Nuria is the only one of her kind. There cannot be anything like her."

"You said she's been here since before you arrived—how long has it been?"

"Too long," he said sadly. "She has been here far too long." He yanked his mask from under his strap and pulled it on.

A man came out of one of those steel shacks in a field to their left. A bucket in each hand, he plodded to the road and trudged toward them. As he passed he raised his hand and nodded at a spot about three feet to their right, as if they were standing on the side of the road instead of only a few steps from him. "Say nothing," Kot said, and Ernie stayed quiet.

When the man was out of earshot, Ernie poked Kot in the arm. "That was seriously weird."

"Where is Woodfin, exactly?" Kot asked, tilting his head as he looked her over.

It instantly put her on the defensive. "Far away from here," she muttered.

"And you came here . . . to find your father."

She shrugged. "It's this way." She pointed to the stone wall she'd walked along to reach the road.

He paused. "Over there? Really?"

"Yeah." She hopped up on the crumbling wall. "You coming?"

Kot slid off his mask and stepped up onto the wall. He glanced over his shoulder at the woods and ran his hands over his thighs, jostling his pockets, which clanked. Then he adjusted the machete strap across his broad chest and let out a long breath. "Lead the way."

"You okay there?"

"Okay," he said slowly. "I'm not sure . . ."

"Are you all right, I mean."

Looking unhappy, he pointed up at the sun, which was now hanging just above the ridge line, then shooed her along the path. "As long as we keep moving, I am."

But by the time they reached the stone-bounded area by the cliff where Virginia had stranded Ernie, Kot was looking even more concerned. "This? *This* is the place? You are certain?"

Ernie nodded. "Do you know it?"

He shifted his weight uneasily. "You expected to find your friend here?"

Ernie's heart sank as she surveyed the empty space. "Maybe if we wait, he'll arrive?" Her fingers twitched toward her pocket. Would his image still be on the Friend-Lover card? Would the others work? Her tattoo throbbed with uncomfortable heat, so it certainly seemed possible, and that gave her some hope, but she couldn't just whip out her cards while Kot watched. She smiled, hating how vulnerable she felt. "I just need a little time for myself, if you don't mind?"

His eyes narrowed, but then he pulled a leather pouch from his pocket. "I will look for water. I think there's a stream that way." He pointed to a dip in the terrain maybe a quarter mile inland. "Please don't do anything unwise."

"Like getting attacked by grasshoppers?"

He gave her a somber look and walked away in the direction he'd pointed.

Ernie watched him go, knowing they were both keeping secrets. She wanted to trust him, but it felt safer to manage alone. Maybe her childhood had prepared her for that, because after her dad had left, she'd taken care of a mom who didn't seem to be there half the time.

But still, it wasn't her preferred state. She craved someone she could trust. All signs pointed to Kot being a decent guy, but Ernie still didn't understand the rules here, so it seemed best to keep him at a distance.

She fished her deck from her pocket, her heart picking up its pace. This place, where Virginia had connected the two dimensions, was where the rubber hit the road.

She flipped the Weapon card, mentally crossing all crossables, and let out a whoop when she saw the image of a machete appear beneath the barbed symbol. She focused hard on it, and the card turned into a small machete, nowhere as big as Kot's, but Ernie was delighted. She'd done it! Being in this spot seemed to help her clear her mind. A conjured weapon could either come directly from the card or manifest from nothing, which was always a little harder, but Ernie was sure she'd been able to do it at some point. Still, with things as they were, she was relieved to have any weapon, any way she could get it. She swung the machete through the air, then knelt on the grass and pulled her Nourishment card. The bread she conjured was a little flat and stale, but it was bread, and it meant her cards were working—*finally*.

She was stuffing the bread in her mouth when she felt the first tremor, when she heard the first shrieking roar, when she heard Kot shouting her name. She jumped to her feet. Nuria had leapt out of the woods and was bounding toward Ernie, covering a dozen yards with each thundering hop, and Kot was sprinting toward Ernie from the field in the opposite direction, his eyes wide and his arms waving. "Run," he shouted.

Ernie drew her Escape card, but it sputtered from warm to cold in her hand. Same with Transport.

"Run," Kot yelled, his voice higher now.

Ernie stumbled back a few steps and scooped the machete from the ground as Nuria landed inside the stone walls. With another leap, the creature slammed into Ernie, knocking her to the ground. Ernie rolled beneath the monster's stomping feet, trying to stay away from its snapping jaws while she swung her machete at its barbed legs.

"No!" Kot thundered. Ernie looked over to see his feet land a yard from Nuria, bringing her within range of his machete—and him within range of her teeth. The beast grunted and let out a shrieking howl. Kot had jumped at her head, and Ernie grimaced as she watched his legs swinging wildly about two feet from the ground. Blood splattered along the grass in front of the beast.

Ernie let out a war cry and sliced her machete along Nuria's belly. The blade glanced off, but Nuria bellowed and jumped away from Ernie. Kot collapsed in a sprawl in front of her.

The ground shook as the creature jumped away, back to the woods, still letting out that earsplitting roar. Ernie crawled over to Kot, who was trying to push himself up from the ground. "Oh my god," she said, "I thought she was ripping your guts out."

"Not quite, but close." Blood welled from cuts across his chest. His jacket had been ripped away, and his shirt was shredded and covered in slime. Kot looked down at himself, groaned, and tore the destroyed garment over his head.

Ernie stared.

On his left forearm lay a tattoo, painting his earth-brown skin vibrant colors of blue, purple, and green.

It was a dragonfly.

CHAPTER NINE

A cold wave spread outward from Ernie's chest, making her lips tingle with the shock. She blinked several times, but the image on Kot's arm didn't change. "You," she whispered.

Kot looked down at his arm, then reached for his jacket, which wasn't as damaged as his shirt. He pulled on what was left of it, yanking the sleeve over the image of the dragonfly, letting the rest hang over his bleeding chest. "We should get back to the cave."

"That's the dragonfly." Ernie rose, weaving unsteadily as her throat tightened. "*You're* the Dragonfly."

Kot acted as if he hadn't heard her. He gathered his scattered possessions, things that had flown from his pockets as Nuria had shaken him. "She'll come back. She always comes back."

"I know what you are!"

He rounded on her. "No, you have no idea what I am," he shouted.

Ernie pulled out her cards, feeling the unsteady, unstable power from them pulsing in her hand. "My father was the Dragonfly! You took his deck, didn't you? You killed him." She pulled her Capture and Enemy cards, crossed them, and slashed her cards at Kot.

He tackled her from behind even before the frayed, slack ropes she'd conjured flew through the illusion he'd left in his place. She hit the ground hard, her breath crushed out of her. He slammed his hand over hers, pressing her deck to the dirt. "Make another play and I'll leave you to die."

Ernie struggled against him, but he outweighed her by about a hundred pounds, and his grip was brutal. "I knew there was something off about you."

"There will not be anything off about me until you stop fighting."

"I meant I couldn't trust you, you idiot!"

"This is mutual," he rumbled in her ear. "Now—I could take the deck from you, or you could do as I say. Choose."

Ernie pressed her face to the grass, frustration running hot in her veins. "Fine. Truce."

"I doubt that, but I'll give you a chance." His immense weight lifted off her back.

Ernie drew in a few deep breaths and sat up. Kot was back to putting his tools in his pocket as if nothing had happened. "You owe me an explanation."

He gave her a half-amused, half-exasperated look. "I'm going back to my cave before we lose the sun. I suggest you follow me. And know that if you play those cards again, she'll find you."

"Huh?"

Kot gestured around the walled space. "I suspected it before, but I know it now. You came from the same place he did. Your cards still smell of that place, and she senses it. She comes when you call on the cards."

Ernie jabbed her finger at his pockets, unsure of where he'd tucked his deck. Now she was sure he'd played them right in her presence, maybe to produce the food or the rope ladder or the liquor, and she hadn't even known—maybe because he'd also played his Conceal card to make sure she wouldn't. It must also be why the villagers always looked through him instead of at him—he was making them see something else. Although she didn't understand why he needed the mask as well . . . but maybe it was for the same reason she'd worn gross, ill-fitting clothes when she was pretending to be a mercenary: just to make the ruse a little easier to maintain. And the cards were possibly how he'd made her fall asleep so suddenly last night. Forget the liquor—all it would have taken was a quick swipe of Rest and Ally—or Rest and Enemy. She didn't know which she was to him at the moment. "*Your* cards come from the same place mine did," she said.

"But my cards have been here for many years," he replied. "The Dragonfly deck has adjusted to its new home, and it does not lure her as it once did." He almost looked sad about that. "Besides—I use them as little as possible. But your deck—it has her in a state. The others can sense it, too. The little ones who serve her."

"The grasshoppers?"

"They infest the land."

"What, is she their mother or something?"

He shook his head. "That is not possible. But she has a strange influence over them." He chuckled. "She is powerful."

"You sound like you admire her."

His eyes met hers. "Because I do." He pulled out a card and pressed it to his chest, and Ernie watched as his cuts healed rapidly. "If you are injured, I can—"

"I'm fine," she snapped.

He stalked over to the stone wall and stepped over it. "Then are you coming or not?"

"How do I know you won't just steal my deck? Seems like you might have a track record there."

He sighed, looking completely exhausted. "If I had wanted to take your cards, I could have done so *just now*. And many times before that."

Ernie looked around at the desolate land. She didn't want to believe Kot when he said her cards would lure Nuria, but it made sense. Almost every time that monster had shown up, including when those grasshoppers swarmed her this morning, she'd been trying to deal. And it wasn't like Ernie's cards were working right anyway—she'd been able to play some of them in this walled space where Virginia had dropped her, but as soon as she tried to play a card that would have carried her *out* of the space, it was a no-go. Which meant she was just as vulnerable as she had been.

Kot seemed to read the indecision on her face. "You'll be safe with me. And your deck will adjust. I promise."

"Yeah, but what does it mean if it does?" she asked quietly. Because a terrible thought had just struck her, one that made her want to stay in the stone-walled area. Was the "adjustment" he was promising also affecting her mind?

She might regain her power, but would the cost be losing herself?

Kot didn't answer. He merely set out walking.

Ernie touched her cards and considered playing Prolong to help her hold on to her memories and herself a little while longer, then remembered that she might end up bringing the monster out of the woods again, which she really didn't need right now. Her eyes stinging, her thoughts a ragged mess, Ernie strapped all her recollections down as best she could and followed the man who had killed her father.

By the time they reached the cave again, the sun had almost set, along with Ernie's coping skills. She followed Kot into his home with a heavy heart and a suspicious mind. As if nothing was amiss, he got out the pickled vegetables just like he had the night before. He also got out several dried cornmeal cakes that hit the metal plate like little bricks. "You've barely eaten today. That is unwise." He offered her water in a metal cup. "You'll need this. The cakes are dry."

Reluctantly, she took it. She didn't want to take *anything* from him, but he'd saved her more than once, and at the moment he didn't seem to want to kill her. "I want to know what you did to my father. You lied to me when you said you didn't know him."

He grunted. "No, I didn't."

"He was the Dragonfly. Now you're the Dragonfly. I know how that works." She tapped her pocket where the cards lay, her brow furrowing. "I think that's how I got my deck," she added quietly. She wished she could be sure.

"You do not know how I got this deck." He poured himself a measure of the alcohol and tossed it back.

"Then maybe you'd better tell me."

"I owe you nothing."

"He was my *father*," she said, her voice breaking. "He left us when I was eight." She let out a bitter chuckle. "I tried to hate him. For years. But . . ." Something had changed. She couldn't remember what. "Now I need to find him—for myself and for my mother." She glared at Kot. "And now I'm realizing he's been dead all this time."

"I think there are *many* things about your father that you do not know."

"I had no idea," she said drily.

"You seem to have many ideas." Kot appeared to be chewing on the inside of his cheek. "I will tell you my story once you tell me yours. Did you travel here to find him using your deck?"

"You're giving me way too much credit," said Ernie, her cheeks heating. "I was stuck here by the Chicken Dealer."

Kot's lips twitched. "A chicken? That is funny."

"Yeah, she's not all that much fun, actually." And Ernie was supposed to make sure she never saw the sunrise—to make sure Gabe got a replacement card from the Forger, she remembered! His name returned to her all in a rush, and her thoughts wrapped around it tightly. He was the man in her Friend-Lover card, but which was he—a friend or a lover? And did it even matter? She was certain she wanted him to have what he needed, though success seemed unlikely at the moment, given where she was.

"Are there many Dealers in this place you come from?" Kot asked, pulling her from her thoughts.

Ernie shrugged one shoulder. "There are probably more here than you'd expect, especially if you haven't used your cards much." Which deck was Gabe's? She tried desperately to recall. Was it a bird, or was she just mixing that up with Virginia's chicken? "Is there something about being here that makes it harder?" She eyed him, wondering whether he, too, had memory issues that might affect his ability to deal the cards.

Kot hunched over the plate and shoveled a few chunks into his mouth. "I don't care about here. I want to hear about *there* and how you traveled between the worlds."

"Okay . . . Virginia has some sort of rune, and that's what she used to strand my father here. That's about all I can remember." She recalled Virginia explaining everything in her sadistic southern belle way once she'd brought Ernie to this dimension, when she'd already had Ernie at her mercy.

"I take it that she is not the friend you were waiting for."

Ernie shook her head. "His name is Gabe. He—I think he might be looking for me." Although all she had to go on was the look in his eyes and a gut feeling that just wouldn't go away. "I hope so, at least."

"I understand this doubt," Kot murmured, pushing potatoes around on the plate. "Even with these cards, we are still men and women. We fail each other sometimes. One can never be completely sure of another."

His voice was so heavy with sadness that it silenced the conversation for several long, painful moments. But then he raised his head. "But if you think he is looking for you, we should make sure you are there when you need to be."

"If it weren't for your monster friend, Nuria, I'd camp there."

"Perhaps we can figure something out," Kot said, scratching at the stubble along his jaw.

"Yeah . . . I'm not sure there's a 'we,' guy. You're wearing my dad's tattoo."

"Ah. Now I will tell you *my* story." He poured her more water and motioned for her to drink. "I had planned to travel east for the winter, to the city of Gelfia. I had heard tell of jobs there in the ports for strong men. I was camped by the coast for the night, perhaps three miles from here." His eyebrow arched. "Close to where we were today."

Ernie leaned forward. "There's something special about that place." She wondered whether it was a permanent connection point between dimensions or whether the rune Virginia had transported the wielder only to that specific spot. Either way, Ernie's cards had worked better there than anywhere else in this world.

"Not sure 'special' is the right word," Kot said. "Cursed, more like. Redmond came into my camp. He offered to share his food and drink with me in exchange for good conversation. Having nothing but corn-meal cakes, I accepted and followed him back to his camp—within those stone walls."

"Where he could use his cards to conjure food. I guess that Nuria thing didn't come running?"

"I did not see her at that time," he said slowly.

Ernie squinted at him. "Okay . . . so you let my dad feed you a free meal."

Kot nodded. "I was too hungry to question how this skinny man, dressed in rags, had such a store of food. Bread, beans, potatoes, and even some pumpkin. He was generous, too, and told me to eat my fill. I wish I hadn't taken a single bite."

"Are you saying he drugged you or something?"

"No, but it lowered my guard, and it should have done the opposite."

Ernie shifted her weight on the uneven stone floor, uncomfortable in more ways than one. "You make it sound like he's the bad guy here. You stole his cards as punishment for a good meal?"

"Yes. That is my custom." Kot rolled his eyes. "He asked me many questions about where I came from and why I had left that place and who I might have left behind. I talked and talked, because my belly was full and the drink . . . ah, the drink. Not piss in a jar like this." He curled his lip as he peered into his empty cup. "It was good, strong ale, the kind you must have silver or state chits to buy."

"You got drunk," she guessed.

"No." He gave her an aggrieved look. "You're eager to believe the worst of me."

She glanced at his left arm, though the Dragonfly tattoo was covered by the bloodied sleeve of his jacket. "I wonder why."

Kot's jaw flexed. "I fell asleep by his fire, and I woke up alone—with the bloody cards in my pocket and *this* bloody thing on my arm!" He yanked his sleeve up to show her.

"You talk about your deck and your animal like that? Seriously?"

"Is there a more proper way to explain that they were completely covered in blood?"

"Oh." Ernie tensed. "What did you do to him?" she asked quietly.

"Nothing!"

"You blacked out. You did something you regretted."

"No!" shouted Kot. He pulled his sleeve down and grimaced as his jacket tore at the frayed shoulder. His hands shook as he poured himself another measure of the "piss in a jar" and gulped it down. "I will admit to you that I do not like that place inside the stone wall. I feel strange whenever I am there, as if my mind is trying to slip away from me."

"Funny. I feel more clearheaded there than anywhere else."

"Because it has touched the place of your birth," he said. "For me, though . . . it feels wrong. But I swear, I did nothing at all to your father. Of that I am certain. I woke up, and Redmond was gone. I had blood smeared all over me. But that wasn't the worst of it."

Ernie was imagining that her father's dead body was the worst of it, but she motioned for him to go on.

"Imagine a great, bloody dragonfly pulling itself off your skin. Imagine that thing attacking you."

"It *attacked* you?" Ernie rubbed her left forearm and received a faint pulse of warmth in return. The diamondback would never do that to her, would she?

"The dragonfly was hurt." Kot shook his head. "He came at me with those jaws snapping, and we nearly killed each other. He finally landed in the grass. Couldn't fly. One of his wings had torn. And he'd nearly ripped my throat out." He raised his chin and pulled the collar of his jacket away, revealing a gnarled scar that extended from one side of his jaw to the other.

"I didn't know dragonflies had teeth."

He snorted. "Worse than Nuria's."

Ernie cringed. "But weren't you immortal by then?"

"I don't know what I was. Only that the cards got hot, and one of them glowed bright. It healed both of us."

"The Healing card," Ernie said slowly.

Kot gave her a dark look. "Then *she* showed up."

"Nuria sensed the Dragonfly cards? Why hadn't she attacked the night before, then?"

His jaw tensed, and he shook his head. "I barely survived that first meeting with her. I guess this old guy"—he tapped his arm—"decided she was more of an enemy than I was."

Ernie's eyebrows rose. "But what happened to my dad? Where did all the blood come from? Was it Nuria? Did she kill him?"

Kot's face twisted like he had a terrible taste in his mouth. "I am certain the blood was his. I assumed he was dead." His eyes met hers. "I was wrong."

"He had to be, though. If you take a Dealer's cards, he dies, doesn't he?"

"If you know that much, then you should understand that what happened was not the natural order of things. Redmond did something,

Ernie. To himself and to me. He left me in that eerie spot with his cards. And he went on his way."

"Casually leaving buckets of his own blood behind. As one does."

Kot threw up his arms and muttered a few words she was pretty sure were curses, though none she recognized. "I never wanted to deal with that man again. Understand?"

Ernie blinked. "Do you know if he's alive?"

"I know he *was* alive. Don't know if he is now."

Ernie was up on her knees now, her heart pounding. "You've seen him? Will you help me find him?"

Kot opened his mouth, perhaps to refuse, then snapped it shut again. He tilted his head and considered her. "You want a favor from me. I would expect you to pay it back." When he saw Ernie nod, he lifted his chin. "I will take you to the last place I saw him. I cannot promise you he'll still be there."

"And what do you want in return?"

Kot looked defiant. Determined. Almost triumphant. "I will tell you when the time comes. Do you accept?"

Ernie eyed him. She didn't like the idea of owing anyone anything, but if her father was alive—and here—it was too enticing to pass up. "I accept."

He put his hand out, and they shook on it. "We'll leave with the sunrise."

"Yeah, yeah, Nuria stalks the night." Ernie reached for the crumpled blanket she'd discarded that morning in her eagerness to escape the cave. "Except I've only ever seen her during the day. Are you so sure she's nocturnal?"

Kot gave her a rueful glance. "Sometimes I think she's more dangerous under the moon than she is under the sun." He pushed the plate of vegetables and cornmeal cakes toward her. "Eat up. Long walk tomorrow."

Ernie chowed down, eyes watering as the vinegar penetrated her nasal passages. It was harsh, gross food, and she didn't understand why Kot wouldn't conjure up something more palatable, but he seemed to have a weird relationship with his deck. That was the least of her concerns, though. Tomorrow, with any luck, they would find her father.

She'd see him for the first time since she was eight.

What would she say to him?

Why did you leave us?

Do you still love me?

Did you ever?

She wasn't sure. But if Kot was as good as his word, the reunion she'd been craving for twenty years might be only a few hours away.

CHAPTER TEN

They reached the village of Fortoba as the sun sank into the hills beyond the town. It was considerably larger and more sprawling than Honeida had been, and the people seemed less wary and hostile. Ernie assumed it was because they were about fifteen miles from the woods where Nuria prowled, but Kot shook his head when she mentioned it. "She has learned to avoid this place."

"They have defenses?"

"There is a danger here to her. She hunts elsewhere."

"Okay . . ." Ernie put her hand over her deck, which was safely nestled in her pocket. It had been pulsing erratically all day, and she didn't know whether that was a good sign or a warning. "So . . . you think Redmond is here?" They had passed a sprawl of tidy one-story homes and had reached a paved main street, clogged with exhaust-spewing cars that looked like they were straight from the forties or fifties. Everything in this place seemed like it was about sixty years behind the times, maybe more, but so many things were the same, including the way people spoke English, although with flat, twangy accents that she couldn't pinpoint. Her father's deep Carolina drawl would have stood out a mile. "How do you know this is the place?" she asked.

Kot pulled his wide-brimmed hat down around his ears. He wasn't wearing the hood today; apparently he saved that for the area around

Honeida because of their paranoid ways. As she'd suspected, he'd explained that it was easier to disguise himself with the cards when he gave them a blank slate to work with, but Ernie wondered whether he needed the extra help in part because he didn't have the closest relationship to Pol, which Kot had warily informed her was the name of the dragonfly. When she'd asked him about his bond with the spirit of his deck, he'd given her a scornful glance and told her that Pol understood why he avoided using his cards, and it was none of her business. He'd been surly ever since. "My search for Redmond ended in this place. After he left me with the deck, I had no idea what was happening, no idea what those cards were. I had tried to leave the card deck in the place I'd met him, but when I tried I felt . . ."

"Awful, I imagine."

"Like I was dying. So I had them, but I didn't understand the symbols or the animal that seemed to have possessed me." He grunted. "I had no idea, then, how gentle Pol was. It wasn't possession at all."

"It's a relationship," Ernie said softly, but it was only an echo in her hollow heart, unconnected to any concrete memories. She rubbed her tattoo, which tingled faintly as they trudged up the crowded sidewalk past food markets, a car-repair shop full of clangs and flying sparks, and a post office of sorts, complete with a wall full of cages that held an array of red-eyed pigeons. The streetlights were flickering on, displaying a crude electrical system. More advanced than Honeida, but it still felt foreign.

"Relationship or not—I didn't want it," Kot said. "I wanted to live my life, and I didn't understand yet that the dragonfly and the cards were anything other than a curse. Every time I looked at them and tried to understand what they were, odd things happened. I thought I was losing my mind. So I followed the trail of dried blood, and when it disappeared, I began asking fellow travelers if they'd seen a wounded man of Redmond's description."

"You could have used your cards."

"Remember that first, I didn't really know how, and second, Nuria can sense them, and she comes for them."

"I don't get that. Why?"

"Does it matter? She does. So I had to find your father in the normal way. I asked. And asked. And the answers led me here."

"You found him alive." Which defied everything she thought she understood about a Dealer's bond with his deck. "Did he explain what had happened?"

Kot shook his head. "He refused to take them back. He said I shouldn't give them to anyone else, either."

"Because it would kill you."

"Just another part of the curse."

"I guess it's easy to see it that way if you get your cards by accident. But I don't understand why my dad would give up the cards, even if he could do it without dying."

"Perhaps you'll be able to ask him." Kot came to a stop outside a rickety wooden door set into a long block of shops. "This is where I found him before."

Ernie pulled open the door, revealing a staircase leading down into darkness. She'd expected to find a library, maybe, or an antique shop full of dusty tomes, as those had been her father's primary habitats when she'd known him. If he'd been trapped here, she was certain he would have sought answers about how to get home through research. But a yeasty, dank smell wafted over them, along with the sounds of shrill laughter and unfamiliar, lilting music. "A *bar*?"

"See for yourself."

Legs pulsed on her arm, and again, Ernie wasn't sure whether it was encouragement or a warning. Warily, Ernie headed down the stairs, her boots squeaking on the sticky floor. When she reached the bottom, she looked through the doorway, beyond which lay the diviest of dives she'd ever seen. It seemed to be a popular place, though, because the wooden chairs were all filled, and most of their occupants were focused on a woman in the back corner dressed in a shirt, corset, and long ruffled skirt, who was plucking at an instrument that looked like a big salad bowl with strings pulled taut across the top. She strutted around her little stage, shaking her hips and warbling about her man keeping her warm in the winter. Everyone seemed mesmerized, except the bartender, whose skin was as brown as Kot's. He leaned around one of his patrons and looked Kot over from head to toe. "No weapons," he snapped, squinting at the machete handle jutting over Kot's shoulder.

"I'll wait outside. I don't want to be here anyway," said Kot. "Good luck." He stomped up the stairs.

Ernie approached the bar as the bartender glared at her. "You got any weapons?" he asked her.

"Nope," Ernie said. "I'm harmless. And I'm looking for someone. Redmond Terwilliger?"

"Never heard of him. Funny name," the guy said as he filled a mug with a thick purple liquid that looked and smelled like cough syrup. He handed it to a man on Ernie's left, whose gray beard was brushing the bar top.

"How long have you worked here?" Maybe the manager could help her out.

"Since I was eighteen," the bartender said. "I own the place."

"Oh." Ernie bit her lip and looked around. Why had she thought this would be easy? She put her hands over her cards. Maybe they would *make* it easy. "You have a bathroom here?"

"You a paying customer?"

"Um . . ." Behind her came a woman's shrieking laughter and a man's hoarse guffaw, along with a smattering of clapping.

The gray-bearded guy lowered his mug to the bar and raised a finger. The bartender nodded and said, "You're good. Yack here wants to buy you a drink. Bathroom's back there." He jabbed his finger at the narrow hallway just beyond the stage corner.

"Thanks." She leaned over the bar and looked at Yack, a man with a sagging pale face, an eye patch, and scraggly hair that covered his ears but left the top of his head bare. "Much appreciated."

Yack, who seemed to be working to keep his teeth in his mouth, gave her a nod. Ernie gifted him with a smile before heading back to the bathroom. To make it, she had to weave her way between tables and chairs, elbows and knees. At one table, a woman with gyrating hips was straddling a man, who clutched his mug in one hand and a gnarled cane with a knob on the top with the other, like he needed help staying upright even though he was sitting down. Right as she passed, another guy smacked the lady on the butt, and she squealed, which all the men nearby seemed to think was really amusing. Ernie looked away and focused on her destination.

The bathroom was a hole in the floor, and the little stall was filled with a stench so foul that Ernie gagged. Still, she shut herself in, glad for a bit of light offered by a thick, buzzing bulb set into the wall. She pulled her cards from her pants and ferreted out the Revelation card, navigating by touch, letting the symbols transmit their meaning right through her fingertips. It was getting easier every time, and she was getting faster. And even if Nuria sensed the cards here somehow, Kot had said she avoided this town, so Ernie figured it was safe. The cards had been signaling her all day, and she hoped that meant they were ready to help.

But as she peered into the card and imagined her father's face, silently begging the deck to reveal where he was, she saw only a shadow. "Dang it," she whispered. "Come on. Is he here?"

The shadow beneath the omega symbol moved and turned, allowing Ernie to view him in profile. Her breath caught. He had a long beard, and the top of his head was smooth. "Yack?"

He'd bought her a drink. She'd looked him right in the face. And neither of them had known the other. Was that because she'd been forgetting things, or had he really changed that much? Her throat tightening—both with emotion and the intense stench coming up from the hole at her feet—Ernie shoved the cards back into her pocket and pushed the bathroom door open.

Yack was standing just outside, leaning on a cane. Stooped as he was, he stood only an inch or so taller than Ernie. She peered at him in the dim light. "Hi," she said unsteadily.

"You're not from here," he said. His voice was rough, and his accent was the flat twang of the area instead of a southern drawl.

But if he'd been stuck here for two decades, maybe that made sense.

She shook her head, her eyes stinging. "Do you recognize me?" she asked, her voice breaking.

He squinted at her with his one good eye. "You do look familiar."

He didn't, not really, but he was still lean and about the right height, with the same long hair. And his eyes were brown like her father's. "Yack isn't your real name, is it?"

His eyebrows rose, the left one arching above the patch. "How did you know?"

She offered him a watery smile. "Do you know who I am?"

He cocked his head back. "You asked for Redmond."

"Yeah." She couldn't believe it. Here he was, after so many years.

"Hadn't heard that name in a long time, but it brought back memories."

"For me, too. And I'm so glad I found you."

She'd been about to embrace him when he jerked his thumb toward the bar. "I assumed you were one of his chickies. Either that or he owes you silver, and in that case, you can get in line, because the old sod owes everyone else, too, never mind that he's always bragging about his treasure. Someday someone's going to stomp the goods right outta him. But either way, he's right over there."

Ernie shook her head, trying to steady herself from the emotional whiplash. "Sorry, what? You . . . he . . . what?"

"Calls himself Laramy, but he told me his real name years ago when he'd had a little too much of the syrup, you know?"

She looked in the direction he'd indicated. "He's out there?"

"Tell him I sent you. And that he owes me forty, and if he doesn't cough it up by the end of the night, he'll be paying with more than coin." And with that, Yack grunted and limped back to the bar, casting a dirty look at the cluster of tables to his right.

Reeling, Ernie emerged from the hallway and scanned the room. Not a single person looked familiar, but then again, she'd been about to throw her arms around some old dude she'd convinced herself must be her father just because he'd bought her a drink.

Clearly she wasn't the best judge of these things.

Maybe she needed a more efficient approach. "I'm looking for Redmond," she shouted. "Anyone here by that name?"

The music stopped, and Ernie looked over to find the singer glaring at her. "Do you mind?" the woman asked.

"No, not at all." Ernie turned to the rest of the room and walked past a few tables, examining each face. "Anyone here use to go by the name of Redmond—"

The lady who had been straddling the guy with the mug and the knob-topped cane let out a squeal and got off him, revealing a face Ernie hadn't seen in twenty years but knew so well that it crushed the breath out of her throat.

"Hi, Daddy," she murmured.

Redmond Terwilliger looked like he'd been clocked in the head with a two-by-four. "What did you just call me?"

"Who is she?" whined the woman who'd been dancing in his lap a moment before.

"Yeah, *Redmond*," said a harsh voice on his other side, owned by a tubby man with a shock of red hair, the one who'd slapped the dancing woman on the butt. "Who is she?"

Redmond's eyebrows rose, and he stroked a trembling hand down his long gray beard. "No idea."

Ernie leaned forward, placing her hands on the table. "You know me," she said steadily. "You left us a long time ago, and I'm all grown up. But you know who I am. And I know you've been through a lot, but—"

"You've been through a lot, *Redmond*?" asked the redheaded guy, his voice all mockery.

"That's not my name," he said, shaking his head. "You know that's not my name! And I don't know what she's talking about." He looked up at Ernie. "Who are you?"

Again, confusion and uncertainty tangled in Ernie's chest. "I'm Ernie," she said. "Ernestine. Your daughter."

"Daughter . . . ?" Redmond stared up at her, and then his face broke into a wide smile as he let out the same guffaw she'd heard earlier at the bar. "I don't have any children," he said. "I can't even get Chessy over here to take me to bed!" He smacked Chessy, the woman who'd been entertaining him, on the thigh, and she shoved him away.

Ernie took a step back and glanced over at the bar.

"Oh," said maybe-Redmond. "Did Yack send you over here to give me a hard time?"

Without turning around, Yack made an okay sign with his hand, and the cronies around maybe-Redmond oohed like he'd just flipped everyone off.

"You have to excuse Yack. Sick sense of humor," said maybe-Redmond, who was seeming more like not-Redmond by the second. His accent wasn't quite like everyone else's, but it wasn't like Ernie's, either. He clutched at his cane and shook it at her in jolly admonishment, revealing the knob on the top to be made of rose-colored glass. "Good one, Yack!" he called out.

Ernie was certain she knew him. She hadn't had to talk herself into this one. "Can we go somewhere and talk?"

The redheaded guy oohed again and leered at Ernie. "Laramy, you'd be a fool to turn that down. There's a beautiful woman under all that dirt. Maybe she'll let you give her a bath. We all know you're fond of the bathhouse."

Unmistakable fear flashed in Laramy's eyes, and he put his hands up. "I'm comfortable right here." He gave her an apologetic smile. "No offense, young lady." He patted Chessy's poufy blond hair. "I'm taken for the night."

"Weed," Ernie said from between clenched teeth. "That's what you used to call me when I was a kid. Weed." She searched his face for any recognition.

His cheek twitched. Then he glanced at his comrades and gave them a goofy grin. "That's cute, but I'm sorry to say it doesn't ring a single bell."

Fury shot up Ernie's spine. "Mom's still waiting for you. Did you know that?" she shouted. "She never got over you leaving!" Before Ernie knew what she was doing, she'd yanked the table away from the group of friends and shoved it to the side, sending mugs and glasses crashing to the floor. "How do you think she would feel, knowing you were *here*?"

A hand clamped over Ernie's shoulder, and she turned to see the bartender standing behind her with a clenched jaw. "I run a peaceful establishment here."

"Kick her out," called one of the guys who'd been grazed by the table Ernie had shoved. Several others voiced their agreement.

Ernie looked at her father. "I can't believe this," she said, her voice trembling. "You know who I am."

"I'm not who you're looking for," he said, not quite meeting her eyes.

Ernie ripped herself from the bartender's grip. "I'm going to find a way *home*," she said to her father.

"This is my home," he mumbled.

Ernie spit on the floor and stalked back to the stairs, stomping her way upward and bursting onto the sidewalk, her breaths coming in sharp little squeaks.

Kot appeared at her side instantly. "You didn't find the person you knew," he guessed.

Ernie looked up at him and shook her head, unable to form words. Kot winced, hesitantly raised his arms, and offered an embrace. Ernie collapsed onto him, sobbing out sorrow and grief as the hope she'd harbored for years fell away and died.

CHAPTER ELEVEN

Ernie came to with a gasp, suddenly awake with very little idea of how she'd fallen asleep. She'd been dreaming of a green expanse, of watching the sunrise. Someone had been sitting beside her, but she hadn't been sure who it was, only that she desperately wanted to see his face. She'd been turning toward him when she'd snapped back into consciousness. Confusion engulfed her. Where the hell was she? How had she gotten here?

She was lying on a wooden floor, next to a wall with peeling wallpaper. Ernie peered up at the window, which revealed only bleak darkness outside. The large room in which she lay was filled with people, many of them snoring. She wrinkled her nose as she inhaled the funk of body odor, feet, and boiled turnips. Craving fresh air and a chance to clear her thoughts, she got up and crept out the door.

She stood shivering on the house's front stoop as the events of the past night slowly returned to her memory. After that reunion, which couldn't possibly have gone worse, Kot had taken her to a different pub and bought her a strong drink and a bowl of cornmeal mush with wilted vegetables that tasted about a week past their peak. Then, as her thoughts turned as soft as the mush and her tears dried to a trickle, he'd walked her to a ramshackle building at the edge of town that seemed to be a crash pad for squatters. Ernie would have loved a hot shower and a warm bed, but what she got was a space on the grimy floor beneath a drafty window. At that point, though, she'd been so wrecked that she lay down and faced the wall, just waiting for morning and wishing she could wake up from this nightmare.

Her breath puffed out in a white cloud as she stepped into the gravel road that ran in front of the house. She rubbed her arms and bounced on her heels, ready to break out into a run just to get away from the raging thoughts in her head. After twenty years, she'd found her father. And he wouldn't even admit that was who he was. Was that because he was hiding something or because he couldn't remember? She could certainly remember him, but her memories were those of a child, her feelings instinctive. Intuitive. Shouldn't his be the same, no matter how long he had been in this place? Some things ran so deep and were so central to who you were that they could never be forgotten.

Right?

Maybe not. Her memories of last night had come back—that had just been a matter of waking up, of separating her mind from the dream long enough to recall where she actually was. She wished she could do the same thing with her memories of where she'd come from. She knew she'd already forgotten so much; her mind flashed with a maelstrom of emotions that she couldn't attach to memories. The gears of her thoughts kept slipping as she tried to recall the people she'd left behind, especially . . . *Gabe*. That was his name, she reminded herself. But that and his eyes and a vague sense of their connection were all she had, and it terrified her. What else had she lost, and how much more would go?

She had to get out of this place, and she needed to take her father with her. Neither of them belonged here, no matter what he said.

Her fists clenched. She was of half a mind to barge into town and try to track him down again, but to keep herself from doing anything stupid, she headed in the opposite direction, walking briskly down the road that led all the way back across the fields to the coast. She felt better when she was moving. Ernie accelerated her pace to a jog, her heel strikes jarring against the rocky road. She didn't plan to go far; Kot had told her Nuria hunted at night. But he'd also said she avoided the town because there was some kind of danger to her here, so Ernie figured as long as she didn't stray past the scatter of buildings marking the final signs of civilization before the road veered toward the sea, she'd be fine.

Sadly, it didn't take long for those buildings to come into view as she reached the top of a rise. Ernie slowed to a walk, then froze as she caught sight of two people huddled under the light of a lantern hanging from the eaves of a metal barn.

One of them was Kot—Fortoba appeared to be home to many people of color, but she hadn't seen anyone else his height since arriving in this dimension, which made him easy to spot. He had his arms circling a tall, slender woman with long black hair cascading down her back. Her arms were around his neck. Ernie stared as Kot dipped his head and kissed the woman, his hand fisting in her hair, his muscles taut as he pulled her against him.

For a moment, Ernie was mesmerized, arrested not only by the passion that emanated from the couple but by an ache in her chest. Blue eyes stared at her from memory, raising a need that rocked her. The sight of Kot and his lover echoed inside Ernie. She could almost feel the rough touch on her skin. She could almost taste earth and whiskey on her tongue. His name was there, right there, but she had to reach for it with both hands—Gabe. This was how she felt for him, and in that moment, even though she couldn't quite picture his face, the longing was a physical pain.

With a ragged groan, Kot turned so that he could press the woman against the wall of the barn. As he began to pull her long, raggedly hemmed skirt up to her thighs, Ernie remembered where she was and how intrusive she was being. She took a step backward, her heel crunching in the crushed stone of the road.

The woman's head whipped around sharply, as if the footstep had been an explosion. Her dark eyes settled on Ernie while Kot, unaware, buried his face in the woman's neck. She looked to be of Asian heritage, with a heart-shaped face and an elegant sweep to her cheekbones, but her expression was all alarm. After a moment that seemed to last forever but was probably only the span of two heartbeats, the woman's mouth twisted into a grimace and she pushed Kot away, then took off running through the field, hurdling one of those low stone walls. She was like a freaking gazelle or something. But it was Kot's reaction that pulled Ernie's attention away. His arms outstretched, he fell to his knees and let out a wrenching cry. He hung his head, as if he couldn't bear to watch the woman run from him.

Ernie scanned the fields for one last sight of the woman, but she'd already disappeared into the darkness.

And it was Ernie's fault that she'd fled. If the woman had been from the town, she was running in the wrong direction, but perhaps she lived on one of the outlying farms? Not that it mattered. As Kot raised his head, Ernie backtracked quickly, not wanting him to know she'd observed him in such an intimate—and then painful—moment. She spun on her heel and ran down the hill, wanting to be back in the village by the time Kot managed to pull himself together and return. When she made it back to the bunkhouse, there was a faint green glow on the horizon, but Ernie slipped through the doorway and found her spot by the window again.

Her whole being was abuzz with what she'd seen. That embrace hadn't been casual. It had been full of a longing so sharp that Ernie could still feel it pricking at her heart, poking at the scars she had there. Was Gabe looking for her? Would she ever see him—or her world—again?

Her throat tight, Ernie rose up on an elbow and turned her back to the room. She fished her deck from her pocket and peered down at the card faces in the green light filtering in through the dusty windowpane. Her Friend-Lover card was easy to find, warm to the touch—but the man who'd stared up at her from within was gone. Ernie stifled a whimper. Why had he disappeared? With trembling fingers, she crossed that card with her Revelation card and put her face close to them, praying to see him looking right back at her again.

But there was nothing but a shadow on the card, a vague, indistinct darkness. Ernie bowed her head and tensed to hold in a forlorn sob. Her cards were working better, but she'd lost *him* somehow. She shuffled through the rest of her deck, hoping to find something, anything, that would bring him back. Her eyes settled on one card in particular—an upside-down check mark and, beneath it, the image of an old tent staked into a leafy clearing. She gasped. "My haven," she whispered, her fingers running over the symbol on the card. "Dreams . . . ?" The card was the Dreams card, the gateway to the realm of dreams. Her fingers closed around it as hope lit up her brain like a sunrise. Could she access her home dimension from *that* realm? Could she even get there, with her cards working so erratically?

The door near her feet creaked open, bringing with it a wash of cold air. Kot plunked down next to her with his cloak wrapped around him. "Hey," she murmured, pretending to have been startled from sleep.

"Be glad they don't work," he muttered when he leaned over and saw her grip on her cards. "When they do, you'll have no connection to your dimension anymore. They'll belong here, and so will you."

"*What?*" A cold shiver passed down Ernie's spine. "How do you know?"

"Redmond told me. When I came here to find him, to ask him why he'd forced the cards on me."

She sat up, looking over the sea of sleeping bodies in the large room. "Did he have a good answer?"

Kot ran a hand through his black hair. "He said that at first, the cards only worked in the connection spot, the place where he'd been stranded. He said he'd been able to send messages through it."

"Did he say how?"

"Never said. Only said the portal closed after a while, once his cards adjusted to this place. And after that he gave up."

Ernie's heart was beating with a painful urgency. "But he knows how to open a window to our world."

Kot shrugged. "Whatever he did, whatever portal he opened, he couldn't use it to get back to your home."

"And no one except Virginia knew where he was. I wonder what would have happened if someone out there knew, you know?"

Kot looked intrigued. "You think there might be a way to reach out across the dimensions and connect them without a rune?" He tilted his head. "Is someone reaching toward you, do you think?"

"I'm not sure." She shoved her cards in her pocket and rubbed her left forearm, which had suddenly rippled with sharp pain. "How would I know if he was?"

"I was born in this place, so I do not know."

She stood up. "I have to find Redmond again."

"Because he was so helpful the first time."

She walked to the door. "Last time, I just wanted to find my father. This time, I need some answers." Even if he'd forgotten some things, maybe she could jar a few memories loose.

"Find 'em some other damn place and stop yammering!" growled a portly guy slumped in a corner. His complaint was echoed by several groggy neighbors.

Ernie inclined her head, inviting Kot outside. He sighed and followed her. If she hadn't known he'd had his heart broken an hour ago, she might never have guessed. He did look careworn, though, with shadows beneath his eyes and a heaviness to his steps. He joined her on the stoop and looked toward town. "This seems like the errand of a fool."

"He was surrounded by people last time," Ernie replied. "Maybe if I can get him alone, he'll admit who he is." Or remember?

"You can try. I'll be waiting at the edge of town. If we leave soon, we'll get back to the cave with plenty of time before night falls again."

"I could use your help."

He crossed his arms. "He won't help you, Ernie. I'm sorry to be saying it, but your father's a bad man. He stuck me with his deck twenty years ago and left me without a shred of understanding what to do with it."

"Seems like you did okay."

"I had help," he snapped. "Just not from him."

For some reason, Ernie immediately thought of the woman he'd been kissing. "I thought you said there weren't any other Dealers around here."

He looked away. "There aren't. Not anymore."

"Wait—what?"

"I'll be waiting," he said firmly, jabbing his finger at the road leading out of town. "And remember you owe me a favor. So be back soon, ready to leave."

He stomped away from her before she could reply. Shaking her head, Ernie hiked back into the town, which was already bustling, people on the sidewalks and exhaust-belching cars on the roadways. No one looked particularly happy, and there was a set in their shoulders and jaws that told Ernie that life wasn't easy here, either. She wondered when and why this world had diverged from hers, or, now that she thought about it, vice versa. How many different dimensions were there, anyway?

When Ernie reached the basement bar where she'd discovered "Laramy" the night before, she found it locked. Of course. Bars didn't open early in the morning even in different dimensions, apparently. Wishing she could rely on the cards to tell her where to find her rogue of a dad, Ernie leaned against the door and looked up and down the street. This wasn't such a big place. If she could find an open shop, she could ask whether anyone there knew him. Yack had said Redmond owed a bunch of people money, and he'd clearly been around for a number of years.

Besides—Ernie sucked at giving up.

She tried a butcher shop, where an Asian guy with thick forearms and a bloody cleaver shouted that if Laramy ever did go in there, the butcher planned to grind him up and make meatballs out of him. Cringing at the imagery, Ernie left while the guy was still yelling something about how Laramy cheated at some game called sic bo. She got a similar response from a blond guy tinkering with a boat of a car sporting an engine so large that Ernie was surprised the tires didn't go flat under the weight of it. The mechanic said that Laramy had stolen coins from the pot the last time they'd played dice, and he seemed to relish the idea of bashing his brains in with his wrench.

And so it went. The package shop. The farm stand. The dentist. The barber. When she finally reached a shop displaying shelf after shelf of books, she braced herself before going in, preparing for the next tirade. Something clattered against the door when she swung it open, almost like a wind chime, except it was made of animal bones. Ernie grimaced and shut out the noise from the street. The musty smell of old tomes instantly pulled her back to her childhood, to sitting on her father's lap as he ran his hands over the pages of historic texts and told her fantastic tales. "Hello?" she called.

She sidled along a narrow aisle to the edge of the room, where she found a table, an open ledger, and a locked wooden box. "Hello?"

A door opened and clicked sharply closed across the room, and footsteps approached. A stocky woman appeared, with leathery tan skin, short gray hair, and a monocle clenched between her right brow and cheekbone. "Sorry about that," she said brusquely, peering at Ernie through the magnifying lens. "What can I do for you today?"

"I'm looking for a man," Ernie said. "I—"

The woman fanned Ernie away. "Matchmaker's down the street." She squinted at Ernie again, taking in her ripped, muddy clothes. "But I suggest you visit the bathhouse before your appointment."

"No, I mean, I'm trying to find someone specific, and I was hoping you might know him."

The woman's head jerked back. "Me? Why would I know anyone?" Suspicion glinted in her eyes. "You new in town? Where'd you travel from?"

Ernie bit her lip. "I'm not staying long. I just wanted to find Redm—I mean, Laramy."

The woman blinked at her. "Who?"

"Laramy? He's maybe late fifties? Bald on top, kind of long, scraggly hair?" Ernie wiggled her fingers around her ears.

The woman laughed at her description. "Sounds like quite a catch. But no, wouldn't know this Laramy from a long-faced sheep. Sorry." The woman sat down on her chair with a solid wumph that created an explosion of dust from the cushion beneath. "If you'll excuse me."

She began turning pages of her ledger, almost like she was looking for something. When Ernie didn't move, she looked up. "Work to do, you know," the woman said. She returned her attention to the ledger and kept flipping pages.

Ernie took a step back. "Thanks," she said. "Mind if I look around? This is a great place. I love books."

"You love books," the woman muttered with a disbelieving chuckle, then seemed to catch herself. "Let me know if you have any questions or need help finding something."

"I definitely will." Ernie tucked herself into an aisle, frowning. Every single person she'd talked to so far had known Laramy—and pretty much hated him. But this woman had denied knowing her dad, and she hadn't even thought about whether she'd seen him when Ernie described him.

It didn't sit right. Ernie trudged slowly up the aisle, taking in obviously hand-bound books . . . with a writing on the spine she'd never seen before. Most of the books here seemed to have been written in Chinese or a language close to it. She thought about her father making this discovery and wondered whether he'd been frustrated or fascinated or both. *He finds an actual bookstore in a foreign dimension, but he can't read any of the books?*

Had he spent the last twenty years teaching himself how to translate?

Or maybe he hadn't cared at all. He was totally different than the man she'd known.

As Ernie wandered closer to the back of the shop, the door to the street opened with another clatter of animal bones, and a man's voice greeted the monocled woman with a gruff "Happy morning." The two began to chat quietly about the weather and whether they'd have a freeze soon. Ernie tuned them out as she reached the end of the aisle and glanced at another door, this one with a sign covered in symbols, maybe meaning "Employees Only." The woman had come through this door when she heard Ernie in the shop. Ernie took a few steps closer and then saw it—on the floor against the wall, nestled in the shadow of a bookshelf, was a small rose-colored glass ball, very much like the one she'd seen at the end of the cane her father had been clutching in the bar last night.

With a glance at the front of the shop, where the monocled owner and her friend were still chatting, Ernie squatted and picked up the ball. Turning it over, she could see a rough, uneven patch on one side. She ran her thumb over it. Was that glue? It could have come off her father's cane.

She turned toward the back door as her suspicion grew. She slowly turned the handle and pulled it open. As the shop owner let out a guffaw at a joke her companion had made, Ernie slipped through the doorway and pulled the door shut behind her, wincing at the slight creak it made before settling into the frame. She was on a small landing at the top of a staircase leading down to what she presumed was the basement. The walls were rough stone, and Ernie ran her hands down them as she descended carefully, edging toward the faint glow of light coming from the hallway at the bottom. "Dad?" she said quietly, then realized how stupid that was. "Laramy? Redmond?"

The hallway was more of a passageway, lit by a few guttering lanterns and leading straight to a high-ceilinged storeroom filled with wooden crates and reeking of mildew. "Redmond?" she said again, already feeling like an idiot for thinking she'd find—

A quiet groan and a shuffling sound came from the back of the room. Ernie jogged the last few feet and rounded the final row of crates. "Oh, man," she whispered.

Redmond-Laramy was shackled to the stone wall with ropes that had been attached to two sturdy metal lantern hooks. His wrists were bleeding from his attempts to free himself, and it looked like someone had used his face as a soccer ball. One of his eyes had swollen shut, and blood trickled from the corner of his mouth. He made a feeble attempt to raise his head as Ernie began to work at the rope binding his left wrist. "Oh," he muttered. "It's you again. I suppose you're after my treasure, too?"

Whoever had tied those ropes knew a thing or two about knots. "I don't care two figs for your treasure. What the heck is going on?"

"I'm not a very good person."

"Obviously," she said, wrestling with the unrelenting coil of rope.

"They want my treasures. Willing to do anything to get 'em."

Ernie groaned. "No offense, but you don't look like a guy with a single treasure, let alone more than one." She grunted as she finally loosened the rope enough to free his hand. As she did, his sleeve slid up his left arm, revealing a grisly, knotty scar that stretched from wrist to elbow. She paused, staring.

Redmond sighed and pulled his sleeve down. His gaze flitted up to her face. "Are you really her?" he asked quietly. "Weed?" For the first time, his voice lapsed into a Blue Ridge drawl that struck a chord deep inside Ernie, as did the nickname that echoed in her memory.

"You do remember me, don't you?" she asked.

He shrugged, grimacing at the pain it caused him. "Yes and no."

"What the heck does *that* mean?"

"I try to remember, but it's all so hazy. You can't blame me for turning you away."

"Oh, I can blame you." Ernie swallowed back the lump in her throat and set to work on the rope around his right wrist.

"How can you be here, Weed?" he asked. "I half thought my broken brain had just made you up. I still do."

Ernie froze as she heard a creak in the floorboards over her head. "I'm not even sure if I should be doing this," she said quietly.

"You are my little Weed, aren't you? You're really her. You really are."

"I haven't been your little Weed for twenty years." Her voice was strained, both with frustration at the stubborn knots and at the pain of wishing for a father it was obvious she could never have back. "And right now, we have more pressing issues to discuss, like how the heck we get out of here."

"I'm never getting out of here," he mumbled. "I tried . . . I tried so hard. *That* I remember. But I'm going to die here." He let out a low whine followed by a sniffle. "I'm so sorry I let you down."

Ernie pulled the final knot loose with an agitated wrench, and her father slumped, heading for the floor. She caught him and pulled his arm around her shoulders, letting him lean his unnervingly thin body against hers. "I need you to focus right now," she told him. "We can't deal with the past if we don't live through the present. Can you walk?"

He stiffened and took a few gingerly steps as Ernie steered him toward the door. "First thing I'd like to know is how in tarnation you actually got yourself here to find me," he said as they reached the corridor. "You're not from here. *We're* not from this world . . . are we?"

Ernie was barely listening; her mind was too full of how she would deal with the monocle-wearing proprietor who either knew who'd tied up her dad or had straight up done it herself. With no other visible exits, the only thing to do would be to barge right through the store and hope they could make enough of a ruckus to escape if anyone tried to stop them. She reached down quickly and touched the deck in her pocket, and it pulsed with a promising heat. She'd use the cards if she had to, but only as a last resort.

With that scrap of a plan in her mind, she pulled her father out into the corridor. A low grunt was her only warning before something slammed into the back of her head, turning everything black.

CHAPTER TWELVE

Ernie came to with her mouth sour and her tongue dry as sand, her head throbbing and her body hanging from the same damn ropes from which she'd just freed her father. Their rough coils bit into her wrists, and her shoulders felt as though they'd been pulled from their sockets. She struggled to get her feet beneath her.

"She's wakin' up." The voice was rough and raspy, and it belonged to the lady with the monocle. Ernie raised her head slowly to see that the woman was holding a tool that looked like a cross between a wrench and an old clothes iron, with a solid handle and a flat, heavy head that was smeared with blood. A wave of nausea rolled in Ernie's belly. "Get in here," the woman shouted. "She's wakin' up!"

"Patience, Maggie, we're coming," came the reply—from the old man Ernie had met in the bar. Yack, she remembered. He shuffled into the room, steering her father by his elbow. "I told you we'd find a way, *Redmond*. Now, if you don't tell us where you've hidden the treasure you keep blabbing about, we'll bash her head in."

Ernie eyed the weapon in Maggie's hand. One hit from that could break bones. It was a wonder it hadn't broken her skull. She winced as she slid herself up the wall. Maybe it *had* broken her skull. "I'm sure we can find a better way to deal with this little disagreement," she said, though her words came out slurred. Her tongue was like deadweight in her mouth.

"Look at her," said Yack, elbowing Redmond, which sent her father off balance. He leaned against the wall, holding on tight. Yack grabbed his arm and yanked him over to stand in front of Ernie. "Look at this young lady," he said. "Come all the way from . . . Where did you say you came from?"

Ernie just glared at him. Her hands twisted against the ropes so she could wrap her fingers around them and pull them tight.

"Just tell us where you're keepin' it," said Maggie to Redmond, brandishing her weapon.

Yack was eyeing Ernie, his gaze focused on her jeans. "Looks like she's got something there." He pointed to the lump in Ernie's pocket. "Let's see if it's valuable."

Ernie jerked her hips away as Maggie reached for her, but she couldn't go far. The woman's meaty paw dove into Ernie's pocket and came out holding the deck. Ernie's stomach dropped as Maggie turned the cards over in her broad palm.

"This definitely might be worth something," she said. "They look handmade by someone who knowed what they was doing."

Redmond's eyes were wide as saucers. "Weed," he whispered, staring at the Diamondback deck. "You . . . ?"

"How did you think I got here?" Ernie snapped as her father's gaze traveled to her wrist, where the tip of a rattle peeked from under her sleeve.

"*Diamondback,*" he said breathlessly. Awe glittered in her father's eyes. "You'd better give that back to her," he said slowly to Maggie. "It's cursed."

Maggie guffawed. "Now I *know* it's valuable." Her grimy fingernail passed over the image of the rattlesnake devouring the world, and Ernie's arm burned with a sudden, sharp agony. Fear pierced Ernie straight through. The thought of losing her deck, her *diamondback*, twisted her heart to the breaking point.

Redmond's eyes were flitting between the deck and Ernie. "I'm telling you, Maggie. Those cards'll kill you if you mess with them."

Yack leaned forward eagerly. "Anything that makes you nervous makes me happy," the old man said as he jostled Redmond, making Ernie's father wince.

Maggie was staring down at the symbol on the Revelation card, and the sight sent a chill down Ernie's back. "Those are mine," Ernie said slowly, concentrating on every word even as it felt like her left arm was about to explode. Every second that Maggie held on to the Diamondback deck felt gut-wrenchingly wrong. "All I did was try to free a man that you're holding against his will. That doesn't give you the right to steal from me."

Maggie let out a wheezy laugh. "Something tells me no one's even gonna notice when you disappear, little girl."

Fueled by a hunger for survival, Ernie gripped the ropes hard for leverage and kicked upward as hard as she could, landing a solid strike to Maggie's crotch. As the woman howled and doubled over, Ernie jerked her knee up to collide with the woman's nose, sending Maggie crumpling to the ground, bellowing and bleeding. The metal club she'd been holding clattered to the ground, and Yack reached for it.

But Redmond Terwilliger was faster. He swiped it up before the older man could, then slammed it into Yack's chest, toppling him backward into a stack of crates, which crashed to the floor. The sound of breaking glass and splintering wood filled the room. Redmond spun toward Ernie, his eyes clear and sharp in a way that told her he'd just been looking for his chance. He gathered up her cards from the floor, elbowing Maggie hard in the face when she didn't move out of the way fast enough. After he'd shuffled them into the deck, he leaned forward and jammed the cards into Ernie's pocket, then began to rummage through Maggie's. The old woman protested and smacked at him, but it didn't stop him from yanking out a small knife. He kicked away her feeble attempts to grab at his legs while he sawed at Ernie's bonds. "How long have you been a . . . ?" He squinted down at the tip of her tattoo, just visible on her wrist.

"Long enough to make some enemies, obviously, seeing as I'm here," Ernie muttered as she finally yanked her wrists free and staggered for the door.

Redmond knocked Yack away with the club and followed her out, bouncing off the narrow walls of the corridor as they rushed toward the steps, chased by the outraged bellows of their would-be captors. "What's your plan?" he asked Ernie as they blundered up the steps.

Ernie's head was hurting so much that her stomach was about to rebel. "Run, basically."

"I have to get some things before we leave."

"Let me guess: your treasure?" Ernie wrenched the door to the shop open and paused to scan the space for potential attackers before walking through. "Not sure we have time for that." She could already hear Yack and Maggie shouting from the corridor. "You don't seem to have many friends in this town."

He grabbed her arm. "The treasure is everything. With it, I can help you—if you help me."

"Already did," she said as they reached the door of the shop, decorated with its wind chime of animal bones. The scene outside looked calm, people and cars bustling along, but Yack and Maggie had reached the top of the steps.

"Don't move!" roared Maggie. Boom. The pane of glass above Ernie's head shattered with a loud crack.

She's shooting at us, Ernie thought vaguely as her father threw the door open and pulled her onto the sidewalk. At the sharp report of another gunshot, Ernie stumbled forward, her shoulder on fire, her arm swinging like a sandbag on a rope.

"Damn," said Redmond as he shoved Ernie to the ground, where she rolled onto her back like a dying bug, gasping for breath. Her father stood between her and Maggie, who had emerged from the shop with what looked to be a rifle in her hands.

"Someone call the constable!" shouted Redmond.

"Go ahead. *He* wants to shoot you, too," Maggie said, scowling as she raised her weapon. "After you stiffed him last week, I'm thinking it's time for your reckoning."

Ernie hissed as she tried to pull herself from the ground. Her right shoulder radiated agony as blood soaked her sleeve. She needed her cards. She had to stop this. People on the street were rushing away from this confrontation, and no one seemed to be interested in intervening. She might be angry with her dad for being such a jerk, but that didn't mean she was going to let someone shoot him. When she tried to rise, though, Redmond shoved her back down, then held his arms out, still shielding her.

"If you kill me, you'll never know where I hid it all," he said to Maggie.

"That's why I'm gonna kill her instead." Maggie moved to step around Redmond, but he lurched to the side. Maggie's arm jerked up.

And the gun went off. Ernie screamed as the world flashed red and white. Then she opened her eyes and gasped—Maggie stood frozen in place, her gun aimed at Ernie, the bullet suspended in midair about a foot from Ernie's face. Yack, who had moved onto the sidewalk, clutched at his chest and blinked at the scene with wide, terrified eyes.

Powerful hands slid around Ernie's torso and pulled her upward. "I had a bad feeling," Kot said when Ernie whimpered and clutched her arm. "And I was right."

Redmond looked from Maggie to Kot, who steadied Ernie against him. "Oh. It's you," Redmond said lamely.

"Get in the auto," Kot said to Redmond, each word clipped with irritation. He gestured toward it, which was when Ernie realized he had his cards out, four of them glowing at his fingertips—Strike, Accelerate, Inverse, and Enemy. As soon as Redmond darted toward the car, Kot pulled Ernie out of the path of the bullet. He picked her up and deposited her in the open carriage of what looked like an old Model T, the kind Ernie had seen only in a museum before arriving in this accursed place.

With a quiet thump, the bullet buried itself in the base of a wooden signpost, and Maggie staggered. Kot swung himself into the car, which seemed far too small for him. It backfired as he spurred it into motion, and they shot into the crowded street with Maggie shouting behind them. Wind buffeted Ernie as Kot accelerated, swerving around slower cars and outraged pedestrians. Her lips tingled with cold, and the searing pain in her shoulder just wouldn't quit.

"Can't you heal her?" asked Redmond.

"I am busy right now," Kot snapped.

"We have to make a stop," Redmond said. "At the bathhouse."

"As much as you stink, that is still a terrible idea."

Ernie moaned. Redmond grimaced as he looked her over. "I have something that can help her," he told Kot.

"Kot can heal me," Ernie said, wishing her ears would stop ringing.

"No," Redmond said, glancing at Kot nervously. "I mean, I think I can help you get out of this *dimension*."

The next few hours passed in a haze. It involved a lot of jostling, a ton of arguing, and a brief car chase that ended with Maggie running her vehicle into a wooden fence at the edge of town. Their own car broke down not long after that, and Kot pulled Ernie out of the back and carried her to one of those steel barns, possibly the same one he'd been leaning against as he kissed his skittish mystery lover. It had been only the night before, but to Ernie it already felt like a year.

Redmond pulled a slender rod from the large pouch he now had slung across his chest. It must have been what they'd picked up from the bathhouse—which meant his "treasures" might be inside, or maybe just the tricks of his trade. He used the rod to jimmy the lock on the barn door before placing the tool back in his bag. Kot slid the door open, releasing a burst of nervous neighs and the smell of hay and horse manure.

"We can't stay here long," Redmond said. "There's a chance Maggie won't give up. She's been after me for the longest time."

"Do you want me to leave your daughter like this so you can save your own skin?" Kot asked as he helped Ernie inside. "You're the one who insisted we stop at that public bath."

"I had to get the treasures!" He jostled his satchel, the contents of which clanked and rustled.

"Pathetic place to hide them," sneered Kot.

"Good enough to keep 'em safe, I'd say, seeing as they were still there!"

"Jeez, stop arguing and patch me up," Ernie muttered. "Please."

Kot settled her into the straw and knelt at her side, his jaw tight. Glaring at Redmond, he pressed his Healing card to Ernie's shoulder. She let out a sigh as the pain faded, then a groan as the bullet pulled itself from her back and fell into the hay.

"Thank you for helping her," Redmond said, sounding relieved as Ernie rolled her still-aching shoulder.

"I didn't do it for you," Kot said.

"That was a nice trick you did back there to Maggie," Redmond offered. "I thought that meant you'd learned to love your deck by now and be grateful for the gift."

"You know nothing about me."

"You could have transported all of us out of there instantly." Redmond didn't appear to notice the clench of Kot's fists as the younger man rose from the hay. "You could conjure up a lovely place for all of us to stay for the night, along with a tasty meal to share while we catch up on old times. And I, for one, could use a drink." Redmond rubbed his belly.

Kot's hand shot out and wrapped itself around Redmond's throat. He whirled and slammed Ernie's father against the metal wall of the barn. Ernie jumped to her feet and stood between them, pressed against the steely muscles of Kot's tattooed forearm. "Hey," she said quietly. "I get that he's a jerk, but please don't kill him before he tells me how to get out of here."

Kot's dark eyes met hers, and his arm fell to his side.

Her father sagged against the wall, coughing. "All I did was give you my deck," Redmond said hoarsely.

"You did more than that, old man, and you know it," Kot growled. He stomped through the doorway of the barn. "I'm leaving in a few minutes, with or without you."

"Whatever else you did, I recommend apologizing," Ernie said to her father after Kot exited.

Redmond rubbed the top of his bruised, bald head. "I've committed a lot of sins, Weed, but I honestly can't recall which one woulda made him hate me for this long." He turned to look at her. "You, on the other hand . . ."

"What happened, Dad? How did you become a Dealer in the first place, and why did you leave?"

"Your mother never told you?"

Ernie thought back but couldn't draw a single memory up from the depths. "I'm not sure, actually."

Redmond sighed. "This place . . . it steals our memories of where we came from. When I first got here, I tried to hold on to all of it. I wrote it all down, as much as I could remember, even as I started to forget." He opened the satchel, revealing a thick sheaf of brown paper covered in tiny, cramped handwriting. "I used to read it every day. Every single day. But the more days that passed, the less real it seemed."

Ernie felt a pang. She'd been here only a few days—but if she sat down to write out her life, her memories, she wasn't sure she could fill even half those pages. "Did you write about us?"

"Of course I did." As he explained how and why he'd left their family, how her mother had been sick, how he would have done anything for her, a flicker of familiarity sparked in Ernie's brain.

It felt like the truth.

Redmond sighed, rubbing his bruised throat. "I was on a hunt after I got my deck. I wanted to find a way back to you. To Mara." He paused, letting his lips take form around her name like it, too, was a treasure. "I couldn't give up my deck without dying, and I couldn't stay without killing her—the Forger had made that clear, the bastard."

"Do you remember him?"

Redmond laughed. "Remember him? He appeared to me—here! Taunted me for losing my memories, for not being able to get home despite all the things I'd found."

"What things had you found?"

"The artifacts. The tools and weapons and toys created by the Forgers since the beginning of history." He touched his writings, calloused fingertips sliding over smudged pages. "I'd hoped that one of them could get me home. Instead, they got me here."

"How, though?"

"I transported myself all over the world—our world—in search of texts that revealed the history of the Immortal Dealers."

"Did you know about the whole multiple-dimension thing?"

"I didn't come by that knowledge in any ancient text." His eyes met hers. "Virginia taught me about them."

"Virginia."

"We were friends."

"Are you being sarcastic?"

"I wish. That evil woman was the only friend I had in those days."

"And did you know she was evil at the time?"

He laughed. "No, at least, not according to what I wrote." He released the pages and let the flap of the satchel fall shut. "I had thought she was the only person who understood how badly I needed to get back to my family. Once she saw that I'd found some of the barrier runes on my own, she agreed to help me. She said she had an interest in certain artifacts, too, and suggested we work together to collect them. I had no idea what she planned to do with all of it. Turns out she was planning to overthrow the Forger."

Ernie blinked. Now it all made sense, how the Forger had told her to make sure Virginia never saw another sunrise, or something to that effect. "You weren't going to help her, were you?"

He shook his head. "But she was using me to find her weapons. I found the rest of the barrier runes in Mumbai, and the antagonist rune, the one that turns an animal against its Dealer, in Siberia. Wish I could remember . . ." He touched his bruised cheek and winced. "Wish I had a drink."

Ernie wrinkled her nose. "Because that would *totally* help you remember."

"Remembering is painful." His head hung back. "Forgetting is worse, when you realize it's happening. You can't blame me for needing some relief."

"Once again, you're underestimating my blame capacity."

Redmond pulled his ratty coat tighter around his wiry shoulders. "It all came down to the Marks. That's why I'm here." He explained what they were, and again, Ernie felt a stirring in her memory, like this was something she should know.

"They were the hardest artifacts to find," he continued. "We knew there were three left, and we scoured the planet for them. She explained what the etchings on those Marks meant."

"The circles etched with the weird runes, all around the one circle in the center," she murmured automatically, then frowned. "How did I know that?"

"Happens to me all the time," he said sadly. "A flash of memory and hope before everything fades into the fog again. But you're right—those runes in the circles represent dimensions. Only the mapped ones, though."

"Mapped?"

"Meaning complete. Whole."

Ernie's brow crinkled. "Huh?"

Her father's smile was ghostly now. "We're not in a mapped dimension, Weed. This place is a splinter. New dimensions are created all the time. Every decision, every accident might cause one to split off, a new branch in the never-ending chaos of the universe. But only some of those dimensions are fully realized worlds. Others, like this place? You can walk it from end to end. North to south, I give it a few hundred miles. And the edge of it is less than fifty miles from Fortoba."

"The edge?"

Redmond shrugged. "A sea like the one we're headed toward."

"Dad," she said gently, "maybe this is just an island?"

"*No.* I actually know what I'm talking about, Weed. Go find yourself a map of this place, and see if I'm not right. You know why you see no boats on that water? No one would dare, because no one has ever returned from an attempt to cross it. And that sea is as dead as a doornail. Not a speck of life in it at all. Does that sound normal to you?" He gestured toward the door. "Kot and all the others who were born here? They have no idea there are bigger worlds out there. This is all they've ever known. It must have split off a few hundred years ago, and maybe this was part of California or something? The history books . . . they don't document anything before then, which tells me there weren't actual history books present in the area when the fragmentation occurred. But it seems the most likely explanation for the types of people who're here."

She held up her hands. "Okay, so this place is a splinter. But other dimensions aren't."

"The place where we come from is a fully realized, mapped dimension. And there are thirty-five others, according to those Marks. And, apparently, countless splinters."

"How did Virginia manage to strand us in this particular place?"

"She's got the fuse rune, the one that stitches our dimension to this one for a short period of time."

"It's pink," Ernie murmured, remembering its vibrant flash and the suffocating darkness that had ended with the appearance of the green sky above.

"That's right," Redmond said. "She used it on you, too, didn't she?"

Ernie nodded. "I'm not sure why, but I'm going to make her pay." She thought back to her conversation with Andy. "The Forger wants her dead, I think."

"Oh, it's mutual. She hates the guy."

"Why? He gave her a deck and a chance to restore her family's wealth, didn't he?"

"Sure, but it came with a price."

Ernie thought back to what her father had told her about how he'd had to walk away from their family. "Was it the same price you had to pay?"

Redmond nodded. "She was supposed to watch from the outside. Leave her family. Except she didn't."

"Okay . . . why didn't he just take her deck back?"

"Because he did worse than that. Plantation house burned down. Most of her kin died right there, but the rest didn't last much longer. Her entire family, every single cousin even, were systematically snuffed out. No coincidence, neither."

For the first time, Ernie felt a pang of sympathy for the Dealer who had trapped her here. "Jeez. I guess I can see why she hates the Forger." Had Ernie known before that the Forger was such a jerk?

"And she did care enough to warn me not to try to go back to you and your mom, for fear the same thing would happen. I wrote it all out myself, in case I ever made it back, in case I couldn't remember. So she did do that for me, and it might have kept both your mother and you alive. But Andy did something for me, too—giving me a chance to save your mother in the first place. So I wasn't about to help Virginia with her coup. Instead, I found myself the only weapon that could stop her once and for all."

He leaned out the doorway to see Kot sitting in his stolen, broken-down car, drumming his large fingers on the small steering wheel. Then he turned back to Ernie and slid his hand back into the satchel. He came up holding a curved golden dagger, which glinted in a shaft of weak sunlight filtering in from the doorway. There were black runes all over the blade.

It looked very, very familiar.

"This is how I did everything I did," said Redmond. "The postcards I sent you, everything. This could deal Virginia out of the game for good."

"You've had it all this time, but you never tried to use it on her?"

"Nope." Redmond looked down at the dagger, then used the edge to push up his left sleeve, revealing the horrific scar there. "I used it on myself instead."

CHAPTER THIRTEEN

Ernie traced the scar with her gaze, following the wide line of flayed skin from his wrist up to his elbow. Redmond pulled his arm out of the sleeve and lifted his grimy shirt, revealing that the scar wasn't limited to his forearm. The knotty, raised mess traveled along his biceps, across his shoulder, and down to the center of his chest, where it took the shape of a silvery-black starburst. "Whoa," she whispered. "What the hell? You did that yourself?"

Her father let his shirt fall back into place. "I'd say the Cortalaza did most of it herself."

"The Cortalaza—that thing has a name?"

"Sure. Like Excalibur."

"Were you trying to commit suicide?"

"No, not really, but at that point, I was desperate enough to try anything."

"You were here already when you did it."

He nodded. "And that means I remember every single second."

She recalled what Kot had said about how he'd spent an evening with Redmond, gotten drunk, and awakened to buckets of crimson. "And you knew it would separate you from your deck?"

Redmond bowed his head. "Hardest thing I've ever done. Or that I remember doing. I imagine leaving you and your mama was just as hard, if my desperate attempts to get back home are any indication."

"If that's true, why did you decide you didn't want to be a Dealer anymore?" Ernie's eyes narrowed, the old resentment rising up. "You gave up."

"Weed, I would have done anything to get back to you. I was willing to try anything, even as my memories left me."

"How does chopping that poor dragonfly off your arm help anything?" she asked shrilly. Her arm was throbbing, and once again it felt like the diamondback tattoo was about to split her skin. Ernie rubbed her forearm in an attempt to soothe her unease.

"I never wanted to hurt him, okay?" Redmond said. "But if I had to choose between my family and the dragonfly, it was an easy choice." His voice was rough, and he was rubbing his forearm, too, wincing as he did it. "The Cortalaza blade was made by a Forger, one before Andy. That one had a different style, I'd say. The legend calls this blade a dragon slayer, like something out of a fantasy. But it does more than that."

Ernie was bursting with questions, but she needed to stay focused. "Seems like Virginia would want the Cortalaza about as much as she'd want the Marks."

"Oh, you're not kidding. But when she ambushed me, I had everything stashed. My writings, my treasures, my postcard collection, anything I couldn't carry with me that I valued. She had no idea she was banishing everything she wanted along with me. She thought she'd be able to find my haven and get to the treasure, but I'd put it in a place no one would ever find."

Ernie thought back to her cards—and the one that had given her that rush of hope that it might be a bridge to her home dimension. "You hid everything in the dream realm, didn't you?" She pulled out her Dreams card and looked down at it, startled as a memory from her childhood came back as she looked down at the image beneath the symbol. "I don't suppose your haven is that old tent with the taped-up rip?"

His mouth hung half-open for a few seconds. "How did you . . . ?"

"In the Pisgah Forest, right where we used to camp? Or the Dreams version of it, anyway."

His face, round eyes and slack mouth, would have been comical if it hadn't made her feel so confused and sad. She waved the moment away, not wanting to admit the connection. "I still don't get why you decided to use that blade on yourself or why you thought that would help you get back to your family."

"That's what I'm trying to tell you." He held up the blade. "It slices through everything—not just Dealers and their animals. It can carve out an opening between the dimensions. A window."

"Then how come you didn't use it to get home?"

He let the blade fall to his side. "The dimensions want to be separate, you know? The window closes fast and hard. So when I couldn't keep it open long enough to get my body through, I started sending messages."

Ernie hugged herself against a chill. "The postcards . . ."

"Do you remember getting them? I sent a bunch of them that year."

"One or two," she murmured. She remembered going out to the mailbox. She remembered knowing the postcards would make her mother cry. She remembered hiding them away.

"I sent the Forger's artifacts that I'd found, too. I had figured out that if I ever could get back through to the other side, I wouldn't be able to risk carrying anything. And I was worried that Virginia would find me in the dream realm—she was getting close. So I was sending everything ahead, hoping she wouldn't realize the artifacts were back in her dimension. And your mother was the only one I trusted." He was watching her closely. "I'm guessing they made it back. I'm even guessing they have something to do with why you're here."

"I can't remember," Ernie said. She growled with frustration. "I can't remember what happened!"

"But you remember getting at least one of them. Maybe the others got stuck in some interdimensional whirlpool or something." He let out a dry chuckle. "Good thing I *didn't* try to fit through myself. I'd probably still be out there in the void."

"How long was it until your deck adjusted and you couldn't open the portal anymore?"

"Completely? Almost a year. I was counting the days as I tried to get my deck to work—I didn't know that would mean I was stuck here forever. And it was dangerous, too, because often, when I tried to play a card, this . . . *thing* would show up—a monster. Like a giant insect."

Ernie glanced out at Kot, who was now leaning against the car, his arms folded and his eyes on the northern horizon. "Apparently her name is Nuria."

"The monster has a *name?*"

"Sure. Like Cthulhu."

"Whatever its name is, when I tried to use my cards, she'd come rampaging out of her woods and make me fight her off." He glanced at Ernie's pocket, where her cards lay. "Barely survived her first few attacks. But every time I used the cards, they worked a little better."

"I would have thought that was a good thing. But Kot told me it meant the cards were adjusting to this dimension."

"Exactly. So every time I tried to open a portal to my home dimension, it was harder. The opening was narrower. The time before it closed was shorter. I sent the last one right after I cut myself, hoping I'd be able to follow. No such luck." His grip on the Cortalaza blade tightened. "But for you, maybe we can figure it out. Your cards still haven't adjusted. You just need one thing, and it would make all the difference."

Ernie leaned forward, her heart skipping. "What?"

"Someone pulling hard from the other side. It's the one thing I never had."

"She may have that," said Kot, looming in the doorway, making Ernie jump. "She told me so herself. A person named Gabe."

Gabe. She'd almost forgotten.

"This was a private conversation," said Redmond, crossing his arms.

Ernie slapped her dad lightly on the shoulder. "Dude. He just saved our lives. He's saved my life probably four times now."

"Exactly," said Kot, eyeing the blade. "And that is why you will do *me* a favor. If your Gabe pulls you back to your home dimension—you will not be the only Dealer who steps through. You understand?"

All he wanted was to go with her? "Hey, no problem," said Ernie. "If we can actually make this work, I'm happy to have you as my ally." She poked her father in the chest. "And you, too. Mom needs you."

For a moment, Ernie could see the thrill in his eyes at the prospect, but then the spark died. "We don't know how long the portal would be open," grumbled Redmond. "It depends on so many factors."

Kot waved toward the road. "Then let us discuss it on the way. We are losing the light and should be at the waypoint between dimensions before the sun sets. Yes?" His gestures and expression were alive with a hope that Ernie hadn't seen since meeting him, and it made her smile.

"Yes," she said and tugged on her father's sleeve. "Let's go and see if we can make this work." She began to hike toward the road, carried forward on a wave of excitement. With any luck, she'd be back home—with her memories—in just a few hours.

"I still don't get why you thought not being a Dealer would help you get home," Ernie said as the dank sea appeared on the horizon. They'd been walking for a few hours, mostly in silence, Kot often several yards in front of them, as if he couldn't stand to be too close to Redmond. But Ernie's brain had been a stew of excitement and confusion the whole time, and it was taking all she had to sort out her thoughts. "I mean, what made you even think of that?"

Redmond prodded a swollen spot on his cheek. He was surprisingly durable despite his completely bedraggled appearance. He had found himself a stick to replace his cane and was limping along at a decent clip. "You ever use your Foretell card?"

Ernie shrugged. "I'm honestly not sure."

"It's a dangerous one. If you try to use it to see the future, that'll lock in whatever you see. There'll be no changing it. But sometimes it's all you've got."

Kot looked over his shoulder at Redmond, then slowed to allow them to catch up. "I used it once."

"And what did you see?"

"Something that gave me hope."

"Did it come to pass?" asked Ernie.

"Not yet."

"It will," said Redmond. "That's how it works. And I was desperate enough and stupid enough to give it a try."

"What did you see in the card?"

"I saw myself using the Cortalaza. I saw the Dragonfly freed." He rubbed his chest. "And I thought, sure, that must be the answer. If I'm not a Dealer, if I'm not connected by the soul to a deck that belongs to this dimension now, then maybe I could finally make it home, even though I could barely remember it at that point."

Ernie thought of that terrible scar. "I don't know how you survived."

"Almost didn't." Redmond glanced up at Kot. "But I found the Dragonfly the strongest, best new Dealer I possibly could." He leaned closer to Kot, who leaned away. "He'd serve you better if you loved him back."

"Whoa," said Ernie. "Kot made a four-card play back there fast enough to stop a bullet from hitting me right between the eyes. I think both of them are doing okay."

"Doesn't mean he couldn't do better if he and the Dragonfly were really in sync."

"It doesn't always happen that way, old man." Kot's voice was cold with rage.

"Oh, you don't have to tell me that. I'm the king of crushed hopes and broken dreams." Redmond's toe caught on a rock, and he stumbled a few steps, the contents of his satchel making a muffled clank. "After I took a knife to me and my deck, it took me months to heal up, but when I did, I went back to the waypoint, inside those stone walls by the sea. And I tried to open a portal again, this time to get home."

"And?"

Redmond grimaced and spat into the weeds at the side of the road. "Turns out, if it's not in the hands of an Immortal Dealer, the Cortalaza is just a knife like any other. A pretty gold-colored one, sure, but it's still just a knife. And *that* was when I gave up."

"But I won't," said Ernie, her strides lengthening as the stone-bounded waypoint came into sight.

"You had better not," Kot replied.

"It's all gonna be about timing, though," Redmond told them. "If you want to get all three of us through that window?" He scoffed. "It's gonna take some powerful pulls from the other side. Especially because *he* is from here." He jabbed a finger at Kot. "And me? I'm just a civilian now." He locked gazes with Ernie. "I might not even survive it."

Ernie pulled her deck and drew Shield, Family, and Strength from the rest. They were warm to the touch. They felt *ready*. "You won't be alone, Dad. Not this time."

For several moments, only the sound of their crunching footsteps hung in the air. Then he let out a shuddering sigh. "I've been alone for so long, Ernie. And that might be best."

"Now you're being a chicken." She gave him a hard look. "She needs you, Dad."

"Do you know that for sure? Can you remember?" he asked, a heartbreaking hope in his eyes. "She didn't get married again? She hasn't just moved on?"

"I don't . . . think so. I just—I was never enough for her. No matter how hard I tried." She tried to blink away the sting in her eyes as her tattoo burned sharply and suddenly on her arm.

He patted her shoulder. "I know it's hard, to feel but not remember. Don't push it. Let's focus on getting back to her. How much of an ally is this Gabe?"

"I'm not actually sure," she admitted. "But I think we're connected. I saw him in my Friend-Lover card. We must be close, right?" She looked at her father, as if he could tell her the answer.

"Friends come and go, and so do lovers. Doesn't mean he was more than a moment in your life. Did you say he's a Dealer? What deck does he have?"

Ernie's chest ached. "I can't remember. But—he has something to do with why I'm here."

Her father's eyebrows shot up. "Are you sure he's not allied with Virginia? Maybe he was pretending to care about you to get to your cards or . . . the Marks I sent your mother?" He looked alarmed, but Ernie couldn't focus on what he was saying, as none of it connected with her memories. All she had right now were feelings.

"I think Gabe is good." Ernie swallowed, caught off guard by a powerful swell of longing. "And that he's my ally, not hers."

"But Dealers play alone, unless the alliance is to their advantage."

"Gabe is different," Ernie murmured, her cheeks hot. Kot was watching her steadily. Unlike her father, he seemed to understand her feelings. Ernie looked away, trying to remember Gabe's face. He had blue eyes. She could vaguely remember them from her Friend-Lover card. He'd definitely been there. "We're connected. More than allies. I think he's looking for me." Ernie pushed her doubts back with sheer will. "Whatever's happening to him, whatever he has to do, *he* wouldn't abandon me."

Redmond flinched at the accusation in her voice. "Well, let's hope so. But the trick will be to sync up with him. Even if he was able to get the fuse rune from Virginia, we'd have to be right here at the waypoint at just the right time to meet up with him."

"Then I'll camp here as long as it takes."

Redmond threw an uneasy glance at the woods at the base of the peak off to the east. "That's risky."

"And whose fault is that?" snapped Kot.

Redmond's brow furrowed. "How 'bout you tell me?"

"You know what you did," Kot said, his voice rising. "Stop telling your pitiful stories and acting so innocent. As far as I'm concerned, you are the author of your own suffering. Every bit of it." He stepped back, fists clenched. "And mine." He spun on his heel and began to stalk away.

Ernie ran after him, putting her hand on his arm to slow him down. "Hey," she said gently. "Don't go."

"I'll get kindling for a fire," he said, looking toward the woods. "It will be a cold night."

Ernie followed the line of his gaze. "Are we going to have to fight her off? Maybe that Cortalaza blade—"

"No," Kot said. "I will deal with her." He shrugged off her touch. "I'll be back soon." He picked up his pace and left Ernie in his wake, feeling as if she were sitting in front of a giant jigsaw puzzle with several key pieces missing.

When she returned to her father's side, he was sitting on a broad, flat rock and looking out at the sea. "When I first got here," he said, "I spent a lot of my time asleep. The dream realm was the only escape. I thought it might be *the* escape. Have you tried it?"

Ernie shook her head. "But I think my haven is there."

"Then you don't know. You haven't figured it out." He chuckled. "The dream realm is the only place your deck will work, no matter where you are. Your brain'll work better there, too. You just have to get there."

Ernie sank to the ground. "Seriously?"

Redmond nodded. "Don't get me wrong—you can't use Transport or Escape cards from there, unless you want to end up right back in this place. But depending on your skill and focus, you can manifest things and bring them back." He chuckled. "Pretty much how I fed myself for the first few months here. I focused on using the Dreams card and nothing else until I got into the realm—to keep from attracting the monster in the woods over there."

"I wondered if I could use the Dreams card to contact Gabe," Ernie said, rubbing her arm. As the weak green sunlight gave way to twilight gloom, she squinted toward the woods. "Seems like a risk, though."

Redmond jostled the pommel of the Cortalaza, which he'd tucked into the belt that held up his sagging pants. "Nah. This thing'd take care of that beast, easy. Haven't found anything it couldn't cut through, even though I'm not a Dealer anymore. Except for this damn dimension."

Ernie wondered whether Nuria could sense the Cortalaza blade, and whether that was the danger that had kept her away from Fortoba. "Except Kot seems to want to handle her himself." She shook her head, thinking of Nuria, the monster that Kot seemed to both despise and defend. He was so strange and secretive about her—and his bond with Nuria wasn't the only thing he was hiding. As she thought back to the Dragonfly Dealer's mystery lover, a creeping suspicion occurred to her. "Are there other Dealers here? Have you ever met one?"

Redmond sighed. "Only one. And I killed her a long time ago."

Ernie rocked back. "Why?"

"She attacked me! First thing I remember about being here. Soon as Virginia dropped me in this place, she was waiting. I think they were allies." He scowled out at the swamp-sea. "I did what I had to do, Weed. I always have." His stubborn, hunched posture told her he wasn't about to reveal any more.

Ernie leaned back against the low stone wall and straightened her legs. "Just wake me up if you hear the monster, okay? She moves fast, so be ready." She pulled out her deck. "I'm just making the one play. Two cards. Maybe it won't ping her radar, since I'll have the cards in the dream realm instantly." She pulled her Haven and Dreams cards.

Redmond sat up on the stone, like he was trying to look tough. "Seems like the most likely way to get through to your ally—if that's really what he is. Watch yourself. The dream realm is a crazy place."

Ernie looked down at her cards. "I'll be back as soon as I can."

"Safe travels."

She crossed the cards and peered at Dreams, relieved to see the image of her tent deep within. After one last glance to reassure herself that a giant monster grasshopper wasn't bearing down on them, she relaxed and let herself tip forward, falling into the card's depths as easily as diving into a swimming pool. A moment later, she was planting her feet in the damp leaves and inhaling the smell of spring in the Blue Ridge Mountains, breathing it in like she'd been underwater for days. Home. This was home.

She looked down at her arm and pulled up the sleeve of her jacket. Legs! There she was, shining and powerful. "Hey! Do you want to come out and visit?" she asked the serpent.

Legs throbbed on Ernie's arm like she wanted to tear herself away, but she didn't emerge. Ernie rubbed the tattoo. "You okay? I've missed you so much."

Legs didn't give her anything to go on, so Ernie headed for her tent, taking in every sight and sound, promising herself she'd notice and remember every detail. Well. Maybe not *every* detail. Her foot struck a pile of rocks that hadn't been there on previous visits, and she stumbled before hopping up and down and cursing. She turned back to see a small cairn, the rocks stacked just so—except for the one she'd kicked off the top. Was that a message from her subconscious? If so, she had no idea how to translate it.

The duct tape was still on the canvas of her tent, patching up the tear she remembered from her childhood. She walked over to it and touched the silver strip, wondering again about how her father had had the same haven. He'd said things were connected in the dream realm—and that Virginia had almost found him here. She'd thought it was all in her head, but the realm must connect *all* dreamers somehow. The thought was both intriguing and worrying.

She gently tugged the zipper up, babying it over the parts where it liked to stick, and climbed inside, where a few of her favorite childhood snacks awaited her. Fruit Roll-Ups, Bugles, and Cool Summer Capri Sun. After a few days of almost nothing but cornmeal bricks and pickled vegetables, Ernie couldn't help herself; she pounced on the food and shoved it into her mouth by the handful, crunching and chewing with a desperation that surprised her. But after a few minutes, her belly sloshing with her third bag of Capri Sun, she tore her attention away from the food and focused on her cards once more.

She had to find the right combination to send a signal to Gabe, one strong enough to act as a homing beacon. Maybe he could find her here. And maybe she'd be able to remember how, exactly, they were connected. The thought made her heart beat faster. He was hanging at the edge of her memory like a word on the tip of her tongue. Here, in the dream realm, it felt like she could make contact, if not with him, then maybe with the memories of how they knew each other and who he was to her.

After shuffling through her options, she settled on the Friend-Lover card, the Aid card, the Amplify card, and the Transport card. Savoring the relief at the familiarity of her card plays, at how natural it felt, she laid the chosen cards out on the floor of the tent next to her sleeping bag, crossing them carefully, and focused as hard as she could on the idea that Gabe could sense her need and reach across dimensions to help her, to get her out of here. Just as she was squinting into the Friend-Lover card on top, a light footfall outside drew her head up.

"You in there, darlin'?"

The sound of his voice, a deep, Irish lilt, so familiar and yet so startling, drew a wrenching cry from Ernie's throat. She tore the flap of the tent open. He stood in the dappled sunlight beneath the trees, his hair long and loose, his blue eyes intense. He opened his arms and welcomed her as she crashed into him, driven by soul-deep longing. "Oh my god," she sobbed against his chest. "It's you, isn't it? It's really you."

He didn't embrace her as she'd expected, but instead simply stood there, allowing her to cling to him. "It's me," he said. "You need to remember this."

He grabbed her left arm and pressed his thumb to the Diamondback tattoo, sending an agonizing jolt along her bones. Ernie yelped and tried to pull herself loose. "Ow! Stop!"

Her head filled with memories all at once—Gabe standing under a white birch, his gaze desolate and devastating. Virginia throwing Trey and Tarlae off a cliff using barrier runes. Andy promising that he'd complete Gabe's deck if Ernie made sure Virginia never saw the sunrise. Virginia standing over her, grinning like a madwoman. Mara Terwilliger *looking* like a madwoman. Legs rattling furiously, fangs bared and dripping, looming over Ernie, ready to strike. It was too much, too confusing.

It was like drowning. She couldn't breathe. "Stop," she gasped.

"I'll never stop," he said quietly, pressing even harder. "You should know that by now."

Tears filled her eyes, both from the pain and from the calm, cool look on his face. "I thought we were—" Agony and confusion momentarily stole her words. What *was* he, really? A friend? A lover? Or something else entirely? Fear bloomed inside her. Had she been wrong about their connection—was it the opposite of what she'd believed?

"Why are you doing this?" she asked. She continued to try to free herself while the memories raged in her head. A white card, a winged snake. Her father fishing in the river. Gabe kissing her. Gabe using his cards to hold a truck over her head. She couldn't sort through it all, and it felt as if her head were about to explode.

Like an idiot, she'd left her cards in the tent. "Who are you?" she demanded.

"You already know." Now his thumb was actually sinking into her skin, making the tattoo waver and ripple like the surface of a lake. "You just haven't been paying attention."

Ernie kneed him in the thigh and jerked herself away, panting. Her left arm hurt so much that she could barely move her fingers. "You're not real," she said between heavy breaths. "You're part of the dream. This is all in my head."

He began to melt like ice cream under the sun. "Does it matter?" he asked, the words gurgling from his throat. "Memories or not, real or not, you know who I am." His voice faded to nothing as his face turned to goo and his body became a crimson puddle on the ground.

Ernie's stomach rebelled at the sight, and she retched and turned her back. She braced her right hand on her knee and tried to catch her breath. When the ringing in her ears subsided a bit, another noise pinged into her awareness. Something huge was crashing around in the woods that bounded her haven.

She ran for the tent, where she'd left her deck. Her left arm was alight with pain, and her skin prickled with cold sweat as she reached inside and scooped up all her cards. She whipped around just as the danger revealed itself.

It was Nuria. Teeth already dripping blood, the monster leapt into the clearing and landed with a thunderous splash in the ruby-red puddle that had once been Gabe. Ernie screamed in spite of herself and clutched her cards to her chest. Was Nuria already there in the real world? Was Ernie already caught in her jaws? Her arm felt like it was being shredded. She had to wake up. She had to fight.

Her body electrified with the need to survive, she jerked awake with her deck at the ready, though she could hold the cards only in her right hand, because her left was twitching uncontrollably.

But it wasn't Nuria who had come for her.

CHAPTER FOURTEEN

Night had fallen, a humid, starless blanket of darkness, but it was filled with flames and shouts and metal clanging. Something hit her in the face and sent her crashing to the ground, where her father already lay. He was struggling to get up, but his head was bleeding. Ernie used her thumb to edge the Shield card up from the rest of her deck and focused her thoughts on a protective bubble around the two of them.

The cacophony went silent except for a few shallow thuds. Ernie raised her head. A mob had crowded around the clear dome that protected Ernie and her father. "Hey," she said, jostling him. "What happened?"

"I was trying to wake you," he said with a groan, cringing as Maggie slammed her club into the bubble, making it buckle inward. "They followed us, I guess, but they must've left their autos far enough away so they could sneak up on us. Waited for nightfall to attack."

The bubble shuddered as several bullets hit its surface, leaving pockmarks that rippled outward. "This isn't going to protect us much longer," Ernie muttered. With a grimace, she got to her feet. "I'm going to have to deal with them."

"The more you play, the more the deck adjusts to this place," Redmond said. He drew the Cortalaza blade and swiped the blood from his battered face with his sleeve. "We might not be able to open the window back home."

"Does it look like I have a choice?" shouted Ernie as the shield popped like a balloon. She played Air and Accelerate, sending a powerful gust outward and blowing several of the attackers off their feet.

"You can't just steal all our money and skip town," bellowed a man with a huge mustache whom Ernie recognized from that morning as the dentist, one of the many who'd complained that Redmond owed him scads of silver.

"Get his pouch." Maggie barged forward with her metal club raised. "That's where he's got the treasure!"

Ernie flipped her Strike and Rest cards, then swept them toward the crowd. Several of the villagers collapsed to the ground, causing their fellow townspeople to yowl with outrage. The sleepers' bodies jerked like they were having seizures, which Ernie hadn't intended, but her cards were pulsing with a strange, static heat. She wasn't sure whether that meant they were adjusting or they were trying to warn her just how wrong it felt to be operating in this dimension.

Yack was shaking a snoring Maggie by the shoulders as a half dozen others brandished hoes and honest-to-god torches. A glint of light off metal in her periphery was the only warning Ernie had before the crack of a pistol. A slice of pain cut across her cheek and filled her ears with a deafening whoosh. Clumsily, her brain scrambling for something to hold the townspeople back without killing them, she dealt Tool, Sea, Accelerate, and Prolong, envisioning what she needed.

A thick fire hose appeared in her hand, one end extending over the edge of the cliff. Bracing herself with the hose clamped under her right arm, Ernie opened it up and sent a blast of stinking seawater toward the mob. Redmond whooped as Ernie drove dozens of people back, but the water pressure faded quickly, leaving her with a dripping length of greasy rope, another signal from her glitching deck. "Stand back," Ernie shouted, though she could barely hear herself. The bullet that had grazed her cheek must have clipped her ear. "We can work this out without violence."

Her words had a startling effect. The expressions of the towns-people, who were gathered on the other side of the stone wall, dripping with swampy brown water, transformed in an instant from rage to ter-ror. Like one being, they whirled around and began to run. Ernie was glancing down at her cards, wondering whether she'd done something terrible, when Redmond yanked her arm. She looked over at him to see the same horrified expression on his face. His lips were forming words she couldn't hear, but the urgency was obvious. Redmond pointed fran-tically, and Ernie turned.

Kot was sprinting toward them, his arms waving, his eyes wide, his mouth moving.

Behind him was the monster, closing quickly. As the Dragonfly Dealer ran, the creature he'd named Nuria leapt into the air and landed on his back, crushing him to the ground before launching itself upward once again. Ernie's left arm exploded with heat as she watched the creature land in the midst of the fleeing townspeople, grabbing one unfortunate man between her jaws.

Faintly, Ernie heard screams, though it felt like her ears had been stuffed with cotton and jingle bells. Several of her cards lay at her feet, and she knelt to gather them up, wishing her left hand would pull its weight.

"Come *on*," she yelled. For the first time, anger toward the dia-mondback on her arm burst into her consciousness. She was doing all the work while the snake did nothing but hurt her.

Kot had gotten to his knees and was pressing a card—Healing, Ernie assumed—to his shoulder. Nuria was chowing down perhaps a hundred feet from where Ernie and Redmond stood, while the towns-people who'd attacked them ran for cover.

"This is on me," Redmond said, right in Ernie's ear. "I'll fix it." With the Cortalaza blade in hand, he stepped over the low stone wall and began to jog toward the rampaging monster, picking up speed with every stride.

Fabulous blade or not, it was painfully obvious that her father didn't stand a chance. Ernie vaulted the stone wall, bloodying her knuckles as she tried to hold her cards and avoid using her disabled and agonized left arm. Off-kilter, she ran after her dad, thinking that for once in her life, she'd love to have a parent who wasn't completely crazy.

The monster tossed her head and turned as Redmond bellowed a war cry and raised the curved blade in the air. Nuria let out one of those shrieking roars and bared her teeth. Ernie shouted at Redmond, but he either was going too fast to change course or had just decided that this was a good way to die. Nuria lunged, and Ernie cried out.

But the beast never got to Redmond—Kot slammed into Nuria and wrapped his arms around her head. His feet left the ground as she tried to throw him off, and one shoe made hard contact with Redmond's face, sending him staggering backward. Nuria roared again, then Kot went flying, too.

Ernie stopped where she was, maybe ten yards from the monster, and flung out her hand, her Death and Strike cards held between her fingers. A few sizzling sparks exploded around the beast's head, but that was it. She was outside the boundaries of the waypoint, and her cards still hadn't adjusted completely.

But she'd given Nuria a new target. The thing closed most of the distance to Ernie with one terrible leap. Ernie backtracked, knowing she needed to get to the waypoint to give herself a fighting chance. Kot was limping toward them, waving his arms and shouting that he would take care of Nuria, but there was no time for that. Ernie whipped around and ran.

The creature jumped over her head and landed inside the stone walls of the dimensional waypoint. Ernie clenched her teeth and climbed up on the wall, which sent another burst of pain through her left arm. More battle with the cards could strand her here, she knew, but it was better than letting a monster grasshopper eat her or anyone else. Air, Sharpen, Strength, Weapon, and the Clay Wild would allow her to shape and direct the attack to her will—it was time for a lightning strike that would blow the damn thing to hell.

Her hair crackled with the charge in the air as she raised her cards to the sky. Kot shouted, "No!"

Nuria roared, an earsplitting sound that was cut off instantly by a bolt from above. Ernie was thrown backward and hit the ground so hard that it knocked the breath from her lungs. Shaking, she pushed herself to her feet to see the effect of her strike.

It wasn't what she'd expected.

There was no sign of the monster, but Kot was within the boundaries of the waypoint now. And in his arms was a naked woman.

As Ernie gaped, Kot tore his long jacket from his body and wrapped it around the woman's slender body. She was trembling, her arms flopping as Kot tended to her. He murmured to her gently, urgently, in a language Ernie didn't understand.

Was that a villager? How had she ended up inside the stone-bounded waypoint?

"What in tarnation?" Redmond muttered as he limped over next to Ernie. His face was ashen, and his eyes were riveted on the woman.

Kot cradled the woman's head against his chest, his face twisted in pain as he rocked her. When he turned to look at Ernie and Redmond, his eyes were filled with accusations. "I told you not to attack her," he said.

"Whoa. What?" Ernie climbed over the wall yet again and walked slowly toward Kot and the woman. Behind her, she could hear Redmond doing the same. "Explain," she said curtly. Her arm was still killing her, and now it was obvious that Kot had been keeping way too many secrets. Or just one very big, very dangerous one.

"Ask your father," Kot snarled. The violence in his voice was completely at odds with the gentle way he stroked the woman's hair away from her face. With a pang, Ernie realized it was the woman she'd seen him kissing the night before. Her delicate face was pale as death, and her eyes were staring up at the sky, wide and dark and deep.

"That's the Dealer who attacked me when I was first stranded here," Redmond said in a weak voice.

"Huh? You said you killed her!"

"You *did*," Kot snapped.

"What did you do to her?" asked Ernie, noting with some relief that the woman was still alive. She appeared to be trying to wrap her fingers around Kot's wrist as he continued to hold her. "I thought you just took her deck."

"No, I used a rune," said Redmond. "I'd had it on me when Virginia ambushed me. She was so fast that I didn't have the chance to use it on her, but when that one attacked"—he pointed at the woman in Kot's arms—"I pulled it out and used it."

"But obviously it didn't kill her."

"I thought it did, okay? She . . . exploded. There was nothing left."

"Wrong," said Kot.

The woman let out a wrenching whimper. She writhed like she was trapped in a nightmare.

"The rune," said Redmond. "It was similar to the one I sent to your mother later, the antagonist rune that turns animals against their Dealers. They were a pair."

One that turned animals against their Dealers. It sounded so familiar. "Let me guess," Ernie said. "Nuria was the Grasshopper Dealer."

"I never knew what she was. It was a shoot-first, ask-questions-later kind of situation."

Ernie's eyes met Kot's. "Instead of making her animal attack her, did it turn her *into* that animal?"

"It's worse than that," said Kot, shifting so he could sit in the grass with the woman leaning against his chest. Her eyes were still unfocused, and her hands were twitching. Kot kept his arms around her, holding her securely against his body. "It merged them. But the two are always at war. And one day, one of them will win." He grimaced. "She is losing herself. She has been losing herself piece by piece for years. More than her memories. Her *mind*."

"She attacked me!" blurted Redmond. "It was me or her!"

"Nuria wasn't attacking you," shouted Kot, making the woman jerk with surprise. "She was trying to get to the Dealer who stranded you here! She was trying to get *home*!"

Ernie's mouth went dry. "Virginia had done this before."

"Nuria had been trapped here for years, trying to get back," said Kot. "She would not give up, even as her memories of her home dimension left her. Like you, she had found a way of remembering things. Unlike you, she was good and exquisite and determined." He glared at Redmond. "And you *ruined* her."

Redmond let out a pained groan and spun around, walking away with his arms up. Ernie took a step toward the cursed lovers. "I saw you kissing her last night," she admitted.

"So that's why she ran from me," Kot said quietly. He looked down at Nuria. "I never know why she runs. Sometimes I think it's to protect me because the grasshopper is taking over again."

"You've known all this time that she was the monster."

He closed his eyes. "She senses the cards. Even the grasshopper is determined to get home. My deck is weaker now, unconnected to your world, and my cards disturb her less. But I still use them as little as possible to avoid agitating her." He looked up at Ernie. "At first, when the deck changed hands, she couldn't stay away."

Ernie turned to Redmond. "I thought you said your deck had fully adjusted to this dimension by the time you gave it to Kot."

His back turned, Redmond shrugged. "It had. She must have sensed a new Dealer. A new energy I didn't have."

"She almost killed me," Kot said, loud enough for Redmond to hear. "Right when the grasshopper had me at her mercy, though, Nuria found the strength to emerge."

Ernie thought back to that moment in the pit in Honeida, when she'd been face to face with the beast. After she'd spoken to it, the creature had paused, shuddering violently, just before Kot drew its attention away. Had Nuria been trying to stop what was happening? "So she's trapped inside that insect most of the time?"

"Inside its spirit as well as its body," Kot said sadly. His thumb stroked the woman's cheek. "She is more like the beast every year, no matter how she fights."

Nuria's gaze was slowly sharpening, and her eyes settled on Kot's face, filling with tears. He hunched over her, again murmuring to her in a foreign tongue. She let out a few faint noises that didn't even vaguely resemble words. "Did she tell you all this?" Ernie asked.

"Many years ago," said Kot. "She has not been able to speak for a long time. The words abandoned her one by one, until she had none left. But before her voice was taken from her, she made me promise." He clutched her head to his chest and looked away. "She asked me to stop her, to keep her from killing, to kill her if it was necessary."

"But you couldn't bring yourself to do it," Ernie said quietly.

He shook his head. "I was already in love with her. She would rather die than kill the innocent. Her heart is true and beautiful, and that is worth saving."

"So you try to stop her when she attacks."

"I am not always successful, obviously. But I try to protect her—and others—from herself."

"Why didn't you just tell me it was her?"

He sighed. "She is ashamed. She blames herself for the deaths she has caused, and she can't imagine others wouldn't blame her as well. Another promise she forced me to make." His gaze settled on a distant point in the field beyond the walls, probably a spot where the monster had left bodies scattered. "And if people knew she is a woman by night, they might try to seek her out and destroy her when she is vulnerable. She has no deck to protect herself—the cards' magic runs through her very veins, but she cannot control it or shape it for defense. The secret has been mine to keep."

"At the expense of half the people in this dimension," said Redmond. He'd come back into the stone boundary with the Cortalaza blade in his hand. "You should have done what she asked—if not for her, for everyone else."

"How about I kill you instead, old man?" Kot asked.

Ernie caught the deadly promise in his voice and took a half step in front of Redmond. "He didn't know what he was doing when he used the rune, just like Nuria doesn't fully comprehend when she kills. Both of them are just trying to survive."

"That is generous," said Kot. "You are protecting a man who is so cowardly that he couldn't welcome you as his daughter. Even as you risk your life to rescue him from certain death, he drags the danger along with him." His gaze settled on Redmond. "You cannot admit the damage you have done. To Nuria, to me, to your own daughter, and to so many others. Which means you will continue to hurt every soul you touch."

Redmond's expression was stony, but the color had gone from his face. Ernie opened her mouth to defend her father but found that she couldn't argue. "My mother needs him," she said lamely. "And that's all I care about."

Kot's stare was unrelenting. "He will hurt her, too."

"Assuming I even have the chance to take him back to her." Ernie looked down at the Cortalaza blade clenched in her father's fist. As her arm throbbed, she thought of the Gabe in her dream and how he had coldly taunted and hurt her. *If* he was trying to pull her back into his dimension, why was he doing it? Misgiving trickled like a mountain spring inside her mind, soaking her thoughts, but now it wasn't just about herself. It was about the people she needed to take with her. "If we do have that chance to get back to my home dimension, are you sure you're willing to leave Nuria and come with us? It might be more than you're bargaining for."

"What?" Kot asked.

"The favor I owe you. You said you wanted to go with me."

Kot shook his head. "That is *not* what I asked. If you are able to open a window to your home dimension, it is Nuria you will take."

CHAPTER FIFTEEN

Ernie rubbed her arm and blew out a long breath. Kot had pulled his deck out and was holding it even as he cradled his love. "She's dangerous, Kot," she said gently.

"It's the one thing that could save her, so you will do this for me. You gave me your word, and I have been your steadfast ally from the beginning."

She had given her word, and she definitely owed him. Maybe he was right—maybe Nuria would be different in her home dimension, more in control, more able to remember. Ernie certainly hoped she herself would be. "What if she starts to forget you, though?"

Kot's handsome face was a mask of determination. "As long as she is safe and alive and herself again, I accept that price."

"Fine. Then I'll try to take her back with me. But I think you should try to come, too." At this point, with her arm feeling the way it was and the fact that her deck seemed to be gathering power in this dimension, not to mention the fact that Gabe might not be who she'd thought, she wasn't sure her efforts would amount to much.

"Did you make contact with your ally in the dream realm?" Redmond asked.

"For a second I thought I had." The hope she'd felt at seeing Gabe standing in the clearing had left a bruise on her heart. "But he wasn't what I expected." His touch had felt like an assault on both her body and her mind. "Maybe it was just my imagination, though."

Redmond's eyes narrowed as he watched her rubbing her arm. "Are you sure?"

"If not, then Gabe is just a pile of goo now. He kind of melted." But only after he had heartlessly told her he'd never stop hurting her. "It definitely wasn't him." At least, she hoped not.

Redmond sat down heavily. "Maybe he's not your friend. Or maybe he's not actually looking for you."

"Ouch," she murmured.

"Sorry, Weed. It's just the truth. Dealers play alone. Always comes down to that. Alliances never last long." He touched his satchel, where his treasured writings lay. "And I know more than most how friends can become enemies."

Ernie leaned against the thigh-high stone wall. "I know." She pulled her throbbing arm against her body, trying to find a position that hurt a little less. "And that means we should be ready for anything—including a duel—if we're able to make it through." She glanced at Nuria. "Are you sure you want to expose her to that danger?"

"There is danger everywhere," Kot replied. He looked down as Nuria sat up, then he shifted his body so she was facing toward the sea—and not the fields where she'd wreaked havoc. He slowly pulled them both to their feet. "You should open that window as soon as you can, if you wish to avoid even more." His thumb nudged a card away from the rest of the deck.

"Is that a threat?" Redmond asked, brandishing his blade.

"No," Kot said calmly, keeping Nuria turned away from them. "It is a statement of concern. We are not alone."

Ernie groaned as her arm pulsed with fire, and a shout from behind her made her look over her shoulder. "Crap." The townspeople had regrouped and were marching toward them with torches raised.

Redmond cursed and shoved the blade at Ernie. "Give it a try, at least. Otherwise we're gonna get burned alive."

Sure enough, one of the townspeople hurled a torch, which landed just inside the walled boundary. With a quick play of his cards, Kot extinguished it, but his face was stiff with concern. "If they attack, she will turn again," he said quietly. He was holding Nuria tightly, clearly trying to keep her from seeing the approaching mob. She seemed to be shaking violently. "She's already on the edge of it. She can't hold on much longer."

Ernie's arm hurt so much that she couldn't use it to hold the blade or her cards, so she shoved her cards in her pocket and used her right hand to hold the Cortalaza. "What am I supposed to do?"

"Carve out the spot where you last saw your own dimension," Redmond instructed, casting a wary eye toward the townspeople. They were milling around about fifty yards away and appeared to be contemplating their next steps, but Ernie saw the long barrels of their guns in the light from their torches. "What's wrong with your arm, Weed?"

"It's the diamondback," Ernie said from between clenched teeth. "It's like she's trying to tear herself out of me, but she can't manage it." She grimaced at the memory of dream-Gabe pressing on the place it hurt most.

"She's been doing that the whole time?" Redmond asked. "Hurting like that?"

"No, it comes and goes." She briefly explained what dream-Gabe had done and how it had disabled her arm with the agony. "He made it so much worse."

Redmond's eyes lit up with a mad eagerness. "What if that's the signal that he's pulling from the other side?" he shouted. "What if it's been the signal the whole time? What if the diamondback can feel him trying to reach you?"

"Oh my god," Ernie whispered, looking down at her throbbing arm, fear and hope braided together.

"Open the window *now*," Kot said, his voice rising. "You must try!"

Despite her fear of what might be waiting for her in her home dimension, Ernie agreed—because the townspeople were coming toward them again, with their guns raised. She gripped the blade and said a little prayer. It felt oddly heavy in her right hand, and as she drew it down through the air, the sensation was of ripping cloth. She gasped as a tear appeared in front of her, and between its fluttering edges, she saw a bright white light.

"Grab the edges and pull," shouted Redmond. "Hurry!" He flinched as the bullets started to fly.

Ernie grabbed one edge of the hole between the dimensions. It seared her skin as she yanked it wide, and what she saw on the other side made her heart gallop.

Gabe stood in front of a stone cottage. He had his deck in his hand, but held between his fingertips was only one card, white and gleaming. The look on his face was as blank as the card and rigid in its focus. Sweat glistened on his brow.

Ernie's cards blazed with heat, as if he'd set fire to them. She glanced down and saw that the diamondback on her cards had been replaced by a hybrid animal, a winged snake, one that stirred in her memory. *Who are you to me?* she thought.

You know me. Step through. Hurry. She heard his reply as if he'd murmured it into her ear, even though his lips never moved.

But she didn't know him. All she had was a pressure inside, a swelling wave of feeling held back by a wall of forgetting—and that forgetting could be the death of her. *I'm bringing allies,* she thought, trying to sound more confident than she felt.

Bring whoever you want—just hurry! His jaw was clenched, and his hand shook as he aimed the card at the window Ernie had opened. Ernie was trembling, too, both with the pain in her arm and with the weight of the window, which seemed to be getting narrower by the second despite her efforts to hold it open. *Why would I help you get back here if I was going to hurt you, love?*

His voice inside her mind was hard but also wry, a dire sort of amusement. And she had to admit, what he was saying made sense, especially as she could hear the shouting of the mob at her back.

"You go first," she said to her dad. "I can't hold this forever, and the opening's as big as it's ever going to be." She glanced over her shoulder and gasped. Everything was on fire. Her father's face was covered in sweat as he took a running start and dove through the window. The other side lit up again, that blinding white searing Ernie's eyeballs. "Kot," she yelled, peering around her in the light and the heat.

She flinched at the sound of gunshots, audible even over the crackling flames that were approaching quickly. Kot hadn't drawn his deck again—he was too focused on Nuria, who looked like she was having a seizure. "Kot, get her through!"

The window is closing. I can't hold it. Come through, Ernie. Now.

"Kot!" roared Ernie. "Now or never!"

Kot whirled around, scooping the flailing Nuria up in one smooth motion. His muscles bulged and strained as he heaved her back and then hurled her through the dimensional window, his eyes glittering with tears.

"You go, too," Ernie urged, even as the ragged edges of the window pinched closer together. She grabbed one side and yanked again, but this time it didn't budge.

Kot jerked and staggered to the side, clutching at his arm. He fell to one knee. "Go," he said, drawing out his deck. "I'll hold them off."

Now, Ernie. Come to me! Gabe's voice was a shout in her mind.

"I'll hold it open from the other side," she promised Kot as the flames crept closer and bullets ricocheted off stone.

As Kot swiped a few cards through the air and produced a wind that blew the flames away from them, Ernie held the Cortalaza blade tightly and flung herself through the window. She hit warm grass and rolled, then jumped up and spun around, ready to pull Kot through.

But there was nothing in front of her except the rough Irish coastline and the crystal blue sea beyond. The pain in her arm had gone, so Ernie whipped her cards from her pocket as she turned back to Gabe, hoping her deck would work properly now and she could defend herself if she needed to. But he had collapsed against his cottage and now seemed to be trying to catch his breath. Redmond lay on the grass between them, looking only half-conscious, and Nuria looked pretty out of it as well.

"Who are they?" Gabe asked, bracing his hands on his knees. The sight of him made for a squirmy mix of feelings and recollections. Memories of him began to return, but the echoes of his coldness in her dream still reverberated inside her. Right now he didn't seem to be a threat, though, and he had just saved their lives.

"That's my father," she said, pointing at Redmond. "And this is Nuria. She was the Grasshopper Dealer."

"Was?"

Ernie walked over to Nuria, who was shaking as she tried to push herself up from the soft grass. She knelt next to her. "You're home now," Ernie said gently, putting her hand on Nuria's back. Kot's jacket was still partially wrapped around her slender body. "We made it."

Nuria sniffed the air, looked out at the starlit ocean, and let out a little cry. She accepted Ernie's support as she rose and swayed. Ernie wondered whether Nuria was feeling a similar mix of the foreign and the familiar as recollections of this dimension returned in a rush, but images of the one they'd just left were still stark and vivid. Nuria swiveled her head around, pausing as her gaze landed first on Redmond, then on Gabe. She frowned and pulled away from Ernie, turning in place. "Kuh-kuh-kuh-kuh?" she stuttered. "Kuh-kuh?"

"Kot?" Ernie's heart sank. "We'll go get him now." Clutching the Cortalaza blade, she swiped it through the air just as she'd done before.

Nothing happened.

"There's no signal to pick up on from the other side," Redmond said, his words slurring as he sat up. "The Dragonfly deck belongs there now. Not here."

Nuria moaned, then ran toward Ernie and snatched the blade from her hands. She carved at the empty air over and over again, tears glittering in her eyes.

"Hey," Ernie said, approaching the woman slowly with her hands up, showing she meant no harm.

"Careful. That blade looks sharp as hell," Gabe said, touching Ernie's shoulder but drawing back when she flinched. "What's wrong with her?"

Nuria dropped the blade as a deep shudder rippled through her body. She turned slowly, and her eyes met Ernie's. Nuria's were ebony all the way through, black and wide and gleaming. She held up her arms as if she were reaching, and Ernie took a step forward to comfort the woman.

Nuria opened her mouth and let out a shrieking roar, veins pulsing at her temples, her teeth growing sharp and protruding from her mouth. Her body roiled and twisted, and her limbs began to lengthen, even as she sprouted two new ones from her torso. Redmond scrambled out of the way, and Ernie pushed Gabe against his cottage as he drew his deck again.

"That's the thing Virginia used to attack me," he shouted as the beast took shape. "She's one of Virginia's allies!"

"No, she's not," Ernie said as a shadow blocked out the sun. She turned to find the beast staring at her and Gabe. The Cortalaza blade lay on the grass between them. Ernie drew her deck slowly, praying her cards would actually work.

She didn't have the chance to find out, because Nuria let out another roar and leapt over the cottage—Gabe's haven, Ernie remembered—landing with a crash on the other side. With one last roar, she headed inland, taking great leaps that carried her over a rise and out of sight. Gabe sprinted around his haven and swiped a card through the air, then cursed. He turned back to Ernie and held up his Revelation card, which showed nothing but fog.

He'd tried to track her, but for whatever reason, it hadn't stuck. "Welcome back, love," he said slowly. "You've just unleashed a monster on my homeland."

CHAPTER SIXTEEN

Nuria had disappeared. In spite of the fact that she badly needed a rest, Ernie spent the next few hours helping Gabe search for the monster, with her father safe in the haven. Ernie had been terrified that the massive grasshopper would rampage through the nearest village, but when Gabe transported them there, they found it untouched. Next, Gabe conjured his motorcycle and took them both on a tour of the countryside, searching for signs of destruction and finding nothing. The whole time, he was quiet. All business. And Ernie fought her growing unease. Not only toward Gabe. Even though Nuria was dangerous, Ernie had still been sympathetic, especially to Kot. He'd sacrificed so much to protect Nuria, to keep her safe, to keep her connected to her soul even as the grasshopper took over. Yes, Ernie had owed him a favor, but she'd also wanted to help him.

In doing so, she'd put thousands, maybe hundreds of thousands, of people in danger.

No matter where they stood or what he was to her—because on that point, she was still confused—she didn't blame Gabe for being pissed. He'd barely spoken to her since he'd used the card that connected them to pull her back from another dimension. The silence settled between them like an infection, deepening her sense of dread.

As the sun began to set, he drove them back to his haven. "She'll come out when she wants to, I suppose," he said. "Not sure what else to do."

"I have to take my dad back home," Ernie blurted. The thought was exhausting. It was December 28, she was pretty sure. She'd been in the other dimension for only a few days, but her dad had been away from her mom for twenty years. Based on the mishmash of what she was feeling, she could only imagine what was going on for her father, let alone how her mother would react to his sudden reappearance. "Will you come with me?" The words came out of her unbidden, like she'd just taken a confident step onto very thin ice.

Gabe looked away and let her fall right through. "I have to stay here. I can't let that thing kill innocent people."

"Of course," she said quickly, reminding herself it was probably better this way—she'd think more clearly if they were apart, right? "I shouldn't have even asked." She bowed her head. "I'll come back and deal with Nuria as soon as I get my parents settled. I'm so sorry."

She stiffened with surprise as he took her hand. He laced his fingers with hers and squeezed. "I know you had a good reason for doing what you did."

Ernie spent a solid minute staring at their joined hands, over-whelmed by her own feelings. Gratitude. Admiration. Fear. Need. She couldn't deal with this now. "Dad?" Ernie called, pulling her hand from Gabe's and walking toward the cottage. "You still in there?"

Redmond staggered out of Gabe's haven, smelling like he'd taken a dive into a bathtub full of whiskey. His hair was even wet. "I'm . . . here," he said, hiccuping between words.

"Completely fluthered," said Gabe, shaking his head.

"Good stuff," Redmond said. "I forgot how good. Forgot every-thing, in fact." He looked up at her with bloodshot eyes. "Now it's all coming back," he added in a choked voice.

Hoping she wasn't making a huge mistake by taking him home, Ernie pulled her Nourishment card and imagined a large mug of piping hot coffee. Legs tingled on her arm, and the mug appeared in Ernie's hand. "Thanks," she said in a clipped voice, still struggling with trusting the cards or Legs. She knew it was totally unfair, but she couldn't help feeling like Legs hadn't been there when she'd needed her. It was a familiar echo of a decades-old pain, a deep scar of fear that had been laid down years before Ernie had become a Dealer, one she'd felt again in that other dimension—and now she had all the memories to understand why. Ernie sighed and closed her eyes. "I mean it, lady," she whispered. "Thanks."

Then she handed the steaming mug to her dad. "Sober up, please. I can't take you back to Mom like this."

"I couldn't face her without a little liquid courage," Redmond mumbled as he leaned against the wall and sipped at the coffee.

Ernie sighed and walked away, looking out at the ocean. She knelt on the grass as her arm prickled, and Legs came slithering off her skin, instantly reminding Ernie how much she'd missed her diamondback. "There you are," she murmured as she sat down, admiring the amber glints of Legs's scales reflecting the moonlight. "No offense, but you've been kind of a pain in the arm lately."

Legs coiled herself around and raised her head, her lidless eyes focusing on Gabe. He walked over and sat down, albeit several feet away. "She hurt you?" he asked, looking incredulous.

"I don't think she did it on purpose. It felt like she was trying to pull herself off my arm but couldn't."

"The whole time you were there?"

Ernie shook her head. "It came in waves."

"I wonder if it was me," he said. "I've been trying to get you back, but I had to stop and rest every once in a while."

"My dad realized that might be what it was." She wrapped her arms around her body. "It's been . . . confusing."

"After Virginia banished you, she bolted again," said Gabe. "I tried to track her but couldn't."

"Are Tarlae and Trey okay?" Ernie remembered them tumbling over the spot where she sat at this moment, pushed by the barrier runes Virginia now controlled.

"They're fine. Trey said he'd help get you back if I needed it."

"In exchange for another favor? I thought you didn't want to be beholden to anyone."

Gabe shrugged and picked at a long blade of grass, twirling it around his finger. "I didn't need it anyway. I set barriers around my haven to guard against further attack, and then I used our hybrid card to call to you. I didn't know what else to do, but it was almost . . ." He glanced at her out of the corner of his eye. "I could feel you. I knew you were alive and that you needed me. That's what kept me going."

Ernie knew she was blushing, so she looked out at the sea. "I hope that wasn't a bad thing." Because she remembered this, too: he hadn't seemed too happy before about being joined to her that way.

"If you're going to take me back," Redmond called, "better do it now, before I lose my nerve." He scooped up the Cortalaza blade and put it back in his satchel, which was slung across his body.

"Are *you* losing your nerve?" Gabe asked quietly as Ernie looked her father over. He looked like a drunk wannabe pirate.

"I owe this to my mom," she said, stretching out her arm to allow Legs to climb aboard. The diamondback rattled, like she was telling Ernie she wasn't ready to relinquish the soft grass. "I'll let you loose as soon as we get back to Asheville, okay? You can go hunt some voles under my mom's porch."

Legs stopped rattling and shimmied onto Ernie's skin. Ernie stood up and pulled her Transport card.

"Summon me when you return," Gabe said. "I'll be on the hunt in the meantime." He drew his deck, pulled a card, and vanished. Ernie spent a moment staring at where he'd been, wishing she could lay aside the uneasiness sitting heavy in her gut.

Redmond seemed mostly steady on his feet as she approached him. "Haven't traveled this way in a while," he said. She took in his damp hair and realized his face was freshly shaven. In addition to getting drunk, he'd apparently tried to clean up at least a little, which made Ernie feel a bit better about what she was about to do. "Do you remember her now? More than just what you wrote, I mean."

His prominent Adam's apple shifted as he swallowed. "It's coming back." He winced. "I'm trying to handle it. I'm just not sure—you think it's okay? I was never supposed to go back to her."

"You're not a Dealer anymore. You're not immortal. Andy has no claim on you."

"But still . . ."

"You can't avoid this, Dad. Just hold on to me, and we'll do it together."

His unsteady fingers wrapped over her arm. "You've really turned out to be something, Weed."

Likewise, she thought as she looked him over, unsure of what exactly that something was. "Here we go." She played her Transport card and pulled them into the void, picturing the driveway of Mara Terwilliger's home and shop, the place where they'd last been a happy family, the place where her mother had been mourning ever since. Her father's hands were like a vise on her arm, and when their feet hit gravel, he spun off and ended up sprawled on the ground, panting and retching.

Ernie watched him for a moment, then looked up at the house. It seemed to be late afternoon, the sun barely clinging to the treetops. She was three days late for Christmas and had broken her promise to be here.

But she'd kept another. She helped her dad to his feet. "I'm going to talk to Mom first, and you wait on the porch."

He nodded, still ashen from the magical transport. Ernie guided him up the steps and deposited him on the porch swing, then tried the door. It was unlocked, and Ernie let herself in with a soft "Mom?"

"Oh! Here!" Her mother came up the hall and into the parlor, and Ernie gaped. She'd expected a wreck. An alcohol-soaked, grieving woman with mussed hair and stained clothes. Instead, the Mara Terwilliger who stood in front of her had done her hair in tidy curls. She was wearing a bit of makeup. Her clothes were clean and pressed, and her fingernails were neat ovals painted a sheer pink. She caught the stunned look on Ernie's face and smiled, her eyes sparkling with tears. "I knew you would come back, even though you were delayed. I didn't want you to return to a mess this time." She gestured at the parlor, and that was when Ernie realized it had been dusted. And vacuumed. "It wasn't only myself that I cleaned up."

"How . . . did you do this?"

"It was that or bury myself in the sheets with a bottle of Jack and wait for death to find me," she said simply.

Ernie let out a choked laugh, suddenly wondering whether she was about to make a huge mistake. "You look great, Mom," she said, walking forward and giving her mother a hug.

Her mom melted into her embrace. "I was so afraid something had happened to you," she whispered. "But then I remembered how strong and clever you are."

Ernie closed her eyes. "Thanks, Mom. I had a little bit of an adventure, and I can't stay. I have some messes I have to clean up. But . . ." She bit her lip and took her mother by the shoulders, looking her in the eyes. Was her mom strong enough for this, or would it break her? Should she just whisk her dad back to Ireland and tell him to stay away from Asheville on pain of death?

No. She owed her mom a choice. "I need to tell you something, but I want you to stay calm, okay?"

Mara's eyebrows rose. "Okay? I—" Her gaze darted over Ernie's shoulder as the door to the shop creaked, and her face paled.

Ernie tightened her grip on her mom as the woman began to sink toward the floor. She looked behind her to see Redmond standing in the doorway, looking sheepish.

"Sorry," he said. "It was either this or running the other way."

"Redmond?" her mother said, voice breaking.

"It's me, honey," he replied, crossing his arms tightly over his chest, making the pouch at his middle clank as its contents shifted. "I . . ." His voice faded away as Mara steadied herself and pulled away from Ernie to walk slowly toward him.

"It's really you?" she asked quietly.

"Yeah," he said, looking uncertain. "I know I don't look that great, but . . ."

Mara Terwilliger began to laugh. "You come home after being gone twenty years, and you think I care about that?"

His arms slowly relaxed to his sides as he watched his wife giggle herself silly. "Well, you look great, and I look like—"

He didn't finish, because she'd thrown herself into his arms. He staggered back as her weight hit him, but he enclosed her in a tight embrace as soon as his back hit the doorframe. Ernie watched her parents embrace, torn between misgiving and relief. The joy was coming off her mother in waves, but Mara didn't know where Redmond had been. She didn't know what he'd done or how he'd lived. She didn't know all the gray areas he'd dwelled in for the last few decades. He'd ruined another Dealer. He'd forced his deck on an unsuspecting man, altering the course of Kot's entire life. He'd cheated who knew how many people out of silver and gathered himself too many enemies to count. They might have left all that behind in another dimension, but that didn't mean it hadn't happened. Though the memories of that other dimension became harder for Ernie to grasp with every passing hour, his slate wasn't wiped clean.

But that didn't mean that Ernie got to decide whether he would be part of her mother's life. Ernie's eyes met her father's as her mother trembled in his arms. She fixed him with a hard look. One that said, *If you hurt her, I don't care* who *you are. I'll murder you.*

He gave her a crooked smile and buried his head in Mara's cloud of curly silver hair. "I've missed you," he said to her. "I've thought about you every day."

Ernie wondered whether that could possibly be true, since his memories had almost completely left him. Had whatever he'd written in those pages he carried really helped him stay connected to her? Watching him embrace her again, Ernie certainly hoped so. "I need to get back to Ireland," she finally said, realizing that this was for her parents to figure out and she had too many other things to worry about to meddle. She edged toward the door.

Redmond kissed his wife's forehead and murmured something soft and sweet in her ear. She nodded and turned toward Ernie, dabbing tears from her eyes. "Thank you," she murmured, hugging Ernie. "Come home soon, okay?"

"I'll be back with you in a second, honey," Redmond said, and Mara nodded and released Ernie before heading down the hall. At the sound of a door clicking shut, Redmond squared his shoulders. "I figured I'd walk you out."

"Okay . . ." Ernie opened the front door and ventured out to the porch. "What's up?"

Redmond heaved a sigh and clutched at the strap of his pouch. After a moment of apparent consideration, he pulled it over his head and offered it to her. "I think you should have all this. I don't need it anymore, and you have the power to wield what's inside—all of it. You can find Virginia. Protect yourself from her when you need to. Maybe even defeat her."

Ernie took the pouch. "You really want me to have your journal?"

"It's more than just my memories of my family, and more than my memories of my time as a Dealer. It's all the research I did before that—I started writing this before I was banished." He eyed the pouch. "Plus the Cortalaza. You'll want to be careful with it."

Ernie lifted the pouch's flap and peeked inside. Her fingers brushed the Cortalaza's hilt and a thick sheaf of crumpled paper covered in her father's slightly smeared scrawl. "I'm not sure I have time—"

"Do your research, and don't be lazy."

She laughed, rolling her eyes. "Whatever, Dad."

"I wish I could keep you safe." His voice was at once firm and filled to the brim with an emotion that threatened to break it. "This is the only way I know to help my daughter, okay?"

"No, it's not. Keep Mom safe, and take care of her."

"She looks pretty good to—"

"I'm not kidding, Dad," Ernie said softly. "She doesn't know who you are anymore. Not really."

He nodded, his gaze on the chipped paint and slightly warped boards of the porch. "I'll make it up to her."

"Just . . . I know it must be strange to be back. I know—"

"I can do this, Ernie. I won't hurt her. I promise."

So he *had* read Ernie's look from earlier. "Good. I'll come back as soon as I can."

"Is that a promise, too?" he asked, that firm tone slipping into a plea. "Because I want to get to know my daughter." He reached out and squeezed her arm. "What I know so far tells me she turned out to be a pretty special person."

Ernie patted his hand. "I'll see you soon." Slinging the pouch across her body, she turned away quickly, knowing she couldn't indulge the pull of emotion right now, knowing she needed to leave her parents to figure themselves out. She tromped down the steps, pulling her deck from her pocket, and within seconds, she'd left Asheville behind once again.

❖   ❖   ❖

As soon as she opened her eyes to stars sparkling over the Atlantic, she crossed Friend-Lover—she paused as she pulled it out, hoping it was the right card to deal—with Revelation coupled with Translate, which she'd learned could be used to transform a simple revelation or tracking action into a signal another Dealer could feel.

Gabe appeared at the doorway to his haven, a few yards from where she stood. "Still no sign of the creature," he said grimly. "Any ideas?"

She put all her cards away except for Revelation. "No luck tracking her?"

He shook his head. "She's a total blank spot."

"Maybe because she's concealed," Ernie muttered. Grasping at her fading memories, she explained what had happened, how Nuria and the Grasshopper deck had melded in one body, how the two were at war for precious turf.

Gabe listened, looking more horrified by the moment. He rubbed his left forearm as she spoke, perhaps imagining what it would be like to lose himself to Caera, the kestrel, the spirit that embodied his deck and protected him fiercely. "Did the Forger do that to her?"

"No." Ernie closed her eyes. "My father did."

"Why isn't he here helping us, then?" snapped Gabe. "I've been dying to ask why the Dragonfly Dealer isn't pitching in."

"Because he's not the Dragonfly anymore." As soon as she admitted it, Ernie clutched at the leather pouch, feeling the weight of the Cortalaza within.

Gabe looked stunned. "But he's alive," he said quietly. "He's alive, and he doesn't have his deck anymore?"

"He gave it to someone else. A man named Kot." A man who had sacrificed everything for his love, whose face she could no longer picture. "I owe him my life."

"Now I understand what your father said about the cards not being connected to this dimension. They were left there—because Kot has them. He's the Dragonfly. But what I don't get—if your father gave up his deck and isn't a Dealer anymore, how can he possibly be—"

"It's a knife, okay?" blurted Ernie. "Something a Forger made. It can separate a Dealer from his deck."

Gabe's gaze dropped to her pouch. "You have it, don't you?"

Ernie took a step back. "Why? Thinking of taking the easy way out?" Even as the words left her mouth, she knew she was being unfair. She'd wanted to ask the Forger to do the same thing for her when she'd first accidentally bonded with a few cards from the Diamondback deck.

"Does it matter what kind of 'way out' is open to me right now?" His expression had hardened. "I'm thinking I have a few messes to clean up first."

They glared at each other, Ernie keenly aware of the blazing heat in her cheeks. The fury in his eyes made it feel unsafe to apologize. She hadn't meant to be so harsh—her fear that Gabe would want to use the Cortalaza on himself had formed as soon as she'd thought about the blade in this dimension. Trey had apparently seen the Cortalaza in his vision, the one he'd had as they'd all dealt their cards in an effort to figure out the best way to help Gabe. Tarlae had seen Gabe's missing haven, and Ernie had seen Virginia, and both of those had helped them find and save him. But the Cortalaza? Was that a sign? An instruction from the cards?

Ernie had no idea, but every possibility made her feel uncomfortable. "I already apologized for Nuria," she said slowly. "And I'm here to help find her. She's unstable, but she's not evil. She doesn't want to kill."

"Something tells me she has, though, in the other dimension, if not here." He grimaced and rubbed his chest, perhaps remembering how he'd come out of his last encounter with the grasshopper monster.

"The best thing for her is if we figure out how to get Kot into this dimension," Ernie said. "If anyone can find and help her, it's him."

"Virginia has the rune that connects this dimension to his."

"And that means we have to find her."

"I'm a bit scant on ideas for that, love," he said, sounding annoyed. "I did try my best."

Ernie put up her hands, forcing down a throb of misery at how distant he sounded. "I wasn't criticizing you, Gabe! Jeez. I'm grateful that you didn't give up on me, I'm sorry I unleashed an elephant-sized grasshopper on the Irish countryside, and I'm worried to death about you, okay? I feel awful that you have to help me with all this, even though I know you will because of who you are." She winced at the lump in her throat. "I'm struggling with memories I didn't have when I was there that came back all in a rush, and I'm struggling with losing memories of what happened over the last few days, even the ones I know are really important. I'm just trying to juggle all that stuff and to do what's right, and I'm sorry if I'm screwing it up."

Gabe's stiff shoulders relaxed a shade as he watched her. "I've been worried to death about you, too," he said after a few moments. "I was climbing the walls with that fear every minute you were gone." He reached out and took her hand, then pulled her gently into his arms. "But I also know who *you* are. And I knew not to give up."

She leaned on his chest, knowing everything was still sideways, but weak in the knees at this momentary reprieve from the tension between them. She wasn't about to ruin it by bringing up anything that would raise it again. "My dad gave me something that might help me find Virginia. At least, that's what he told me."

Gabe leaned back so he could look her in the face. "What is it?"

Ernie reached between them and opened the pouch, revealing the hundreds of pages of her father's writing. "I know we have to patrol in search of Nuria, but I think we might need to take a couple of study breaks."

CHAPTER SEVENTEEN

For the moment, Nuria seemed either able to control her monster side now that she was back in her home dimension after so long away, or so incapacitated that she wasn't even able to ravage the countryside—because she was nowhere to be found. She'd thundered off as the giant grasshopper, but no one she or Gabe checked with—not the barkeep at a nearby pub or the farmer a mile down the road or the baker who seemed to have a massive crush on Gabe and practically stumbled over herself to give him free bread when he stopped by to inquire—had seen anything unusual in the last day or two.

Gabe poked at the logs in his fireplace as Ernie rubbed her eyes and tried to bring her father's untidy scrawl into focus. "I don't know where else to look," he said.

"Maybe she'll come to us," Ernie suggested. "She knows where we are. At this point, I think she knows we're not the enemy." She frowned. "Unless she's forgetting."

"Because she has the mind of an insect?"

Ernie shook her head. "Because forgetting is part of what happens when you get stranded in another dimension."

She could feel his eyes on her but couldn't meet his gaze. "How much did you forget?" he asked.

"Too much," she whispered. "I didn't even realize how much until I got back. And now it all feels . . ." She had no idea. She'd thought it would all settle into place, but she felt more on edge, especially about him. "And now I'm forgetting things about what happened when I was there, I think. Except I don't know what they are."

"Kot, the Dealer you left behind," Gabe said. "I saw him throw Nuria through the dimensional window."

"He's in love with her," she said slowly. "They're in love. But she was originally from this dimension."

"There were rumors that the Grasshopper had been defeated by another deck, but no one ever owned up to it," Gabe said.

"Did you ever meet the Grasshopper?"

He shook his head as he set the poker on the hearth. "I had heard of her, though. She was active in the early twentieth century, I think. Never faced off with her, but the Brahman Bull mentioned her once."

"The Brahman . . ." Ernie chuckled, remembering how the other Dealers had described him, an old man with questionable mental stability. "Lawrence, right? Virginia seemed to be a fan of his. She got mad when Trey made fun of him. Remember how Trey told us he once tried to steal a few of the Brahman's cards, and the old guy hit back pretty hard? Seemed to be part of why Virginia hates Trey so much."

Gabe swiped a bottle of whiskey off a shelf next to the fireplace and poured himself a slug. "She and Lawrence might've been lovers at one point. Not sure, but those things can be fleeting among Dealers. Few are like Trey and Tarlae."

It hit Ernie like a slap. Hadn't her father said something like that to her about Gabe? And maybe he'd been right. She felt too raw to think about it too much.

"Lawrence and I brushed shoulders at the end of the First World War," Gabe was saying, "and at that time he said the Grasshopper was causing trouble in Germany."

Ernie's eyes narrowed. "Isn't Virginia kind of a Germanophile?"

Gabe shrugged as he considered the amber liquid in his glass. "You think she tangled with Nuria?"

"Oh, definitely. Virginia's the one who stranded Nuria in that awful place."

Gabe sat down next to her and lifted one of the pages laid out on the tabletop. "Any luck here? Do you even know what you're looking for?"

Ernie's thumb stroked her father's notes. "Dad said it would help me find Virginia, maybe even defeat her, but I've read about fifty pages so far, and all I've gotten is a tale of searching for a genie."

Ernie braced, almost expecting Gabe to laugh and confirm that her dad was crazy as a soup sandwich, but instead he tilted his head and said, "People find lots of ways to explain us, and the modern idea of a genie makes a kind of sense. It's an old legend of demons made of fire, yeah? But at some point, some of the tales became more about beings that might grant wishes if you asked the right way. Like an Immortal Dealer might, if he or she were feeling generous or had taken a liking to a mortal player."

"That's exactly what Dad was thinking. He was certain this genie was either the Forger or another Dealer and that they'd left some sort of treasure in a place he calls the Red City. No idea where that is, but it sounds like it might be in the Middle East, the way he describes it?"

Gabe leaned forward, scanning the pages Ernie had already read. "He's got to be talking about Marrakech. The walls around the city are made of a red sandstone. Did he find what he was looking for there?"

"No. He was convinced someone was following him, maybe Virginia—in one passage he says it was after he stole the Marks from her but before she ambushed him. He was on the hunt for more of those artifacts, to keep her from getting them, when he found reference to a treasure in an ancient archived text at the Mustansiriyah University library in Baghdad." Her eyes skimmed the page, looking for the place she'd left off. "He'd gone to the Red City to try to find it, convinced it was one of the Forger's toys."

"If it was that ancient, it might not have been made by Andy. I don't think the Marks were, either."

"Minh told me they were made by the Forger before Andy. Her name was Phoebe. I think the artifacts she made had a very different purpose. Like she was trying to lift Dealers up instead of pitting us against each other."

"Well, that makes sense. He's never really seemed the soul of generosity. More of an eye-for-an-eye sort of fellow." Gabe knew that firsthand; Andy had let Duncan, Gabe's younger brother, kill the only family Gabe had left besides him.

"He . . . he offered me a deal," she said, reaching for exactly what he had offered her. "He wanted me to make the sun set on Virginia—or something like that?"

Gabe rolled his eyes. "And let me guess—he made some tricky, barbed offer in return?"

She stared into his eyes as the memory floated beyond her grasp. Then she looked away. "Probably."

"He likes to watch us twist in the wind. It's why all the artifacts he's made are like booby traps. The Marks were different. They seem designed to give a Dealer more power over his own future." His gaze slid to the pouch that held the Cortalaza.

"Or the power to destroy himself," Ernie snapped.

"That might not be all that blade does," he said mildly, "seeing as it can also open dimensional windows."

"Only in certain circumstances." She crossed her arms, knowing she had no right to be feeling this grumpy.

Gabe turned to look into the fire. "So your father didn't find this treasure," he said after a few seconds, "which means Virginia might already have found it, or it might still be in Marrakech. Does he offer any details about where to look?"

Ernie didn't protest the change of subject—it was a relief to stay focused on the hunt and not remind Gabe of the blade that could give him back his mortality and end his existence as a Dealer. She didn't want to think about whether he should use the Cortalaza. She didn't want to think about what it would do to him and Caera, the kestrel he'd shared his life and body with for the last century and a half, or how alone Ernie would feel if he took that way out. She didn't want to consider how her feelings might be completely selfish or how, if Gabe asked, she probably couldn't refuse to give it to him. Better to keep the both of them moving, searching, fighting for something. "I'm still trying to finish the passage. His writing is so, so dense, and his handwriting is awful. But he mentions a place called Dar El Bacha, or maybe it's a street? His contact was named Belkacem, but for all I know, that might be the Moroccan version of Smith."

"But it gives us something to go on. Did he describe this person?"

"It's a guy . . ." Ernie reread her father's messy handwriting. "I think that says 'chipped tooth.' Should we go to Marrakech and try to find him?"

She'd been half joking, certain Gabe would refuse. Instead, he said, "I don't know about you, but it might make me feel a shade less helpless."

She couldn't help but smile as he stood up and drew his deck. "Let's hit the road, then."

Gabe had been to Marrakech before, so he transported them to the old medina. Ernie leaned against his body as they slipped through the void, happy for an excuse to be close and relishing the solid strength of his arm as it anchored her to his side. With so much feeling off, this, at least, felt right. They appeared in an alley, right in front of an extremely startled donkey-cart driver, who shouted something in Arabic as his donkey brayed. Both creatures' eyes were round with terror. Gabe let his hands fall to his side, his deck held in his left, and began to speak in French. Ernie watched his fingers draw up two of his cards, one of which she recognized as Warp. The other might have been Translate—either that or Gabe actually knew how to speak French—but it could have been Negotiate or even the Inverse card, because the elderly driver's expression smoothed as the seconds passed, the anxiety sliding off his face. Gabe asked him something, and when the driver switched to French to answer him, Ernie played her Translate card.

"—perhaps half a kilometer that way," the driver was saying, pointing to the left while his donkey, who had calmed as soon as his owner had, nudged its nose against Ernie's pant leg as if it were searching for apples or sweet hay. She edged away; she'd felt dirty for days, and now that she had had a chance to take a shower and put on fresh clothes, she wasn't eager to get grimy again. "Many shops of antiquities beyond the old palace of Dar El Bacha," the man continued. "You will find many good things to buy." He looked them over with interest, tugging at his long, loose robe with nervous fingers.

"I'm not tourist," Gabe said. He really was speaking French, Ernie realized as she listened to the translation. *Bad* French. "I look for good treasure. Real treasure." He rubbed his fingers together, indicating he had money to burn. "*Genie* treasure."

The driver chuckled, mimicking rubbing a genie's lamp, his eyes rolling comically. "You want to find the lamp of a djinn? This is the best place. It's very close." He pointed to the left again. Then he held out his hand. "For twenty dirhams, I can take you."

"Do you know someone named Belkacem?" Ernie asked.

"Belkacem?" asked the driver, already nodding. "Oh, yes. I can take you."

With a sidelong glance at Gabe, she played her Discern card, an oval with a straight line down its middle. "Yeah?"

"Yes, yes."

Ernie felt the pulse at her fingertips that told her the old man was lying. "Uh-huh."

The old man seemed to perceive her doubt, for he put up his hands. "Maybe not the Belkacem you know. Maybe we know a different Belkacem. There are many. But in the market, there are many treasures, and one place known for special things. Old things."

This time, he was telling the truth—or, at minimum, something he *believed* to be the truth. A few minutes later, after a surreptitious swipe of Gabe's Coin card, they squeezed in next to the driver's load of overripe fruit, and he shuttled them through the busy streets, past souk after souk crammed with haggling merchants, confused tourists, and savvy locals. Gabe told her that this was the medina at the heart of the city, its oldest part, where the roads were too narrow to accommodate cars, and sidewalks were nowhere to be seen. Pedestrians had to dodge growling mopeds, bicyclists, and carts like theirs, which were apparently not often used as taxis, given observers' shouts, laughs, shaking heads, and waving hands as Ernie and Gabe bounced along. It clearly wasn't a ritzy area, but it was rich all the same, with vibrant scents and so many colors, and Ernie was struck by how, just a day ago, she'd been stuck in a dour splinter dimension with a green sky and only a faint hope of escaping. The sun had risen over the close-set buildings, and she shed her jacket, enjoying the warmth. "This isn't too bad. I thought it'd be even hotter, since it's the desert."

"Well, it's December, isn't it? Probably the coldest month," Gabe said, turning his face to the sky. "But it is nice to feel the sun."

Ernie watched the slight smile pulling at his lips. "Yeah. It is. Do you think we're actually going to find something?"

"We have to start somewhere."

Yes, they did. And something about the sunlight, the smells of cinnamon and cumin wafting out of stalls at the roadside, and being next to Gabe in a random donkey cart in Morocco, a place Ernie had only ever dreamed of visiting someday, had put her in a good mood.

She knew this might be a wild-goose chase, but it felt better than sitting around helpless. Gabe seemed a little less careworn, too. She put her hands firmly over the pouch that held her father's notes and the Cortalaza, hoping more clues lay within and wondering where they might lead.

After several bumpy minutes, the old driver pulled his donkey to a halt in front of a door identical to several they'd passed, completely nondescript and set into a dusty mud-brick building. The donkey driver confidently told them that the place was around here somewhere, but he wasn't sure exactly where. Another pink ten-dirham note shoved into his palm earned a definitive point at the door he had pulled up right next to. Ernie groaned and got out while Gabe chuckled.

As soon as they'd gotten out of the cart, the donkey man jerked the reins. It took him only a second or two to disappear around a corner. "Did you check to see if he was telling the truth just now?" Ernie asked.

Gabe shook his head. "Let's just see what's here." He tried the door, which swung inward, revealing a sight that made Ernie gasp. They were peering into a long, narrow room, a corridor almost, and every inch of space was packed with colorful lamps. Shiny globes, glittering teardrop-shaped orbs cradling amber flames, intricately hammered and punched panels fused together and lit from the inside, some hanging from chains, some crowded onto shelves, some set on the floor, all glowing merrily. It was like a passageway into a different place, maybe into a different dimension, only this one offered sensual delights instead of horror. Ernie felt a tug on her sleeve and looked up to see Gabe smiling at her. "Remember why we're here?" he asked softly.

She nodded mutely and followed him inside, her gaze devouring every sight as they walked along the black-and-white tiled path toward the back of the space. Gabe had to duck his head to avoid getting beaned by a few low-hanging lamps, and Ernie was so distracted that she ran right into his back when he paused. She leaned around him to see that the space had opened up and that the ceiling was now only slats of wood letting in slanted beams of sunlight. This room was lined on either side with merchants' booths, each a world unto itself. Hand-woven baskets, colorful ceramic bowls, jars and pots of spices and can-dies, hanging rugs, shoes, nuts and dates, purses, tea sets, and countless other goods lay tempting and gorgeous while shoppers hovered and touched, haggled and paid.

"I've got at least a century on every item in this place," Gabe said, striding through the center of the space and firmly waving off a woman trying to offer him a length of gauzy fabric while nodding back at Ernie as if suggesting he buy her a gift. "None of it looks even vaguely ancient."

Rebuffed by Gabe, the woman approached Ernie, smiling hope-fully. Ernie smiled back and shook her head, but this seemed only to encourage the lady, who took Ernie by the wrist and tugged her toward a booth hung with hundreds of other fabrics, a patterned, shimmering rainbow of cloth. Gesturing at the satchel Ernie was carrying, the lady seemed to be suggesting she'd offer a good price and that Ernie should get out her wallet. Grasping the bag's strap protectively, Ernie looked over her shoulder to see Gabe talking to a young man who was watch-ing over the scene with a stern expression and folded arms, perhaps standing guard.

When the guard guy pointed to a door at the back of the cavernous room, Ernie pulled herself away from the eager saleswoman and trotted over to join Gabe. "He said there's a guy named Belkacem in a souk across the way," Gabe told her.

Ernie reeled with the sensory onslaught of the last few minutes. Everything in Morocco seemed like that—an overwhelming, chaotic, delightful surprise—and she was still trying to adjust. "How many souks *are* there?"

"You're joking, yeah?" Gabe chuckled as he led her through an alley and an open doorway into another mud-brick building. This one was more closed in, more cavelike, more hushed, more what Ernie had expected of a place where an ancient artifact could be found. The ceiling was low enough to make Gabe bow his head to avoid brushing the silky fabric that had been stapled overhead in billowing folds.

Ernie squinted as her eyes adjusted to the low light. "This reminds me of my mom's shop," she muttered, taking in the jumble of goods—stacks of books, beads and jewelry, embroidery, clocks, a few toys, boxes of loose ceramic tiles, and several oil lamps that looked like they'd been pulled straight out of a retelling of *Aladdin*.

"I wonder how much of this is really old as opposed to reproduction," Gabe muttered, making a beeline for a man rising from a stool in a shadowy corner. A soot-stained robe hung from his wiry frame, and he wore an embroidered skullcap on his head. "Are you Belkacem?" Gabe asked.

The look of bland interest on the man's face instantly turned into a mask of suspicion. "Who is sent you?" he demanded in heavily accented English. His eyes narrowed and scanned the room, taking in the three other customers browsing nearby.

Ernie peered at the man's mouth, looking for a chipped tooth that might identify him as the guy her father had described in his notes. But as the man grimaced, it was apparent he had few teeth at all, and the ones he did have didn't appear to be chipped. Gabe was casually asking about the antiques in the man's shop, saying he'd heard that the man had an excellent reputation, but his compliments just seemed to make the guy more defensive.

"Hey," Ernie said. "Did you ever meet a man named Redmond Terwilliger?"

The man recoiled. "If you are not here to buy, you go now! Go now!"

Gabe began to reach into his pocket for his deck, but this caused the man to shout with alarm, drawing the attention of everyone in the place, and then some. A door opened a few feet away, and another man leaned in from the alley, his intonation suggesting he was asking the skullcap guy whether everything was all right. Ernie tugged on Gabe's arm as he began to argue with his hand still in his pocket. But with every passing second, the skullcap man seemed to become more vehement that Gabe and Ernie needed to get out, and finally, he stormed out into the alley, still waving his arms and shouting. Gabe and Ernie followed him into the narrow space between buildings, past a few entrances to other souks on the way to a wider thoroughfare jammed with mopeds and carts and a few actual cars. Ernie was picking up her pace to keep up when she felt a tugging and heard a quick metallic snip.

Slender hands shot between her arm and her torso, wrapping around the strap to the pouch and yanking it off, spinning her in place in time to see the thief, a teenage boy in jeans and a ratty T-shirt, fleeing the other way with his stolen treasure cradled to his chest.

"Stop," Ernie roared, starting after him with dread nearly choking her. The Cortalaza blade. Her father's writings. Both irreplaceable. Both getting farther away by the second. With Legs tingling on her arm and reminding her that she had a lot more to work with than just her mediocre sprinting ability, Ernie halted in place and pulled her deck from her pocket, relieved she hadn't stuck it in the pouch. The Draw and Tool cards leapt to her fingertips, and she played them with a frantic swipe, not even caring who could see—a few witnesses were nothing compared to losing those treasures.

The thief yelped as the pull of the bag swung him around, but he maintained his grip on it even as the satchel dragged him back toward Ernie. Already seeing that the kid wasn't going to let go, Ernie drew the Rend and Sharpen cards and wielded them like a scalpel, cutting both sides of the strap and causing the pouch to fall to the ground. Both she and the annoyingly persistent thief dove for it, but Ernie flung out her Shield card before either of them could reach it. The thief bounced off her invisible, flexible shield and landed on his butt on the dusty ground, looking dumbstruck.

Ernie scooped the satchel from the ground and glared at the thief, who scrambled back like a crab before darting away. Her heart still pounding, she brushed dust from the pouch, relieved to hear the clank of the blade inside. She turned around to see Gabe staring at her. "Sorry," she said as she approached. "I couldn't risk losing him."

"More than okay." Gabe seemed to be suppressing a laugh as he stepped aside to reveal the wide-eyed skullcap man who had just been trying to get away from them.

"I know what you are," the man muttered, his mouth barely opening. "Tonight, midnight, my shop." He inclined his head toward the doorway he'd stormed out of not three minutes before. "When no one is here." His gaze darted nervously to the curious bystanders. "You meet me?"

Ernie nodded.

"Good," the guy said, his English suddenly smoothing out into a suave British-sounding accent. "I've been hoping to safely unload this thing for nearly twenty years."

CHAPTER EIGHTEEN

After agreeing to meet up that evening, Gabe transported himself back to Ireland to see whether Nuria had made an appearance, and Ernie went back to Asheville to check on her parents—and try to get a little more info from her father about what, exactly, Belkacem might be offering them. She figured it would be easier than trying to wade through her dad's confused writings. She'd also learned enough about Marrakech to know that it was all about the bottom line, and the Moroccans she'd met were pretty savvy. Was Belkacem messing with them, just trying to get some cash out of them because he sensed there was something they wanted? It hadn't seemed that way—he hadn't wanted anything to do with them until he'd seen Ernie's deck in action. But Ernie was still cautious.

When she arrived at the shop, though, it was locked up tight, and the "Closed for Family Time" sign had been put out, something her mother almost never did. Unable to forget how her mother had been brutally kidnapped from that very house, Ernie took a quick peek into her Revelation card—and suddenly experienced a feeling she hadn't had since she was a child, when she'd gone into her parents' room to complain that she couldn't sleep and witnessed them engaging in what her mother had later explained as "Mommy and Daddy having cuddles."

She decided to leave them alone and returned to Marrakech. By then it was late afternoon, and she spent a few hours trying to stay awake as she perused her father's notes, then another few hours slumbering heavily after surrendering to her body's demands for sleep. Now, long after the sun had set beyond the walls of the old city, she was dining on the rooftop terrace of the lovely riad Gabe had checked them into before he left. Sitting alone at the table, Ernie felt a pang, a restlessness she couldn't quite shake. She'd escaped from a hellish splinter dimension, gotten her father back, and reunited her parents. But Kot had been left behind, Nuria was an ever-present danger, and Virginia . . . well. Hopefully they'd be able to draw her out and eliminate her once and for all. She decided that threat was the reason for her squirminess. It was hard to sit still when so many wrongs needed to be put right, and even harder now, because she knew she couldn't even remember all those wrongs. Her memories of her own dimension had all returned, gradually sorting themselves and settling, but her recall of what had happened during her exile in the splinter dimension had faded quickly to a blurred and confusing tableau of feelings—fear, longing, hope, fury—without clear events to pin them to. She'd discovered things there that she needed now, she was sure—but they were slipping beyond her grasp.

Ernie sat on the rooftop terrace, full from a delectable veggie tagine with almonds and chickpeas, trying to plow through a few more droning pages of her father's notes. It wasn't just that they were boring—his determination to remember things he knew he was forgetting made her chest ache. The pages were full of notations like *Have to get this down before it's gone* and *Not sure if this really happened but I think I remember* and *I know there's more than this, but I only have this piece of it*. Reading those sad, desperate phrases awakened her own fears that she had forgotten something important.

She let her head hang back and rubbed her eyes, remembering what her father had said to her—*Do your research, and don't be lazy.* She'd gotten only about a quarter of the way through the pages, and what lay within had brought her and Gabe to Marrakech. In a few hours they'd meet with the man who had promised them some artifact he'd had for twenty years, one created by a Forger, according to her dad—and it would be awesome if she could figure out what the artifact actually was before the meetup. Ernie knew from experience that some of the rune tiles Andy had created did terrible things to Dealers and their animals, and if Belkacem's artifact was one of those, they needed to be prepared.

Unfortunately, her dad's journal seemed to contain one golden nugget of information for every ten pages of useless detail, and the last several had been about Belkacem's family drama, how his father had just died and left him the shop, how there'd been a feud with Belkacem's uncle and some hunt for a key that had been lost or maybe hidden by a peevish and jealous cousin, and how Belkacem—whose mother had sent him to London for college—didn't buy into his own family lore about their encounter with a djinn over a hundred years earlier. Redmond clearly took every word as gospel, though, and had convinced Belkacem to sell him anything connected to that family legend. She blinked and focused on the words at the top of the current page: *Got to the medina before the souks opened and went to ask Belkacem about the Sunrise, what it looks like, its approximate size, where he's keeping it, how he's containing it.*

Ernie squinted at the words, trying to make sense of them. Her dad wanted to ask Belkacem about the size of the sunrise and where he was keeping it? What the heck? It was tempting to dismiss the words as more crazy prattle from a man who was losing his grip, but something about them snagged in Ernie's mind like a fishing hook. *Went to ask Belkacem about the Sunrise . . .*

Gabe appeared a few feet away. His hair was loose but brushed, and he looked like he might have snuck in a nap at some point, as the circles under his eyes seemed to have faded slightly. "Could the old man give you any help?" he asked, taking a seat at her table for two.

She shook her head. "He and my mom are . . . getting reacquainted. I'm not sure how much he could have told me that isn't in here anyway." She looked down at the stained, worn pages she'd just read. "He definitely thinks Belkacem has at least one of the Forger's artifacts."

Gabe's eyebrows shot up. "Does it say what it is?"

Ernie read a little farther on the page. *He says it's more than it seems in the right hands, but even he's not convinced it's the truth. But what he's told me makes me even more afraid Virginia will get to it first. The Sunrise could make all the difference.* Ernie frowned. "The sunrise," she murmured.

Andy's face flashed in her memory—his black eyes, his devilish grin. *Keep your eye on the sunrise, dear.* "Oh my god," she whispered, her eyes riveted on the word. "Sunrise. The thing we're looking for is called 'the Sunrise.' And Andy told me to get it." She closed her eyes and tried to pull more of the memory up from the depths. "He was offering me a deal."

"If he offered you something in exchange for this 'Sunrise,' our little treasure hunt could be a trap."

"No," she said, but couldn't draw a single recollection to support what she was almost certain was true: "I think he's trying to use me to stop Virginia."

Gabe touched her hand. "This artifact could be dangerous."

"I'm certain it is," she said, keenly aware of his fingertips brushing her skin. "But if we can use it against her, maybe we could get the dimensional rune from her. Heck, maybe this thing opens dimensions! Seems like something a 'Sunrise' could do, right?"

Gabe focused on the pages with a welcome energy. "Maybe, but I can think of a few other things. Altering time. Or setting the entire horizon on fire and causing a total apocalypse."

Ernie snorted. "Well, that would be a downer. But either way, it doesn't seem like something we want in Virginia's hands, does it?"

"Not at all." His eyes were still scanning the notebook in front of him. "Especially if it's something she could use to defeat the Forger."

"My dad thought she was aware of the Sunrise." A chill passed through Ernie. "Do you really think this thing could be used against Andy? Why would a Forger create something like that?"

"Andy wouldn't," said Gabe. "But his predecessor thought differently about us. The Marks weren't intended to be used against a Forger, either, but in the wrong hands . . ." Gabe looked around and gestured for the attendant, asking for tea. "I suppose we'll find out very soon."

"I hope so," Ernie said quietly. "Hey—before we go to meet Belkacem, I need to put this stuff away." She touched the pouch. "Mind if I—" She pulled out her Dreams and her Haven card. "I won't take long."

Gabe nodded for her to go ahead, and Ernie made the fastest trip ever to her tent haven, where she stashed the blade and her father's writings, all tucked into the satchel she'd stitched up with a quick swipe of her Repair card. With a forceful push of her thoughts, she jerked upright in her chair just as the attendant came over with a full tea service, causing the poor fellow to yelp with surprise. Once the sweet, minty concoction had been poured into etched glasses and they were alone again, Ernie asked, "Any sign of Nuria?"

Gabe sniffed at his tea and took a sip. "Not yet. But I summoned Minh to keep watch tonight."

Ernie's eyes narrowed. "You offered him a favor, didn't you?"

Gabe was very focused on his tea.

Frustration and worry got the better of her the longer he remained silent. "Are you actually planning to stick around long enough to pay off all these favors?"

Gabe's fist came down on the table with a bang, rattling the silver teapot and threatening to overturn their glasses. "I pay my debts, and I don't appreciate the suggestion that I wouldn't."

"So, what—you're just going to pay up and hand over your deck? Is that how this is going to go? What would happen to Caera? Does she get a say?"

"It's after eleven," Gabe growled, taking one last gulp of his tea before standing up.

"We could just transport there."

"You can go ahead. I need to walk." And he began doing exactly that, heading for the stairs.

Ernie jumped up from the table, wishing she could take back what she'd said to trigger his anger. After her horrific initial handling of his announcement that he was considering ending it all, and after her realization that despite those feelings, he still hadn't given up on trying to get her back, Ernie had been trying to figure out the right way to broach this particular topic. Even with everything else going on, her feelings for Gabe had shaped her thoughts. She'd been trying to work up the bravery to ask him not to go, trying to figure out a way to remind him that there were still good things in the world to see and experience and do. But finding the perfect words at the perfect time had never been her strength.

"I'll come with," she announced as she caught up to him. "I'd love to see more of the city."

Gabe was silent as they descended to the street and set out. His pace was brisk. Impatient. His expression was stony. Ernie trotted along next to him, biting back stupid chatter about desert sunsets; the melodious calls to prayer flowing forth from the minarets; the idea of buying her mother a few lengths of a pretty fabric she'd seen as she walked through a souk before dinner; silly, ordinary wishes and wants even when the world seemed to be falling apart. But when the road opened up as they reached a broad, wide-open square, Ernie was too fascinated to be nervous. Street vendors of every possible food and item stood by their carts, calling out to anyone who looked even remotely like a tourist, including Ernie and Gabe. As they strode deeper into the square, Gabe firmly shook his head at the offerings, but Ernie's head was on a swivel. Up ahead stood a man with a monkey on his shoulder, and beyond that . . . Ernie squinted through the smoky night air. "Are those snakes?"

"They're a fixture in Jamaa el Fna," Gabe replied. "Cobras, water snakes, vipers . . . take a look."

Ernie did. Wide-eyed, with her racing heart reminding her that before Legs had come into her life, she'd had a serious snake phobia, she stopped several steps from a hooded black cobra that had to be at least fifteen feet long. Other snakes, fat ones with dusty tan scales and patterned backs, slim and whippy grayish-green ones, and one that looked like an honest-to-god anaconda, were coiled into piles nearby while a jaunty man played a pipe and danced before them. Then he stopped playing and leaned forward to chuck the cobra under the chin. The thing stared at him impassively. He poked at the thing again, and it lurched forward like it wanted to strike him before rearing back and swaying ominously.

Ernie gasped as a slight weight was slung around the back of her neck, and she looked around to realize that another man had draped one of the slender snakes around her neck. As Gabe stood a few feet away, smirking, the man made a gesture suggesting she take a selfie with him and the reptile.

"He wants your cash," Gabe warned.

"No, thank you," Ernie said as Legs tingled hard on her arm, maybe jealous, maybe annoyed. She picked up the snake and handed it back to the man. He was smiling and weaving to the music, holding out the reptile in an effort to entice her. Ernie took in the moment and the fact that Gabe was no longer looking supremely irritated at having to be in her presence. She moved a few steps closer to the horn-playing snake charmer holding his creatures in thrall—and had a wild idea.

She turned around and knelt, then stroked her arm. Obviously reading her mind, Legs came slithering off her skin, perhaps five feet longer than she usually was. Ernie grinned and picked her up, fake groaning under the weight.

She spun around. "I brought my own," she announced, smiling as she went over to stand near the charmer, who'd stopped his playing and was gaping at her. He scanned his snakes as if wondering whether she'd stolen one of them, then squinted at Legs, as if trying to recognize her. "Mine," Ernie explained, which of course seemed to baffle the poor man. She motioned to him to keep playing his horn, then set Legs down at the front of the pack.

Even the other snakes seemed a little intimidated. Ernie bent down and looked her reptilian partner in the eye. As the man began to play, his music more tremulous and squeaky than it had been, Ernie shook her hips, and Legs lifted her head from the ground, rising as high as Ernie's thigh and swaying in perfect time. "How am I doing?" Ernie asked the snake charmer, and the man laughed and shook his head.

Gabe laughed, too. Ernie turned her head to see him watching her with a bemused smile on his face, like he didn't quite know what to make of her. "Show-off," he called out as a few people around them clapped.

"You could try it," she said, giving him a wink. "If you and your kestrel care to impress."

He arched one eyebrow, and after a moment of staring her down, he did a quick turn and smoothly pulled Caera from under his sleeve like a rabbit from a hat, drawing delighted oohs from the little crowd that was gathering. The kestrel flapped and let out a soft shriek, perhaps irritated to be in the presence of so many snakes. Gabe raised her to his face and whispered something to her before his eyes strayed again to Ernie, making her breath hitch. His gaze was full of mischief and challenge, and it sent electric excitement surging along her limbs. With an upward swoop of his hand, he launched Caera, who soared through the haze with a cry loud enough to carry over the music and the shouts of the vendors.

The kestrel returned a moment later with a gold coin, which she dropped into Gabe's palm as she streaked by. It earned Gabe a cheer or two and made a few of the other performers glance around as they realized a tourist was stealing the show. Caera landed on Gabe's shoulder, nipped at his ear, snatched the coin from between his fingers, then flew low over the snakes and disappeared into the haze again.

This time, when she returned, she carried a flower in her beak. She landed on Ernie's shoulder, poked it into her hair, and returned to Gabe's wrist to wild applause. Ernie offered the pair a slow clap, working to suppress a giddy, girlish thrill.

Not one to be outdone, she squatted in front of Legs and stroked her fingertips up Legs' exposed underside, up to her triangular head. Then she leaned forward, close enough to bump cheeks with her magnificent diamondback.

"We've got Gabe smiling," Ernie whispered. "Thank you, lady." She gave Legs a quick peck on the top of her head before standing up.

The laughing snake charmer, apparently getting the idea that this giant viper was docile as could be, reached out and tried to pet Legs under her chin.

Legs reared back, and the air filled with the loud, menacing buzz of her rattle. She seemed to grow in length and girth as she raised her head even higher. When she bared her fangs in threat, she was rewarded with gasps and little screams from the crowd that had gathered. The snake charmer quickly stepped behind Ernie.

"It's okay," Ernie said, mostly to Legs, who was on the verge of causing a panic in the square.

"Need some help?" asked Gabe. He came forward as everyone else took a step back, with Caera comically perched on the top of his head. He bowed, and Caera flew toward Legs. She fluttered in front of the agitated diamondback while Legs glared at her. Although maybe it wasn't a glare. Legs never blinked, so it was hard to tell. But whatever look it was, the two animals seemed riveted on each other. When Caera listed one way, Legs bobbed in the same direction, as if they were dancing. And finally, Caera came down for a light landing right on Legs's scaly body, which had slowly contracted to her normal but still considerable size. Legs coiled around so they could continue to stare at each other. Watching it was utterly hypnotic, and Ernie was alight with the intensity between the two powerful animal spirits. She tore her eyes from them to find Gabe staring at her with the same kind of look, and it almost melted her nerve endings on the spot.

"We should go," he said quietly while a few observers tossed coins onto the worn woven blanket the charmer had laid out, apparently believing that Legs and Caera had been part of his show.

"Okay," she murmured. She knelt down and picked Legs up, and Caera flew back to Gabe. The charmer chattered at her, clearly wanting her to leave her beautiful diamondback behind, and the audience looked on. Ernie and Gabe carried their animals through the square and took the first chance to duck into an alley to let Caera and Legs disappear back onto their arms. As soon as the spirits of their decks had become swirls of ink on their skin, Ernie looked up at Gabe, and they both started to giggle.

"I think I might give up trying to get paid as a Dealer and take up a new career as a snake charmer," she finally managed to say.

"That was brilliant," he said, wiping a tear from the corner of his eye. "But that old man is lucky Legs didn't eat him for dinner. She has a low tolerance for disrespect."

"As she should." Ernie bit her lip. "But it looked like Legs and Caera have developed an understanding."

"Yeah?" Gabe took Ernie's hand and pulled her toward him. "Do you think it's just the hybrid card?" His eyes were full of fun, absent the grim, weary look that left a bad feeling in the pit of her stomach. Somehow, the last few minutes had awakened him, arousing something hungry and hopeful inside Ernie. "Or maybe they sense something here." He pressed her hand to his chest.

His heart beat against her hand, fiercely alive. Ernie pushed down the fear that he would ever allow it to stop. And when his lips touched hers, she rose on her tiptoes and welcomed it, stomping down that nagging whisper not to get too close. It was easy for a moment, when his arm slid around her back, when her tongue ran along his bottom lip and made him groan. This was something she'd craved for months, something she'd dreamed about.

Dreams. Suddenly, the memory of dream-Gabe rose up like a specter, his hard grip . . . and the way he'd melted away a minute later. Sure, it had been a message from her subconscious. *He's reaching out to you. He's trying to get you back.* That had been the pain in her arm—Gabe pulling from another dimension. But what about the melting? The way he'd been there and then sunk into the ground, forever gone? What had her mind been trying to tell her then?

Once he gets you back, he's going to fade away?

Her father's disappearance had left her mother in ruins, and Ernie couldn't imagine living like that. She sank onto her heels and pushed gently on Gabe's chest, pulling her lips from his and bowing her head. "I—" she began in a shaky voice. "I think we should focus on our meeting."

"Are you all right?" he asked. "I'm sorry if I—"

"No." She took his hand and squeezed it, not wanting to let go of this suddenly *alive* Gabe. "No. I wanted it, too." It wasn't his fault that she was confused as hell and scared to death of too many things to name.

"Then we'll revisit this discussion later," he said, his tone still light. "But I suppose we should turn our minds to the Sunrise and how to make it ours."

Holding hands, they stepped back onto the narrow street and headed for their meeting with Belkacem.

The souk where they'd found Belkacem was locked when they arrived, but after Gabe pounded on the door a few times, the man himself pulled the door open. His gaze darted up and down the street, then he yanked the door wide to let them in. "Did you bring money?" he demanded.

Giving Ernie a sidelong glance, Gabe reached in his pocket and pulled out a wad of dirham twice as thick as his deck. "More where that came from, but I'd need to know what we're buying first."

Belkacem nodded. His brown skin was creased with lines that appeared deeper than they had in daylight, and he looked as if he'd consumed enough caffeine to make a camel dance on a table. "Not sure I should be doing this." His fingers skittered along the doorframe, and then he leaned out to scan the street again.

"You said you'd been wanting to sell for twenty years," Ernie said as he motioned them inside.

"This artifact's been in my family for over a century," he explained as he escorted them down the lamplit passageway, pulling a lantern from the wall as he did. "I'm not superstitious, but my mother always thought it was bad luck."

He led them across the now-quiet room full of wares and through another door, which led through a series of dark, low-ceilinged chambers that smelled of cinnamon and must. The lantern light bounced off the rough plaster walls in crazy patterns, and Ernie's stomach was in knots as she lost track of the turns. She pulled her deck from her pocket just in case, although the entire place was silent as a grave, with only their footsteps disturbing the quiet.

Finally, they reached a corridor, and Belkacem unlocked a door. Ernie was glad, thinking they had reached their destination, but then she nearly groaned when she rounded the door and saw a staircase leading down into a barely lit cellar. "Gabe . . ."

"I know." He had his deck out, too.

"My grandfather told me the Sunrise could never be sold to anyone but a card Dealer," Belkacem said over his shoulder as he descended the steps. "He said it would kill a mortal man who tried to use it. He said if I ever gave it to the wrong person, I would have death on my hands."

"Redmond Terwilliger is my father," Ernie explained. "He mentioned you in his journals."

"Many years ago, I thought he could be the person to sell this item to. But before I could, he told me to go into hiding, to be careful, to deny that I knew him. And then he disappeared. No one came after that, until now."

"But what *is* it?" Gabe asked.

Belkacem paused as they joined him at the base of the steps, from which Ernie could see little more than yawning darkness. When he lifted the lantern to look at them, she saw fear in his eyes, a sheen of tears. "I do not pretend to understand the games of immortals," he said, his voice shaking.

"Whoa. Are you okay?" Ernie asked.

Belkacem winced and shrugged. "This has been a long time coming." He turned quickly and ventured down the corridor. Gabe nudged Ernie in the darkness, as if warning her to be ready.

After passing a few closed doors, Belkacem paused at one on the left and pulled a key from within his robe. With shaking hands, he unlocked the door and pushed it open. Inside was a small chamber, and he motioned for them to wait as he went inside. Ernie leaned into the doorway and watched him kneel in front of a case, which he unlocked with a second key. He stowed his key ring in his pocket, pulled an object out of the case, and cradled it against his belly while he stood up slowly and turned around.

He was holding what appeared to be an egg the size of a chicken's, white with deep, sparkling orange and gold veins tracing across its surface. "This is the Sunrise," he said in a hushed, tremulous voice.

"Finally," someone replied, but it wasn't Gabe.

Ernie gasped as three men appeared in the corridor with them. She recognized two of them—Rupert, the Hyena Dealer, and Ruslan, the Dealer of the Komodo Dragon, had both tried to help Duncan get ahold of the Marks. They were positioned at either end of the hallway with their cards drawn. As for the third man, the one who had spoken from just a few feet away—

"Brahman," Gabe said, his voice level as his gaze swept the scene. "I wouldn't have thought you'd want to get involved."

The Brahman Bull Dealer, who Ernie remembered was named Lawrence and had been described by the other Dealers as more or less completely batty, was a barrel-chested old white guy with a thick, steely-gray beard and mustache, and he wore a striped Moroccan robe, worn slippers, and a skullcap that couldn't quite contain his impressively thick, wavy hair. He looked like a man who had been a total lady-killer in his day, but with a wild and weird edge that had only gotten weirder as he aged. He held his deck in hands tipped with long, tobacco-stained fingernails as he smirked at Gabe and Ernie.

"Kestrel," he said to Gabe in an accent that sounded very New Jersey to Ernie's ears. He jerked his chin toward her. "Who's the chickie?"

"Seriously?" Ernie scowled at the old man. "I'm holding a freaking *deck*. Show a little respect."

"When you earn it, baby Dealer, I will."

"You might regret saying that, *elderly* Dealer." Ernie shifted a few of her cards to the top of her deck. She hadn't really full-on dueled since having a complete deck, but now Legs was pulsing on her arm, and her heart was pounding in her chest. It felt as if she were about to start a Spartan Sprint, all pistons firing. Gabe had shifted so they were almost back to back, so he could keep an eye on Rupert at the end of the hallway, and the solid feel of him against her shoulder only made her feel stronger.

Lawrence coughed and spit on the ground. "Go ahead and talk, little girl," he said, sounding bored. "I'll let you, as long as you keep being so very easy to track." He glanced at her deck and winked.

Dread billowed inside Ernie, and she nudged at her Strike card. "Gabe, I'm sor—" she began.

"Focus," he barked. "Doesn't matter now."

The Brahman Bull Dealer chuckled as he watched Ernie's grip on her cards. "I have a no-regrets policy when it comes to dueling, but I'm not interested in fighting tonight."

"But she's the *Diamondback*," Rupert said, staring daggers at her as he fidgeted with his deck. He looked like he still bore a grudge from when Ernie had used the antagonist rune against him and his hyena. "And I'm going to make that little snake suffer."

"Can it," Lawrence snapped. "We're here on a fetch-it and that's that."

"I didn't know you were Virginia's errand boy," Ernie said.

Lawrence smiled, whistling in admiration. "I'd run a lot more for her than just errands. Quite a woman."

"Let's get it and go," Ruslan grumbled. He was standing on Ernie's right, near the base of the stairs that led up to the street level.

"You're going to have a very bad night," said Gabe, fanning his cards.

Lawrence regarded him with a spark of cunning in his eyes. "I hear you're down a card, Kestrel. Does it hurt? I've always wondered."

Gabe tilted his head. "Would you like to find out?" he asked, the Irish lilt of his voice laced with quiet menace.

The Brahman Bull Dealer twitched at his sleeve, revealing a flash of hooves and horns. "I believe my lady Virginia would like to speak with you again, boy, so maybe we'll be taking you with us."

"Not likely." Ernie fanned her cards as well, then glanced into the little chamber across the hall where Belkacem was cowering, looking as if he were about to explode with terror. "Hey," she said to him. "Just—"

Belkacem let out a squeak and slammed the door in her face.

"Get the relic," Gabe instructed. "I'll—"

He didn't have the chance to finish his sentence.

CHAPTER NINETEEN

With the swipe of a few cards, Lawrence blasted the closed door to bits, sending splintered wood flying in all directions. Ernie threw up her shield a moment too late and staggered back when the shrapnel shredded her pants and legs. Reeling as the corridor filled with noise and smoke, Ernie played her Draw card, hoping to snag the Sunrise, only to see it zoom over her head toward Ruslan, who had beaten her to it. Gritting her teeth against the pain, Ernie played Capture and Tool, and the egg-shaped treasure flew back in her direction. She was about to jump on it when she felt a whoosh of air and found herself plummeting straight toward a stormy ocean through howling wind.

Someone must have played Transport, Enemy, and Sea against her.

A split second before she splashed into the churning water, Legs burned on her arm, and two cards leapt to her fingertips—Transport and Friend-Lover, to carry her straight back to Gabe. After an instant in the void, she appeared in the corridor between Gabe and Rupert just as the latter loosed his snarling hyena. The creature leapt for Ernie's throat but fell to the floor in a metal dog crate before it reached her, thanks to Gabe.

"Get to Lawrence and stall him," he snapped as he forced Rupert away from her. "I've stuck the Sunrise here for the moment, but as soon as the Brahman gets it, he'll be gone."

Ernie looked past Gabe to see Lawrence floating in midair, clawing furiously at the artifact, which appeared to have superglued itself to the ceiling. Gabe was dealing in both directions as he tried to hold off both the Komodo and the Hyena, who were doing their best to capture him. Fear for him, along with the memory of his tortured body after Duncan had kidnapped him, made it hard to leave his side. She flung Warp and Enemy toward Ruslan, temporarily twisting him into a pretzel and sending his cards fluttering out like dying butterflies. Ernie was about to use her Draw card to collect a few of them—maybe the Wild card Gabe was missing—but then Rupert hit Gabe with a strike that momentarily shrank him to the size of a small child, and Ernie dove in front of him to shield him from the hyena, whose cage had disappeared with Gabe's concentration lapse. She played Transport and Air against Rupert to give him a taste of skydiving without a parachute. He blocked the strike but was distracted long enough for her to kick the mangy, growling creature away while Gabe played his Amplify card to restore himself to his normal size.

"Stop protecting me and get the Sunrise!" roared Gabe, hitting Rupert with a blast of air that slammed the snarling Brit against the wall, leaving a sizable dent of crushed plaster and stone as the Hyena Dealer slid to the ground, stunned. Gabe whirled around and flung another strike at Ruslan, twisting him up again just as he'd managed to reach the cards to fix himself.

Gabe did seem able to hold off the two Dealers, so Ernie blocked a careless strike Lawrence hurled her way before playing her Strength card and barreling into the old man, throwing them both to the floor—at which point, he loosed the bull. The droopy-eared, humpbacked white behemoth came charging off his body and crashed into her. While the strength from her card play was still surging through her body, Ernie dug in her heels and halted the thing's momentum before he could interfere with Gabe's fight. With a desperate flick of her cards, she played Pleasure and Nourishment on the bull itself, resulting in the appearance of a lovely cow, which blocked her view of Gabe just as Ruslan charged past, seemingly determined to destroy him. The bull let out a bellow of interest as Ernie turned her attention back to his Dealer, who had risen from the floor, laughing.

"Nice one, young lady," said Lawrence. "But I'm afraid *nice* is hard to take seriously." He bared his teeth and slashed his cards. Ernie went down hard as agony exploded through her entire body, as if nuclear bombs were detonating in every cell. She writhed, breathless, trying to play her cards but too overwhelmed with pain to manage it. Lawrence casually stepped over her and played another few cards, and the Sunrise artifact fell from the ceiling into his open palm.

With a cry, Ernie played Case and Enemy, enclosing Lawrence in a gluey, airless bubble that melted quickly because of her lack of concentration. She could hear the terrible rumbling of the building around them as Gabe's battle with Rupert and Ruslan continued. Neither enemy Dealer had much finesse, and they appeared most focused on crushing or perforating Gabe, judging by the shouts and crashes. The lady bovine Ernie had summoned to distract Lawrence's rampaging bull had disappeared after the Pain strike Lawrence had hit her with, and now the bull was charging up and down the hall while its owner shouted for him to return because they had to get going.

He was going to escape—with the Sunrise. Still crackling with the aftershocks of pain, Ernie rolled onto her stomach as chunks of ceiling began to pelt her from above. The building, having been shaken to its foundations, was about to come down. Ernie peered across the hallway, into the small room where Belkacem had been hiding when Lawrence exploded the door. The elderly mortal lay sprawled across a jumble of artifacts and splinters, bleeding profusely and seemingly unconscious. He needed help, but first she had to stop Lawrence from taking the artifact to Virginia.

She played her Shelter card in Belkacem's direction, hoping to protect him from the building's imminent collapse, and pushed herself to her feet in time to see the bull disappear onto Lawrence's arm. Ernie played Capture, but the Brahman Dealer neutralized it with a quick swipe of his Shield card. He sent a rain of barbed arrows at her, but she blocked it—barely—with *her* Shield card. She played Draw and Strength, which was enough to cause the artifact to jump to his finger-tips, but because she'd played both cards earlier, they didn't have enough power left to rip the precious object from his hands. As he grabbed it back and shoved it in his pocket, she made other plays, but he blocked every one or stopped her in her tracks with strikes she had to protect herself from.

"Boys," Lawrence called, amusement in his voice, "grab the damn Kestrel and let's go!"

Just as the final word left his lips, that end of the hallway collapsed with a thunderous roar, and a thick, gritty cloud of dust blinded Ernie. She could hear Lawrence coughing in the darkness and aimed a clumsy Inverse-Transport play in that direction to attempt to hold him there before he escaped with the Sunrise. But the sound of him went silent a moment later, telling her she had failed. Completely.

"Gabe?" she called out, inhaling a huge lungful of dust that sent her into a fit of uncontrollable hacking. "Gabe!"

She played her Light card, creating a bright glow from its rune that revealed nothing but rubble between her and the other end of the hallway, where Gabe and his two opponents had been. Frantically, she played Land, Rend, and Friend-Lover to shift the crumbled sandstone away, but the debris barely twitched. When she looked down at herself, she understood why and began to sink to the ground. Her legs were too injured to hold herself up, and the pain caught up as the adrenaline faded. She pulled her Healing card and lay still for a few minutes, focusing her whole self on becoming strong enough to find Gabe. Whom she'd failed. If they'd captured him along with the Sunrise, she'd never forgive herself.

When the wounds on her legs had closed up, she began to rise. The light from her card had faded, so the only illumination came from within the small chamber where Belkacem lay. One look inside reminded Ernie of how vulnerable mortal bystanders were in fights between Immortal Dealers. Grimacing, she leaned into the room, where the old man lay in a circle of relatively dust-free space, maybe because of the shelter she'd put up to protect him, one that must have disappeared as she focused on herself. At first, she thought he might be dead, but then his chest shuddered, and she knelt at his side. His eyes opened, and when he saw her, he whispered, "You have the Sunrise?"

She pressed her Healing card to his body. "No. The enemy has it."

"They were in the market today, asking many questions. I was afraid . . ."

As he trailed off, Ernie realized his wounds weren't healing. She'd completely burned out the card on her own injuries. With a lump in her throat, she played Transport and pulled Belkacem out of the suffocating basement that might collapse at any moment, through the void, and into her room at the riad. She carried him to the bed, his body wiry and light in her arms.

"I'm so sorry we brought this fight to you," she said. "And I'm so sorry we lost." She couldn't think about just how much she'd lost right now, though. She needed to keep moving, keep fighting. She needed to get Gabe back, just like he would have done for her.

"You did not lose," Belkacem said, his voice hoarse and wheezy as his breathing faltered.

"Some very bad people have that very powerful artifact," Ernie argued, wondering whether she should call a doctor or try to transport the man to a hospital. His skin had gone pale, and he grasped for her hand.

"That may be . . . true," he said. "But . . . they do not have . . ." He guided her hand to his pocket. "They do not have . . . the *key*."

Ernie pulled the key ring from Belkacem's pocket, and his trembling fingertip touched a small, intricately crafted key made of black metal that sparkled in the light. But when she looked up to ask Belkacem more about it, he had already taken his last breath.

Gathering her energy once more, Ernie transported Belkacem's body back to the wreckage of his souk building and gently laid him among his treasures. She wondered whether he had family or friends, people who would celebrate his life and mourn his death. She wished she had been strong and skilled enough to save him. She spent a few moments by his side, wishing him well and vowing not to let his sacrifice go to waste, before searching the rubble for Gabe and finding nothing. That meant he either had been taken by the enemy or had escaped. With nothing more to do in the rubble, she returned to her riad to clean herself up and get ready for a fight.

After a quick shower and change of clothes, she dipped into her Dream world to retrieve the pouch containing her dad's notes and the Cortalaza. She was considering popping a handful of the peanut M&M's stocked in her tent when she felt a strange tug at the center of her body. She glanced at her Revelation card to see Gabe sitting on the edge of her bed in the riad, pushing her hair away from her face as she slept.

She awoke with a start, the satchel clutched against her body, Gabe looking down at her. "Where have you been?" she blurted out, loudly enough to make him wince.

He scooted over as she pushed herself up. "I tried to track Ruslan, the big oaf, but he got away from me."

"You do realize they wanted to capture you, right?" She punched him in the arm. "It could have been a trap!"

He laughed. "Which is why he got away from me. He was a little too obvious about it, which told me how badly they want what I have. Speaking of, did you get the Sunrise?" When she shook her head, his smile died. "I should have been there. I should have helped you."

"Nope," Ernie said. "We're a team, and that job was mine to screw up."

"Lawrence is old. He's powerful. And—"

"And you told me to handle him, and I tried," said Ernie, pushing away the stinging memories of the old man's smirk, the way he'd utterly dismissed her and then demonstrated why she didn't deserve much more than that. "I'm not sure what happened tonight."

"Maybe you were more worried about me than you should have been."

"You were dueling two Dealers at once."

"I'm not weak, love."

"Sorry if I can't quite forget how beaten up you were the last time you were captured!" She tried to read his expression, but he wasn't giving much away. "Are you saying you weren't worried about me?" she asked quietly.

He looked away. "Now Virginia and her minions have the Sunrise."

Was he blaming her for that? "You didn't play the hybrid card while we were dueling those guys. How come? We might have been able to beat them."

"I don't keep that card in my deck," he admitted.

Something hard and heavy seemed to have lodged itself behind Ernie's breastbone. "Oh." She would *not* get into this now. If he didn't want to keep that little piece of her with him, he didn't have to. It was his choice. "Belkacem told me that they can't use the Sunrise without a key, by the way. So the apocalypse isn't imminent. Yay?"

Gabe stood up. "Yay indeed. Did he say where that key was?"

She pulled it from her pocket and held it up.

"Fair play," he said, offering her a gorgeous smile and his hand. As he pulled her to her feet, Ernie's thoughts rolled on a wave of confusion. The whole night had been this way. One minute he was dire and weary and detached, and the next, he was electric and vital and touching her in a way that made her melt. One minute he was acting like he cared, and the next, he was as distant as the moon. She couldn't wrap her head around it and didn't have the time to try right now.

"I guess we should go back to Ireland and see if Nuria's crawled out into the open," she offered, feeling awkward as she stood there, holding Gabe's hand, when he'd just told her that he didn't bother to carry with him the powerful card that connected them.

Gabe nodded. "And gather our allies again."

Ernie put the Sunrise key in her pouch of treasures. "It won't take Virginia long to realize she only has half of what she wants. Maybe that's the way to draw the Chicken out of whatever coop she's hiding in."

"Especially because she still wants the Marks as well. But you have that blade. The one that cuts through anything, right?" He poked at her pouch. "We could beat her this time. Permanently."

He sounded almost eager, and she wasn't sure—was he eager to end the threat Virginia posed? Or eager to right every wrong so he could slough off his immortality? She wanted to ask, but the last time she had, it had gone nowhere good. So she just said, "Let's go."

He nodded. Then he leaned forward, touching his forehead to hers. "Do you trust me, Ernie?"

"Yeah," she said, confused again. "Why?"

He pulled her against him and stepped into the void, where he whispered his plan into her ear, words that terrified and exhilarated her. By the time they came out on the other side, Ernie knew she had no choice but to focus on defeating Virginia and getting Kot reunited with Nuria. Everything else had to wait.

CHAPTER TWENTY

Minh was waiting in front of Gabe's haven, his angular face lit by a glimmer of firelight filtering through the windows of the cottage. "No sign of a monster bug, but a farmer halfway up the road to Clifden had some sheep go missing, and her neighbor reported one slaughtered in the field."

"That has to be her, right?" Ernie asked. "Where is she hiding, though?"

"Up to the north, it's not just fields and coast," said Gabe. "There are wooded spots and marshlands."

"Hard to understand why no one would have seen an elephant-sized grasshopper emerge to kidnap a sheep in broad daylight, though," Minh replied. He didn't really look dressed for a hunting expedition; he was wearing his usual slick outfit—black pants that hugged his narrow hips, silky shirt left unbuttoned at the top. Even his boots were free of scuffs and mud. And his expression suggested he didn't quite believe he was doing this when he could be pursuing other, more lucrative sports. "You didn't describe her as a silent killer, so why isn't anyone telling me they heard something unusual?"

"She isn't just an animal," Ernie said, thinking over what had happened to Nuria. "She's a Dealer and a deck combined. Maybe she's somehow cloaking herself?"

"Could be." Gabe ran his knuckles along his stubbly jawline. "So is she out of control, or is she intentionally hiding?"

"It's possible she's both." Ernie adjusted the strap of the pouch; the contents were heavy with possibility and risk. "But the only one who can help us really figure it out is the Dragonfly. He's been her guardian and lover for years." Ernie remembered that much, even though she couldn't remember Kot himself, not his face, not his voice. But she knew he was important to stopping Nuria. "To get to him, we have to go through Virginia or find some other relic that can get us to that specific splinter dimension." She looked down at the bag slung across her body. "I can do some more reading if I have enough time." And if their other plans didn't work.

Gabe sighed. "I hate that Virginia's got some obnoxious rune the Forger planted here just to make everyone's life more difficult."

"We're doing his cleanup work," said Minh, his eyes flashing with irritation. "You guys sure this is how you want to spend your time and energy? Isn't this chaos what he wants? Isn't us fighting each other his best advantage? You ever think about that? We're playing his game. And those Easter eggs your dad was after—that plays right into it."

"My dad was just looking for a way to get back to his family," Ernie said, feeling a swell of protectiveness toward him despite his failings.

"That explains the Marks," said Minh. "But what about this other stuff he sent your mom? The barrier runes? Having that stuff out in the open is just temptation to Dealers like Virginia, who crave power more than peace."

"We can't go back and change that," Gabe argued. "All we can do is try to fix what's in front of us."

"Why, though?" asked Minh. "I'm here because you traded a favor, Gabe, but if you hadn't made me such a nice offer, I'd be in Singapore making a few thousand bucks an hour. This isn't my problem. And it's not really yours, either."

"This is my homeland," Gabe shouted. "I won't leave these people to fight off a monster I helped loose on them!"

Ernie cringed. She was the one who had unleashed the beast, and Gabe's only fault had been trying to save *her*. But Minh had squared off with Gabe, shaking his head. "These mortals will die one way or another."

"But it doesn't have to be today, because of something we did," Gabe thundered. "I'm so fucking *sick* of this!" With sharp, agitated movements, he pulled a tie from his pocket and restrained his wind-blown hair. "Why the hell are we given this power? Just to cause misery and chaos? I won't. Not anymore. Never again."

Minh shook his head. "You may not have a choice."

"I will always have a choice." Gabe took a step back from Minh, his attitude, his outlook, but Ernie leaned in.

"It's easier to be detached than to care, isn't it?" she asked Minh. "You must have learned that a long time ago. It keeps your heart from being broken."

He rolled his eyes. "Ernie, may you someday experience the exquisite comedy of having someone a twentieth of your age try to fathom your mind."

"I think she more or less got it in one," Gabe said. "You didn't feel this way fifty years ago, and I don't actually believe you feel that way now."

"I'm here, aren't I?" The words burst from Minh like a gale, ready to lay waste. "But I don't have to care. And if that's the membership requirement, I have better things to do."

With a sudden flick of his Transport card, he vanished. Ernie gaped. "Are you freaking kidding me? Since when is he such a mercenary?"

"Since always," Gabe said mildly, playing a few cards. "I'm summoning Trey and Tarlae."

The couple appeared very near the spot where Minh had been standing. Trey, dressed in board shorts and an open short-sleeved button-down, brushed sand from his clothes and came forward to greet them while his lover hung back. Tarlae wore a maxi dress, and her thick hair was braided. She looked like she belonged on a beach with an umbrella drink—and as if the last place she wanted to be was there, with them. But as Ernie approached her, she saw something else: circles under the Coconut Octopus Dealer's brown eyes that hadn't been there before. She was still down her Shelter card, and it looked like it was slowly taking a toll.

"Thank you for coming," Ernie said.

"We are not staying. Trey is telling Gabriel now."

Ernie looked over her shoulder to see Gabe in somber discussion with the normally jokey Raccoon Dealer. "This is important, Tarlae."

"You think everything is important, Diamondback. You have not yet learned. And you saw what happened the last time we helped the two of you."

"We're all here and alive, aren't we? And we have a chance to beat Virginia and fix some of the suffering she's caused."

"Why must we beat Virginia?" Tarlae crossed her arms over her chest and cocked her hip. "Why do you think our Forger is so wonderful that he must be protected like this? What would he say if you asked for the same protection?"

Ernie had to give her that one. "He'd say that if I needed it, I didn't deserve to live. But that's BS, and you know it. This isn't about him! It's about Virginia and what she'd do if she were the Forger."

Tarlae gave her a contemptuous look. "What has this Forger done? Look at the things he creates! The runes that threw us over that cliff's edge—wielded by another Dealer! The rune that banished you to another place. The tools that let us hurt and destroy each other. And now you ask me to protect this being."

"He's helped us all at one time or another," Ernie said, thinking of the hybrid card the Forger had given her. At the time, she'd thought it was less than what she needed, but it had turned out to be the *only* thing she'd needed. "I don't think he's perfect, but I don't think he's evil. Virginia, on the other hand . . ." Virginia had grudges to settle. She might go after Ernie's father. Or Gabe.

"This is not your job," Tarlae said as Trey returned to her side. "And it is not ours, either. We do not care who the Forger is!" Her voice rang out almost unbearably loud, almost as if she'd amplified it with her deck. When Ernie winced, she lowered her voice. "And we simply wanted to do you the courtesy of telling you in person."

Trey wouldn't quite meet Ernie's eyes. "Sorry, Ernie," he said, his eyes fixed on something behind her, maybe Gabe. "No hard feelings."

They disappeared, and Ernie stared at the place they'd been. "What is *wrong* with them?" she yelled, throwing her arms up and turning to Gabe. "Is there anyone else we can ask to help us?"

"None that would say anything different than what you've heard in the last hour. I think we're on our own."

Ernie opened her pouch, and her fingers closed around the Cortalaza blade. Her heart thudded in her chest. "Okay, then."

"Am I interrupting your couple time?" came a saccharine voice. Virginia appeared on the low stone wall about twenty feet away, her white cloud of hair bouncing around her wrinkled face, her gauzy gown billowing in the wind. In one hand was her deck, and in the other was a rune, though which one, Ernie couldn't be sure. "Too bad all your allies abandoned you." Her gray eyes settled on Ernie. "And baby snake, you've *got* to learn to conceal yourself. It's pathetic how easy you are to track."

Ernie felt Gabe at her back as Virginia looked beyond them and said, "Don't attack until I give the word."

Ernie leaned around to see Rupert, Lawrence, and Ruslan perched on the opposite wall. She and Gabe were surrounded. She kept her hand in the pouch, her palm sweating over the hilt of the blade. This would be enough. It had to be enough.

"I hear that your father has come home," Virginia called, drawing Ernie's attention back to her. "Did he bring his thieved treasures with him?" Her eyes darted to Ernie's pouch, and she smiled. "I believe I'll pay our Dragonfly a visit after I deal with you."

"I will straight up kill you if you mess with him," Ernie said. "He dealt himself out of the game."

Virginia arched an eyebrow. "And how did he manage that?" she asked. "Something he found in the splinter dimension?" She batted her eyes in an apparent—but failed—attempt to look like a harmless schoolgirl. "Maybe I don't want to 'mess with him.' Maybe I want to offer him a job. He was always good at fetching."

"I've got all his notes," Ernie said. "Give us the dimensional rune, and we can negotiate." She took a step forward, shuffling the pages in the bag so Virginia could hear. She just needed to be close enough to strike.

Virginia played a card and floated theatrically down from her perch on the wall. She held up the tile in her right hand, revealing the glittering pink rune branded into its surface. "I suppose I won't need this soon. I'll trade it to you for the Marks. As for the pages . . ." She smirked. "Maybe I'll just take them."

Ernie pulled the Cortalaza from the pouch. "I had something else in mind."

"You think you can beat me with *that*?" Virginia fanned her cards. "You're such a peach. Boys?" Her voice abruptly became loud and harsh. "Let's clean this up."

Ernie let the blade fall back into her pouch and dove to avoid the first strike. The area around Gabe's haven had once again become a war zone as Virginia and her allies sought to press their advantage, confident they could defeat a pair with their quartet.

Which was what Ernie and Gabe had been counting on. Right on cue, Trey and Tarlae appeared on either side of the cottage, cards drawn, and threw themselves into the duel. Ernie lost track of time as she made play after play, just trying to hold Virginia back and do her part, wishing Minh would appear and help them out, too. That had been the plan. As they had traveled from Marrakech back to Ireland, in those moments with the void pressing in on them, Gabe had explained what he had set up to lure Virginia to them. Ernie had deliberately left herself unconcealed so Virginia could locate her, and Minh, Trey, and Tarlae had agreed to put on a show so that Virginia would think Ernie and Gabe were easy prey. But Minh was supposed to be back by now to help, and they needed his strength and skill badly.

When Virginia had pretended to be their ally, she'd played up her batty-old-lady schtick, but now, as they fought, Ernie could *feel* how strong she was. Despite a few assists from Tarlae, who had repeatedly disappeared Rupert—he kept reappearing covered in something that Ernie was pretty sure was cow manure, more pissed every time—Ernie could barely hold Virginia off. And finally, the older Dealer hit Ernie with a strike that slammed her into one of the stone walls so hard that everything went black.

When she came to, Gabe stood in front of her, playing cards with both hands, his deck glowing so fiercely that it surrounded him with a halo of blinding light. Trying to shake off the fogginess and pain that threatened to pull her back to the ground, Ernie shoved herself up and blocked a strike Lawrence had aimed at Gabe's flank.

As Virginia taunted Gabe about the last time they'd fought, inviting him to surrender to her in exchange for his life, Ernie charged at Lawrence before the Brahman Bull Dealer could help his mistress gang up on the Kestrel. Once again, she wished that Gabe had kept the hybrid card handy, but she had to push that thought aside when Lawrence covered every inch of ground between them with metal bear traps, the kind with jagged teeth, just as she barreled forward. A moment before Ernie fell into their open jaws, Legs brought three cards to her fingertips—Alchemy, Warp, and Tool. Ernie played them without a single conscious thought.

The traps melted and re-formed as a hard tiled floor between her and Lawrence, who promptly made another play, which threw Ernie into the air and brought her down hard on the unforgiving surface. She landed right on the pouch and felt the bite of the blade, her thoughts refocusing like a laser. "You broke my leg," she cried out, sobbing, groping at the satchel.

"You were never worthy to have that deck," Lawrence said as he walked toward her. "It has a proud history, and Duncan was a worthy Dealer. You're nothing but a—"

Ernie jumped to her feet and slashed out with the Cortalaza blade, cutting deep along Lawrence's left arm as he held it out to make another play. The cards fell from his fingers, and the bull came charging off his arm, bleeding and in a rage. Ernie gripped her weapon, ready to strike out again, but as Lawrence clutched at his chest and sank to his knees, his eyes bugging, she knew the damage was done. The other Dealers looked around in stunned surprise as the bull thundered through their battlefield, bleeding profusely from a terrible, huge gash along its side.

When Virginia saw it, she paused midplay, two cards poised at her fingertips. "Cecil?" she asked, looking around. "Where's Lawr—" She screamed as she saw him collapsed and gasping a few feet from Ernie, who didn't know whether to offer CPR or aim a death strike. A jumble of feelings coursed through her. She wasn't a killer and hadn't expected this to kill, but it looked like the shock of being separated from his bull had given Lawrence a coronary. Mortal again, he didn't look so good.

Part of her was defiant. He'd taunted her for being too nice. He'd planned to kill her for being so weak. All she'd done was get to him first.

But part of her was ashamed. Was she any better than him? Any more merciful or ethical?

Didn't look like it from where she was standing. The other Dealers stared at the blood dripping from the curved blade of the Cortalaza while Cecil the bull let out pained bellows as he, too, collapsed in the grass.

"What did you do?" Virginia asked in a high-pitched voice as she ran to Lawrence's side, turning him over. *What did you do?*

"Virginia," Lawrence said with a moan, reaching for her with his flayed arm. "It's-it's in my—"

She looked down at him in horror. "Look at you," she murmured. "You're about as useful as tits on a bull."

With a flick of her Draw card, Lawrence's scattered deck zoomed into Virginia's hand before any of the other Dealers could pull themselves together and make a play for them. She slashed a card at Lawrence, cutting him off midbreath. "And that's for failing me twice."

Lawrence slumped to the ground, obviously dead, as she shuffled the Brahman Bull deck into her Chicken deck. The bull let out a horrible choking noise and disappeared. Virginia's cards lit up bright, enough for Ernie to feel the heat from their glow. She watched in awe as each card found its match and each pair combined. Virginia's hair blew back, and she raised her head, every wrinkle illuminated.

She looked absolutely delighted. "I think you need a spanking, little snake," she said to Ernie. "Children aren't supposed to play with knives."

"Ernie," shouted Gabe, "get—"

Ernie lunged for Virginia with the blade, but she was hit with a suffocating force that stopped her in her tracks and knocked the Cortalaza from her hand. It landed in the grass a few feet away. The sounds of the other Dealers renewing the brawl cut out, and her nose filled with a thick, briny funk that was sickeningly familiar. Ernie scrambled to her feet as soon as she could move and took in the dead brown sea and the mountains in the distance, bathed in pale green moonlight.

She was back in the splinter dimension.

No way would she be stranded here again. No way. She looked around for the Cortalaza, but it had been left behind.

Holding the pink rune with her spindly fingers, Virginia stood nearby, framed in firelight from Gabe's cottage instead of the eerie green of the splinter dimension. "Where's my old friend Nuria?" Virginia asked, turning in place. "I bet she's hungry."

Virginia shrieked as she was tackled from behind by a dark blur. It was Kot. The rune flew from Virginia's hand, and Ernie dove for it, landing next to the struggling Dealers.

"Get her cards," Ernie cried. "Check her pockets!"

Kot shouted as Virginia threw him off her. When she got up, still standing in the patch of earth that connected the two dimensions, she was her monster self, jutting jaw and limbs with too many joints. Ernie tried to play her Shield card, but it sparked and faded almost immediately outside the range of her home dimension. Luckily, Kot produced a shield large enough to cover them both, and the barrage of spikes Virginia sent their way lodged in its thick wooden slats. Then he charged into it, launching it forward and sending it crashing into Virginia. Ernie scooped the rune from the damp grass, squeezing it in her hand and feeling its heat.

After a moment of crushing pressure, her home dimension engulfed all three of them, and Kot's broad wooden shield disappeared along with the stench of the dead sea. Kot staggered, hit with the crush of the transport to a foreign dimension. Virginia doubled him over with a Pain strike an instant later, and his Dragonfly cards scattered in the grass. Ernie jumped in front of him and called out for Trey, who was nearby, to protect Kot. She used her Warp card to avert Virginia's next strike, but it was so strong that it knocked her back. Virginia's lips were peeled away from her teeth, and her face was alight with fury. "You keep ruining things," she hissed at Ernie.

Trey's raccoon, Terrence, grew to the size of a buffalo, barreled past Ernie, and hit Virginia before she could make another play. "Use that dimension rune to get her out of here," Trey shouted.

"Not if Terrence is with her," Ernie said as Trey reached her side. She glanced around to see Gabe and Tarlae dueling with Ruslan and

Rupert while Kot, still stunned, knelt in the grass, trying to gather his cards.

Trey whistled, and Terrence turned to run back to him. Ernie stepped to the side to use the rune. But Virginia played her Draw card with such ferocity that the tile pulled Ernie's fingers out of joint as it was ripped from her hand. Virginia caught the tile as Ernie instinctively cradled her mangled fingers to her body. Seeing that Ernie was injured, Trey stepped in front of her.

Tarlae screamed his name.

Virginia grinned and slashed a few cards through the air, and several of Trey's zoomed from his hand and into the old woman's deck. She hit him with her Rend card, and he crumpled. Ernie fumbled with her deck, but her fingers were too injured to allow her to play quickly. She watched in horror as the pink rune glowed and Trey and Virginia vanished, right before Tarlae hit the place where the Chicken Dealer had just been with a strike.

Virginia reappeared a moment later, but Trey was nowhere to be seen. "He was a pest," she said, casually shuffling a thick stack of stolen Raccoon cards into her deck. She calmly threw up a clear shield as she was hit from three sides by strikes from Gabe, Tarlae, and Ernie.

Virginia held up the pink rune tile. She grinned and waved two cards over it. Tarlae crashed into the shield, pounding on the barrier as the tile flashed with blinding light and burst into flame, reduced to ash in a matter of seconds.

Ernie scanned the ground and dashed for the Cortalaza blade. With it, she could open a window to the splinter dimension, big enough to pull Trey back. Maybe Virginia hadn't taken too many of his cards. Maybe he'd be okay. All those thoughts were in her head as she reached for the blade. But a shrieking roar and a shout pulled her up short. She gasped as Nuria abruptly appeared in their midst. Minh was on her back and looked like he was holding on for dear life.

"Can't control her," Minh shouted as she crashed into the space between the cliff and the cottage, tossing him to the ground, her roar drowning out all other noise except for Tarlae's furious shrieks as she attempted to get through Virginia's shield. Rupert and Ruslan disappeared, perhaps too frightened to stay. Gabe ran forward to help Minh with Nuria. Kot struggled to get to his feet, Nuria's name on his lips.

Ernie's focus had to be on helping Tarlae and rescuing Trey. She reached for the Cortalaza blade.

But it spiraled away from the outstretched fingertips of her uninjured hand. Virginia, who had now imprisoned Tarlae in a metal coffin, caught it easily. She winked at Ernie and patted the shiny casket, which was very similar to the one Ernie had used to imprison Alvarez in one of her first duels. "Thought I'd take a page out of your book."

With a flash of her supercharged cards, Virginia disappeared.

CHAPTER TWENTY-ONE

While Minh, Gabe, and Kot tried to subdue the rampaging monster grasshopper that had appeared in their midst, Ernie ran over to the casket. Tarlae was shrieking and pounding from inside, obviously too panicked and traumatized to free herself using her deck. Ernie clumsily played Escape and Ally, and the coffin disappeared, dumping Tarlae in the grass. The Coconut Octopus Dealer looked around wildly, seemingly unable to comprehend what was happening in front of her.

Ernie grabbed her arm and hoisted her up, pulling her away from the struggle. She guided a dazed Tarlae to the other side of the stone wall that bounded one side of Gabe's property, and pushed her down to the grass. Tarlae shuffled almost blindly through her cards, as if looking for the right play to bring her lover back to her. Ernie's heart felt as if it were clamped in someone's fist. She didn't know whether to touch Tarlae, to offer comfort, or to leave her alone for fear she'd lash out. She felt utterly helpless.

The shrieking roars abruptly subsided, and Ernie looked over the wall to see that Nuria had reclaimed her human form. The three male Dealers around her seemed to be in a race to see who could clothe her first. Gabe used his deck to conjure a blanket while Minh produced a fluffy bathrobe. Kot gently pulled the trembling woman from the grass and accepted the gifts with a grateful nod. When she realized Kot's arms were around her, Nuria pressed her face into his neck and began to sob. Ernie had no idea how much Nuria had already forgotten from her time in the splinter dimension, but it was obvious that her love for Kot remained deeply embedded in her soul.

Ernie sank down next to Tarlae, knowing such a reunion might be impossible for the Coconut Octopus and the Raccoon. It looked like Virginia had taken a huge chunk of his deck.

Tarlae was muttering to herself. "He's not here," she whispered as she peered at her Revelation card. "He should be here."

Ernie touched her arm, but Tarlae jerked away with a snarl and pulled her Strike card from her deck. "We should never have helped you."

Ernie raised her hands, the fingers of her right throbbing and mangled. "We'll do everything we can to—"

She didn't get a chance to finish—Tarlae hit her with a blast of wind that knocked her off her feet. Ernie tried to right herself and cried out in pain when her swollen, out-of-joint fingers caught her weight.

"Tarlae." It was Minh, who was now standing on the wall with his deck drawn. "This isn't the way to get him back."

Gabe vaulted the wall and landed next to Ernie. He pressed his Healing card to her damaged hand as he lifted her from the grass. "It's all right," he said in an unsteady voice. His arms were a vise around her. "You're all right."

Ernie wasn't all right. She squeezed her eyes shut and pressed her face to Gabe's chest as Tarlae began to wail again. "I lost the blade," Ernie said in a choked voice. "And the rune—"

"I'm taking Tarlae to my haven," Minh announced. He had gotten the grieving Dealer to put away her cards and was holding her in much the same way Gabe held Ernie—keeping her from falling to the ground. He looked over his shoulder at Gabe. "You know what you have to do."

Gabe nodded. Minh flipped a card, and he and Tarlae stepped into the void.

Her fingers healed, Ernie moved away from Gabe's embrace and scrambled back over the stone wall. "We have to get that blade from Virginia," she said.

Gabe paused next to her as they surveyed the scene of the battle. Only blood and churned-up earth remained. Lawrence's body had turned to ash, and bits of him were blowing out to sea. "She has nearly three decks merged into one now," he said. "She'll be hard to outduel."

"We can't just give up! Trey might be dying *right* now!" Or he might already be dead.

He took her by the shoulders. "I have to make sure Nuria doesn't lose control again. Then we'll go." He released her and headed for his cottage with Ernie trailing behind. Too much had happened for her to wrap her head around all of it. The only thing she had to hold on to was her determination not to leave Trey behind.

They entered the cottage to find Kot and Nuria sitting on the bed. "Dragonfly," Ernie said, "This is the Kestrel."

"Dragonfly," Gabe said with a nod at Kot. "My haven is yours. From what Ernie's said, your deck may need some time to adjust to its new home."

Ernie approached the bed and put her hand on Kot's shoulder. In a way it felt like meeting someone for the first time, but in another, it felt like she'd known him for ages. "You were right there when I needed you. Again."

Kot stroked Nuria's hair. She seemed to have eyes only for him, perhaps afraid he'd disappear if she blinked. The only sound she made was a soft, lilting "kuh-kuh-kuh," as if she was trying to say his name. He kissed her forehead and said, "I knew she needed me, and I knew you understood that." His dark eyes rose to Ernie. "And I believed you would not abandon me there."

"We were trying to get the rune from Virginia when she almost stranded me again."

"It worked, all the same." His brow furrowed. "But the other Dealer, the man with dark hair . . ." He shook his head. "It does not look good for him."

Ernie hugged herself against a sudden chill. "We're going to get him back, too."

"Can you keep her calm?" Gabe asked Kot. His gaze was on Nuria, like he thought she might become the grasshopper again at any moment.

"Now that she is back in her home dimension, it may be easier for her to control it," said Kot, looking down at his love. "But I do not know. And it will be harder for me to help her until my deck adjusts to this world." He chuckled. "Until I adjust to this world."

"But your Dragonfly deck was made for this dimension," Ernie said, "so maybe Pol and you will get used to it quickly."

He looked down at his arm, where the dragonfly glittered in swirls of blue and green. "Perhaps you are right." He frowned. "Will I forget, as you did?"

"I didn't forget everything," said Ernie. "Some things I had known long enough to remember, like my parents. You've loved Nuria for a long time."

"I could never forget that. It is knit into my being."

Biting her lip, Ernie glanced at Gabe. She'd forgotten him, in a way. But even then, their connection had called to her. She wished she knew what it meant now.

"My haven will shelter you," Gabe told Kot, playing his Aid, Strength, and Shelter cards. "We'll give you some time. But summon one of us if she . . . well . . ." He turned in place, crossing his Draw card with his Ally card. "Because this cottage is an extension of me, I will feel it if you summon me."

"I will," said Kot. "And thank you."

"We'll be back soon." Without explaining further, Gabe took Ernie's hand and played his Transport card. Her cold fingers clutched at his, the question of where they were going frozen in her mouth.

They appeared in darkness, but Gabe flipped his Light card, revealing a space somewhat similar to his haven. Ernie thought she could hear the ocean outside. "Is this another haven?"

"This one is simply a home," he said, turning on a nearby lamp with a twist of its antique switch. They were in a cramped living room containing a few squashy chairs by a cold woodstove, a tiny kitchenette against the wall, and a doorway through which Ernie could spy a bedroom.

"Where are we?"

He pulled the tie loose from his hair. "Still in Ireland. Just farther to the north. I like the wind off the ocean."

The wind rattled the window frames as if it liked him back. "Why are we here, Gabe? I feel like we need to be doing something."

"I'm going to get the Marks." A shadow of something—maybe fear, maybe doubt—lay behind his eyes. "And I was wondering if you would go with me."

Her satchel, with her father's notes, was still hanging from her shoulder. "You don't think I should stay here and try to see if my dad described any other way of opening a dimensional portal?"

"You could. But . . . I am asking you to come with me."

"Of course I will," she said, compelled by the need in his voice. "Are they around here?"

"They're in my dreams. It was the only place I could think of where no one could take them from me, even if my body failed." He walked over to the stove and tossed small kindling logs inside, then lit it.

"You think Tarlae could use one to ask the Forger to bring Trey back."

"Maybe he'll show a bit of mercy. And Kot and Nuria could use the other to ask him to restore her health and her mind, perhaps to separate the animal from the Dealer and deck. There are two Marks left, and I can think of no better use for them."

"Not to mention it would stop Virginia from coming after you, and remove the Marks from the game," Ernie said, watching him closely.

He glanced back at her before putting a larger log into the stove and closing its door. "I'm not doing this to keep Virginia from attacking me."

"Do you think the Forger will grant their requests?"

"If they can convince him that the threat of Virginia is real, maybe he'll see the value in a strong alliance of Dealers to stop her."

"And will you be a part of that alliance?"

He stood up to face her. "What are you getting at?"

"You're joking, right?" She stared at him in disbelief.

He exhaled, obviously annoyed, and muttered, "I'll go get the Marks myself."

"Why did you ask me to go in the first place?"

"Because I trust you to watch my back," he snapped. "With a bit of know-how, an experienced Dealer can push her way into another Dealer's dream space, and I'm thinking Virginia might give it a try."

"Fine," she said. "I'll come."

He stalked into the bedroom. "A bit more comfortable in here," he said gruffly, as if he could crush the obvious and awkward intimacy of the situation with a change of tone.

Her heart pounded as she followed him into a spare-looking bedroom occupied by a double bed with a rough-hewn wooden frame, covered by a simple quilt. He kicked off his boots and scooted back so she could join him. It seemed so simple and so easy, as if they were getting into bed for a nap, except the tension between them was so thick that she wondered whether she'd even be able to relax enough to enter the dream realm in the first place. But regardless of what was going on with Gabe, both of them owed it to their allies—their friends—to bring the Marks back to them. She lay down next to him. "How do we do this and make sure we end up in the same place?"

"Bring out your Dreams card. And . . ." He seemed to be avoiding her gaze. "Friend-Lover."

She laughed. "You sure?"

He rolled his eyes. "Just do it, Ernie."

She pulled the cards, ready to snap with irritation, breathing slowly to try to defuse the bomb of emotion ticking in her chest. With impatient movements, he crossed his Dream card with hers and his Friend-Lover card with hers so their decks were meshed in a little pile between them. "Be ready for things to get—"

"Weird? I already know the drill."

"Good."

They glared at each other for a moment. Then they peered into the cards and let the realm pull them in. After a moment of dizziness, Ernie blinked up into a haze of rainbow-tinged mist that hung over an emerald countryside. Next to her, Gabe immediately walked forward. They were on a narrow gravel path that led toward the base of a hill. She had to jog to keep up with his rapid pace, but she scanned her surroundings, partly because the new realization that Virginia might be trying to find Gabe's dream stash was freaking terrifying, and partly because she couldn't help being just a little bit curious about Gabe's dreamscape.

It looked like a slightly more lush and wild version of Ireland, but the farther she walked, the more she noticed the ground slowly shifting beneath her feet, as if they were on a large boat in a rolling sea. And when they passed a burbling stream, Ernie realized it was strangely deep. She paused, leaning over the water, trying to see the bottom.

"Don't get distracted."

His voice brought her up quickly. She'd been in this realm before. Many times. She knew better than to lose herself. She jogged to catch up, ignoring the sudden appearance of a small flock of blue sheep that ran by in the other direction, two by two. "Where are we going, exactly?"

"It's right up here." He sounded incredibly irritated, just like he had in Marrakech before they'd walked through the square, when she'd accidentally broken the tension with her silly antics.

She doubted silly antics would work right now, so she trotted along behind him, taking in brilliant sunshine and rainbows hung between fluffy clouds hovering over this strange, unsteady, mist-covered land. "Have your dreams always been like this?"

"Not really your business, is it?"

"Okay, are you gonna tell me what I did to earn this attitude from you?" She poked him in the back. "I'm trying to help you out!"

He whirled around. "If you want to help, stop treating me as if you think I'm going to off myself at any moment."

She pulled up short. "Jeez, Gabe—you're the one who told me you were considering it! Are we just going to ignore this? A week or so ago, you told me you were thinking of giving up your deck!"

"Things have happened since then that made me reconsider."

"Another wrong you have to set right?" She raked her fingers through her tangled, damp hair, not sure where to aim the worry that had been coiling inside her for days—and that had been pulled to the breaking point by what had just happened to Trey. "Is that the only reason you're here anymore? To balance the ledger?"

His brow furrowed. "Obviously not."

"Obvious?" Ernie scoffed. "Nothing is obvious with you! One second you make me think you don't give a damn about yourself—or me—and the next I'm thinking the opposite. You fight like a freaking warrior but then talk about letting go. You seem like you're done one minute and ready for a fight the next!" Frustration made her eyes burn with tears. "I don't get you, I *don't* know how to help you, and it's driving me nuts."

"You don't have to help if you don't want." His voice had gone cold.

She waved her arm. "See? This is what I'm talking about! You ask me to come with you, like you need me, like I matter, and now you're acting like we're just allies. Or maybe strangers."

"What the hell do you want from me, Ernie?" he shouted. "I don't have everything figured out. I'm not wise—I'm a fecking fool, and I never meant to love you!"

"I don't want to love you, either, you big jerk!" she yelled. "If you think I'd give my heart to someone who's willing to walk out on me, you *are* a fecking fool." She swiped a hot tear from her cheek, and her fingers came away smeared with silvery glitter. Just another reminder that they were standing in a dream, but right now, the only thing that seemed real was Gabe. "I don't know what you want from me. I don't know what to ask from you. All I know is that this is driving me crazy. I don't want to let you hurt me, but I know it's going to happen anyway."

"I'm not trying to hurt you." He turned around and began walking again, reaching a steep set of grass-covered steps that descended into the hill but were invisible from just a few feet away.

Ernie shook her head and trailed after him. "But even if you don't want to hurt me . . ." She let out a shuddering sigh. "Did you see Tarlae earlier?"

"You think I don't understand how that feels?" They'd reached the bottom of the steps, and the path opened up to a sort of cave, except it was still grassy and sunlit despite there being no discernable sun. Meadow flowers carpeted the ground, but the ceiling was covered in knifelike glass shards that wobbled with every eerie roll of the terrain.

As Ernie watched, one of them fell, embedding itself in the soft earth below. Gabe barely seemed to notice. He stopped on the edge of a crystal clear pond and looked over the seductively dangerous landscape of his own mind. "I've lost one family already, Ernie. Not just my mother and sister but also my wife and my child. They're buried not three miles from my haven." He was quiet for a moment. "I visit their graves every chance I get, and I never want to feel that pain again."

Ernie stared into the water, still trying to find the bottom. "So you're trying to keep your distance from me."

"I don't know what the hell I'm trying to do! I never planned to care about anyone ever again. I was just living to right the wrongs I'd done. And I was looking for a good excuse to give up." He cursed and then chuckled. "And then I met a woman so damn obstinate and determined that even the idea of giving up is foreign to her."

"I think about giving up all the time," she said quietly. "But then I decide not to." She slowly turned in place, understanding how fragile and perilous and beautiful the space was, how unsteady but vast. "The idea of you giving up hurts my heart, Gabe. Enough to make me want to keep *my* distance, just to protect myself from that." The last thing she wanted was to be impaled by one of the glass knives that hung above them like guillotine blades.

"Look at me," he said quietly, drawing her attention away from the glittering threat. "Do you know why I don't carry the hybrid card that connects our deck?"

"Because you never had a choice about it in the first place," she mumbled.

"Wrong." He brushed a strand of hair from her cheek. "Because I knew Virginia was after me, and I knew she was strong. If she ever got my deck, she'd get that card—and then she'd be able to summon you. Get into your head. Feed on your power. Hurt you—and Legs. And I couldn't risk that. So I hid it here, knowing it would be much harder for her to steal."

"Oh." That had never occurred to Ernie. She glanced above their heads and wondered whether the shards of glass were less of an unstable danger and more of a trap, in case the wrong person tried to invade. "But Gabe, what do you think would happen to me if you gave up your deck? Whether you carry that card or not, it still exists. It still connects us. I know you didn't want it, but—"

"It's not that I didn't want it. I wasn't sure I was strong enough to be worthy of it."

She put her hand on his chest. "You are the strongest person I've ever met."

He gave her a crooked smile. "Have you met you?"

"I've never felt stronger than when we fought Duncan *together*. Even though both of us were almost dead at the time."

"I felt the same," he murmured. "And that was a hard truth to swallow. It's easier to be alone."

She laughed, but the sound was strangled, cut off by fear and sorrow. "Don't I know it? Then no one can walk away from you."

"I won't walk away, not from you. And you know that."

She looked into his eyes. He'd already proven that when he'd refused to abandon her or take her cards when she'd fought to earn the Diamondback deck. And again when he'd worked tirelessly to pull her back from the splinter dimension. But—"Do you actually *want* to stay, though?"

"I don't want to lie to you—sometimes I'm not sure. This work of creating chaos just to fuel more chaos . . . I question it all the time." He touched her forehead with his. "But I'm not sure I've ever felt more alive than when we were in that square in Marrakech. If I could have more moments like that . . ."

She smiled, remembering the playful spark in his eyes and how it had wiped the shadow of weariness from his face. "I think Caera and Legs had fun with it, too."

"And that makes me want to stay. I want to preserve a world that makes those moments possible. That's worth fighting for, if we did it together. If that's what you wanted."

Together. She nodded, though it drilled her fear of losing him even deeper into her heart, and tilted her face to his to welcome his kiss, lingering and tender. Yes, the knives still hung over their heads, ice blue and razor sharp, and yes, the ground slowly shifted beneath their

Sarah Fine

feet, rising and falling like a breath. But it was no different in any other realm. Everything could be taken from them in a moment, just like Trey had been taken from Tarlae. She could lose him in an instant, an existence cut short with the slice of a knife or a slash of a card, and a bottomless hole in her heart would be all that remained.

Ernie wrapped her arms around his neck and kissed him back. Gabe Carrig was worth the risk.

CHAPTER TWENTY-TWO

One moment there was nothing but Gabe, and the next, the blades began to clatter over their heads and then to fall in a jagged but clear perimeter around where they stood, only a few feet away from them. Gabe pulled away and whispered, "I think that's my mind telling us it's time to go."

She flinched as a long shard of glass sliced into the soft earth beside her. "Your mind is terrifying."

"Sometimes I'd agree with you." He looked around, calm as a few more blades of glass plummeted from the ceiling. "It wasn't always like this." He steadied them while the ground rolled lazily but surely beneath their feet. "The earth didn't use to move, for one."

Ernie took in the uncertain look on his face and felt a deep pang in her chest.

"Are you all right?" he asked after he brushed a kiss across her knuckles.

"I'm not sure," she murmured. "I think I'm good. I just . . ." Her brow furrowed as unexpected tears stung her eyes.

"This means something," he said to her, taking her face in his hands and making sure she was looking at him. "For me, at least."

"Same," she whispered. "But now—"

"Now we fight together, and we watch each other's backs." He gave her a firm, lingering kiss on the forehead. "Like we have ever since we met."

Ernie couldn't get Tarlae's tearstained face out of her head, so she simply closed her eyes and nodded. "Are the Marks nearby?"

"Very." He pulled his deck from his pocket. With the casual sweep of one of his cards, the glass knives scattered across the grass immediately pulled themselves from the soil and replanted themselves in the ceiling.

"Whoa," Ernie whispered. "Do you have control over all this?"

"I've spent a fair bit of time here," he said as he squatted in front of a boulder on the bank of the pond. As he reached for it, a knob appeared on its surface. He gave it a twist and pulled open a small door, revealing that the rock was hollow and glowing from within. From inside it he plucked the hybrid card and the box containing the Marks.

The whole cave shuddered, making the jagged ceiling sound like a dozen wind chimes, exquisite but alarming. From outside came a peal of thunder, even though abundant sunshine streamed in rainbows through the mist at the entrance to the cave. "Another warning?" Ernie asked.

Gabe frowned as he reached her side. "Virginia is looking for this place."

"Have you ever met another Dealer in this realm? Or another person? I thought I was alone in my dreams."

"Most of the time, you are, if you don't leave the territory of your own mind. But it is possible to travel and explore beyond those boundaries."

"Have you done it?"

He gave her a sheepish smile. "I tried, when we were separated and you were in the splinter dimension."

"How?"

"Using our card. But nothing was as clear or safe as it is here, and it was hard to stay there, because my own dreams kept wanting to pull me back." It looked like he was biting the inside of his cheek. "But I may have found your haven."

"Whoa. Did you happen to leave a message for me?"

"The cairn?"

She nodded. "That was you. And you did find my haven."

"I'm sorry—"

"No. It's just . . . I thought I was safe there, and now I'm not so sure."

"Any haven can be found. But it wasn't easy, and I don't think I could have done it if we hadn't been connected the way we are. Virginia, though . . ." He took her hand as the earth rumbled again, nearly knocking them off balance. "We should go."

Ernie pulled her Revelation card and looked at it. Her cheeks warmed, and Gabe chuckled as he looked at his. In the waking world, they were no longer lying side by side, separated by the cards. Instead, she was in his arms, her head on his shoulder, his arms around her, one hand in her hair. She let herself be absorbed by the sight, and in the next moment, she awoke right there, inhaling his masculine scent and feeling his stubble scratch her forehead.

As he stirred and his eyes opened, Ernie looked down at herself. "Was that real?" she asked quietly.

"If it wasn't, then I just had a damn good dream," Gabe said, rising from the bed. He winked at her. "And first chance we get, I say we see if this realm compares."

She couldn't suppress a smile. "If you play your cards right."

He shuffled his deck, letting the cards fly from hand to hand. "Good thing I'm a pro, then."

She drew her Transport card. "Minh said he was taking Tarlae to his haven. Want me to take us there? I know where it is."

"Glad to hitch a ride." He took her hand as she played the card, and a moment later they were standing at the edge of a thick tropical jungle, birds cawing in the trees and the thick humid air throwing Ernie's hair into an instant frizz.

Minh came to the door as they approached, his expression grim. "She's touch and go," he said. "Just be ready with a few defensive plays, okay?"

Ernie's fingers closed over her deck. "Is she really attacking you?"

"She's just struggling to control all of it, and she's used to having Trey with her, like a counterbalance. It's likely that either one of them would be out of whack without the other."

Ernie swallowed hard. Was that what it was like to be connected? Did you lose your balance if the other person wasn't with you? She avoided looking at Gabe as they entered Minh's hut. Tarlae sat at the table with a cup of clear liquid in front of her. Her normally lustrous skin looked dull, and like Ernie's, her hair was in a frizz. She didn't look up as Ernie and Gabe sat down across from her.

"Tarlae," said Gabe. "Trey is a friend of mine, and—"

"You killed him," she said in a flat voice, her gaze riveted on the liquid in her cup. "I knew it would happen. I just didn't know when."

"He's a solid Dealer," Gabe said. "And he knows his own mind."

"He looked up to you, Kestrel. He would have followed you into hell, and he did. And then you left him there."

"He sacrificed himself in a battle," Gabe said. "And I would never leave him."

Tarlae raised her head and glared at Ernie. "He sacrificed himself for you, Diamondback. Because you are too weak to defend yourself." Her hand twitched over her deck, which lay on the table between them, and a shimmering tentacle pulled itself from her left arm and knocked over her cup.

Ernie scooted back from the table, her Shield card at her fingertips.

"I think Rika is telling you that you've had enough," Minh said softly, moving to Tarlae's side. He dropped a cloth over the spreading liquid, which Ernie could smell now—gin.

"Get on or get off," Tarlae snapped at the waving tentacle extending from her skin. "I don't care."

The tentacle curled around Tarlae's wrist, as if trying to pull her hand away from the cards. Tarlae rolled her eyes and moved her hand, and the tentacle sank back into her arm. Then her face crumpled, and she bowed her head.

"Tarlae—" Gabe began, but the Coconut Octopus Dealer let out a growl and shoved back from the table, staggering backward until her back hit the wall.

"I'll get her myself," she shouted. "I'll find her, and I will kill her."

"That won't get him back," said Ernie.

"Nothing will get him back!" Tarlae's beautiful face was strained with rage and grief. "Trey is gone. Did you not see her take his deck? Did you not see what happened to the Brahman?" She let out a wrenching sound, and she grabbed her deck from the table. "Dust," she screamed. "Only dust was left!"

"She didn't get all his cards," Gabe said, holding the box containing the Marks. "And that means there's hope."

"What hope?" she asked, shaking her head. "He is somewhere out there, alone, without his cards."

"He's not alone," Ernie said. "Terrence is with him."

"Suffering!" screamed Tarlae. "If he had stayed with me, listened to me—" She grimaced and let out a sob.

Ernie was trying not to cry herself. Seeing Tarlae like this felt like a punch in the heart. "This was your worst fear," she said. "But do you remember what you said to me a few months ago? Loving him meant letting him be himself, and that meant letting him be brave, letting him take risks to defend and protect whatever was worth fighting for. You knew that loving Trey fully meant taking those risks, and you did, because you're brave, too."

"No, I'm not," said Tarlae as she slid down the wall. Her knees curled to her chest, and she covered her face with her hands. "If I could go back and do it again, I'd tie that damn Raccoon to a bed and never let him loose."

"Liar," Ernie said quietly. Her chest was tight with sorrow. "You would let him be who he is, and you would never give up and never rest until you'd done all you could to save him."

"There is nothing," Tarlae sobbed. "Nothing."

"I have a Mark for you," said Gabe. "Yours to use as you wish. If you think that Trey is gone forever, you can use it to ask the Forger for a different favor." He opened the box and set a Mark on the table with a heavy clunk. "Or you can call the Forger to you and ask him for Trey."

Without uncovering her face, Tarlae asked, "And do you think he will grant a favor of that size?"

"There are no guarantees, but he will be required to help you in some way. It's up to you what you want to ask for."

Tarlae spread her fingers, revealing her dark eyes. "What if I ask for a death instead of a life?" she whispered.

Gabe met her gaze steadily. "That is your choice. And if it's my death you seek, he may very well grant it."

Something inside Ernie went as hard as a diamond. "But if you ask for that," she said to Tarlae in a low, deadly voice, "then you will have earned yourself an enemy who will dog you for the rest of your freaking existence."

Minh, who had been standing quietly against the wall, whistled.

Tarlae's eyes locked with Ernie's, and Ernie didn't have a bit of trouble staring her down. "I mean it," she said through clenched teeth. "You want to choose some twisted revenge? Go ahead. But I will, too."

Gabe's hand closed over Ernie's shoulder, but she shrugged him off. "If you decide to try to rescue Trey, though," Ernie said to Tarlae, "then I'll help you in any way I can."

"I'll take the Mark," said Tarlae.

"We're going to give the other to Kot and Nuria," Gabe said. "Come with us back to my haven, and you can all summon him together."

"Safety in numbers," said Minh. "Nice."

Gabe arched an eyebrow. "Perhaps I could be forgiven for hanging back, though."

"Fair enough," said Minh. "But we can use the audience as a chance to warn the big guy about the very real threat Virginia poses now."

"Shouldn't he know that already, though?" asked Ernie.

"He doesn't pay attention the way he should," said Tarlae, who had regained her feet and was using a card to smooth her hair and clean her soggy, stained maxi dress. "We will make him understand."

Together, they traveled to Gabe's haven. Kot and Nuria were there, and to Ernie's relief, Nuria looked slightly steadier. "I've been working with the cards," Kot said as he emerged from Gabe's cottage. "They are starting to respond." He put his arm around Nuria's shoulders. "But for her it is still very hard," he added softly.

Gabe held up the box containing the one remaining Mark. "With this, you can ask the Forger to help her. Or you can ask for a different favor entirely."

Ernie watched as Gabe gave Kot the final Mark and explained all his options, and Kot listened with surprise written all over his face. "You give this to me, a stranger," said Kot. "Why?"

"Because you're an ally, not a stranger. And because you're worthy of it," said Gabe. "You protected and sheltered the Diamondback in your dimension, and we will protect and shelter you in ours."

A wild mix of emotion flickered across Kot's usually impassive face. "Thank you," he said in a strained voice.

"Maybe we do this now," said Minh. "Before Virginia regroups."

At Gabe's suggestion, they moved from his haven to a high mesa in the middle of Utah, on neutral, unpopulated ground. Ernie looked around her as they all appeared on the red earth. The Kestrel. The Pot-Bellied Pig. The Dragonfly. The Grasshopper. The Coconut Octopus. And the Diamondback. They were wounded and grieving, but they weren't defeated. And with the help of the Forger, maybe they could be whole again.

Ernie tugged on Gabe's arm as the others scanned their surroundings. "You need to be somewhere far from here." Her fingertips found his face, skimming over the crinkles at the corners of his eyes, the few gray hairs at his temples.

He pulled their hybrid card from his deck. "I won't be here, but I'm not leaving you alone, either."

"Will Andy grant the favors they want?"

She couldn't read his expression as he said, "That would be the easiest way forward."

"Do you think I should try to tell him about the Sunrise? Or will he know?"

He pulled her into his arms. "Don't give him a reason to focus on you, love, especially because you didn't do what he asked. Trust me." He kissed her hard and disappeared.

"That's what I thought," Minh said, smirking at Ernie.

She was torn between a grin at the idea of being with Gabe and a sense of dread as she remembered what Minh had said about foolish Dealers who were connected by the heart. "Shut up."

Ernie walked over and sat down next to Nuria, who was watching her man intently while she rocked back and forth. "How are you?" Ernie asked her.

Nuria looked over at her, seemingly surprised that anyone had acknowledged her. "Ah-ah . . ." she said. "Fuh-fuh-fuh . . ." Her exquisite face twisted with frustration.

"It's okay," Ernie said. "With any luck, we'll get what you need. Kot won't rest until it happens."

Nuria's gaze darted to the Dragonfly Dealer, and a rippling shiver passed through her body, tensing every muscle in Ernie's. If the grasshopper took over at the wrong moment, it might take all of them to subdue her. Ernie touched Nuria's arm. "Hey, it's going to be fine."

Tarlae and Kot sat down on a flat expanse of slick rock as the moon hung over the harsh landscape. Minh conjured a knife, and the pair of lovelorn Dealers shed blood over the two Marks, focused on what they needed. Ernie knew from experience that the Forger would choose his own method of making contact. When she'd used a Mark, he'd called her on the phone and set up a date at a local brewery.

But not even a minute after the Marks had absorbed the blood of the Dealers, the figure of a man materialized at the edge of the table rock. He walked forward slowly, taking in the scene. Andy crossed his arms and stroked his beard. "Since when is this a team effort?" he asked.

"Only two of us requested a favor," said Tarlae. She and Kot stood up.

"Yeah? And you just needed a little moral support, like a gaggle of ladies in a restroom?" Andy spread his arms. "Am I really that scary?"

Kot took a step forward. "It is an honor to meet you, Forger." He bowed his head. "I am the—"

"I know who you are. The guy Redmond shoved in his loophole."

"I have accepted my deck," said Kot. "And now I have but one request."

"I have one as well," said Tarlae.

"Got it," said Andy. "Just one problem."

Ernie's heart sank as she saw the Forger's eyes go from blue to black in the space of a second.

"You're all just a little bit too organized," the Forger said, black bleeding across the whites of his eyes. "And that's the opposite of what I created you for." Strands of blue lightning sizzled between his fingers, and he smiled. "So before I grant any favors, I'm going to offer you a lesson on the nature of chaos."

Before any of them could play a single card, the Forger did exactly that.

CHAPTER TWENTY-THREE

Ropes of blue fire lashed from Andy's fingertips and wrapped around each Dealer on the mesa. Searing pain traveled along Ernie's limbs, melting her focus. All she could do was hold on to her deck. Her tears turned to steam as she glanced around to see all her allies in the same predicament.

His arms outstretched, strands of power extending from each fingertip, the Forger clucked his tongue and turned to Minh. "I thought you were smarter than this, brother. Remember the promise we made to each other?"

"I'm not interfering with your rule," Minh ground out. He was writhing in the grip of the blinding blue light tangling around his limbs, trying to reach his cards in his pocket as the Forger turned to Kot and Nuria.

"You never even appreciated what you had, Kot," said the Forger. "You use all your power to protect this abomination." His black gaze focused on Nuria, who had been cursed by a rune Andy himself had created. "I used to hear stories about you from other Dealers, did you know that? I thought you were going to be one of the greats. And look at you. Maybe the favor I should grant is putting you out of your misery."

Kot shouted and slashed one of his cards at the blue ropes of electricity around him, severing it. He landed in a heap but jumped up immediately—only to be snapped back into the grip of the blue lightning before he could do a single thing to help Nuria.

The Forger moved on to Tarlae. "And you. I thought you were clever and strong, but what you really are is pathetic. Your sentiments for the Raccoon made you weak. You don't even deserve to have a deck, let alone the Coconut Octopus."

"You have to grant a favor," Tarlae shrieked, fighting furiously against the bonds.

"Sure, and here it is," Andy said. "Trey is *dead*. I've rescued the raccoon and am in the process of building a new deck and choosing a better Dealer for it. Now get over it and do your *job*."

Tarlae jerked like she'd been slapped, her face a mask of pain and horror. Ernie grimaced as the Coconut Octopus wailed with pure grief, but all she could do was try to stay conscious as the blue coils around her tightened. The Forger had turned his attention to her. Legs surged on her arm as if she wanted to break free, but the sizzling bonds seemed to have immobilized her as well.

"I gave you one job, Ernestine," the Forger said, his deep voice thundering across the desert. "I thought that I could trust you to stay focused, given the stakes for Gabe." His obsidian gaze streaked over the mesa. "Where is he, by the way? I'm thinking it's time we had a chat."

Ernie squirmed in the agonizing grasp of the lightning coiled around her, unable to find her words. *What's happening?* asked Gabe's voice in her head. *Are you all right?*

He was using the hybrid card to keep tabs on her—and he could feel that something had gone wrong.

Stay away, Ernie thought, pleading. If Gabe showed up, the Forger would probably destroy him. *Stay far away.*

Do you trust me? was his only response.

"Your mission as Dealers is to sow chaos in this universe, or at least in this dimension," roared the Forger, wiggling his fingers and causing the ropes of blue lightning to grow barbs that dug into their skin. "And suddenly, you're all hanging out together, having dinner parties and coupling off and acting like ordinary humans! What the hell has gotten into all of you? Do I need to take all your decks and hand them over to people who would actually use them the right way? Should I turn you all to dust right n—"

The blue lightning disappeared abruptly, and the Forger staggered back, his arms reeling. Gabe stood a few yards away from him, his cards fanned in one hand, a few of them held between his fingertips, glowing brightly. Terror for him brought Ernie scrambling up.

The penalty for Gabe's interference would be death. She ran toward Gabe, feeling all his thoughts and intentions. He was ready to sacrifice his deck and his life to protect all of them. He didn't care what happened to him. He didn't care, if it meant others could live.

Andy regained his balance and faced off with Gabe, his eyes black, his body glowing, his smile lethal.

Goddammit, Gabe, she thought as she played Lock, Prolong, and Accelerate, hitting the Forger with enough power to temporarily slow his arms as they rose from his sides, crackling with power. She glanced around to see the other Dealers playing cards of their own—except for Nuria, who was shuddering on the ground while Kot stood in front of her, ready to defend his lover.

"Enough!" shouted Gabe, pulling Draw and Amplify and Strength. He reached forward with those cards and then yanked them back toward his own body.

Ernie gaped as a line of blue lightning shimmered from the Forger's chest and hit Gabe, who gasped. His head snapped back, and his hands went rigid. His eyes opened wide, sending up beams of light to the sky. The Forger shouted and struggled, grabbing the blue stream of power with both hands and trying to pull it back. It snapped loose from Gabe's body, but the Kestrel's eyes were still alight with the power.

"You've bullied us all for too long, just to entertain yourself," Gabe said, his voice carrying clear and powerful across the mesa. "No longer. This is the last day of your reign."

Ernie's entire being buzzed with the power coursing through Gabe. His mind was blinding and bright and singular in its purpose—he'd had enough of the callousness, of the pettiness, of the cruelty. And she found herself agreeing. Why had they protected a tyrant? Maybe Duncan and Virginia had been right, in this way at least—maybe it was time for a revolution.

The Forger laughed. "You come for the king, you best not miss—"

He snarled as Minh hit him with a sharp blast of wind that blew Andy right over the edge of the mesa. "Gabe, gotta say," Minh said as he moved to stand next to them. "Never thought you'd make this move, but it makes sense."

Gabe looked around with glowing eyes. "We haven't won yet."

"I'll help you," said Kot.

"Only if we can make him suffer," growled Tarlae, joining them as the ground began to shake.

"Kot, Minh," said Gabe, widening his stance. "Try to immobilize him. Tarlae, strike him however you want. Just make sure your aim is true."

"And me?" Ernie asked quietly.

Forgive me. His words in her mind were tender and devastating.

She looked around to see the Dealers readying their cards, even as a crack tore the mesa in two, threatening to throw them off their feet. Her mind was a storm, consumed with the intensity of Gabe's determination but also the doubts growing rapidly in her own thoughts—if Gabe became the Forger, what did that mean for him? And for them?

She pushed the fears away as the Forger floated up above the mesa, looking like the lord of chaos that he was. He didn't look human anymore. Veins of black ran under his now-translucent skin, and his heart pulsed with shimmering power. He landed on the edge of the rock, his arms wide, his palms turned to the sky, drawing crackling streams of electrons from the heavens. "I make the cards," he said in a monstrous voice. "If you think this is all it takes to defeat me, you're more foolish than I even imagined."

Gabe threw a strike, but the Forger turned it back on him so fiercely that it sent Gabe crashing to the ground and skidding all the way along the rock, leaving a trail of blood in his wake. His connection with Ernie went silent with a deafening crack between her ears.

Andy walked forward, seemingly immune to the strikes from the other Dealers. "I should have done this years ago," he said, reaching toward Gabe's unconscious body. Ernie cried out as Gabe's cards flew upward in a stream. She sprinted forward, only one thought in her head. The cards leapt to her fingertips—Sacrifice, Aid, and Friend-Lover. Gabe's cards halted in midair even as Ernie's were torn from her pocket and began to flutter through the air.

Andy began to laugh. "Have it your w—" he began before being crushed to the ground by a grasshopper the size of an elephant. Ernie's cards floated to the ground, and she scrambled to scoop them up before running to Gabe. Behind them, the massive insect roared as it snapped at its prey, but then a shadow passed over the rising sun. Ernie played her Shield card just fast enough to protect her and Gabe from the creature's body as the Forger hurled it away. The grasshopper hit the crumbling mesa with an earth-shaking crash and skidded toward the edge of the rock.

Andy rose to his feet again, snapping his arms back into proper position. "Here's your favor, then, Nuria," he shouted, clawing his fingers through open air. With a terrible ripping sound, the grasshopper's body was torn in two. The sound that came out of Kot resonated inside Ernie's chest. Next to her, Gabe stirred and opened his eyes. Ernie helped him to his feet. All around them, Tarlae, Minh, and Kot were hitting the Forger with all they had, but Ernie's world was completely silent. The look she shared with Gabe was the beginning and the end, and she knew what had to happen next. He handed her the hybrid card as his next plays leapt to his fingertips. "It has to end here," he said simply.

Ernie couldn't think about what she was about to lose, because either way, it was everything. Her own cards glowed as she prepared to help her love fight his final battle. The Forger's attention was on the others, his teeth bared, his power drawing down thunder and lightning from the sky.

"We have to combine our power," she shouted, offering Gabe her hand. "It has to be one strike." The hybrid card between them, Ernie felt the connection between her deck and the Kestrel's surging up her arms and selected the cards that matched his. Dealing as one, the two of them raised their arms and hurled the strike. Rend, Amplify, Strength.

The Forger jerked as it hit, his hand going to his heart, his eyes going wide, his mouth falling open. Black blood trickled from his lips.

For a moment, Ernie thought they'd done it. But then Andy's hand fell away, revealing a curved blade protruding from his chest. He looked down at it in surprise and began to sink to the dirt, revealing Virginia standing behind him. She wrenched the Cortalaza blade from his body with a look of vicious satisfaction, and Andy pitched forward, flopping to the ground face-first. Black dust streamed from his body, sparkling as the sunlight caught every shimmering particle. The stuff spiraled in the air before arching downward and flying into Virginia's wide-open mouth. Her arms rose from her sides, and her hair floated away from her shoulders. Her feet left the ground.

Andy let out a final shudder as his face crumbled away, decaying into ebony and blue powder that gusted upward before disappearing into Virginia's glowing body. And when there was nothing left, Virginia touched down on the ravaged mesa, looking a little stunned.

Gabe's grip on Ernie's hand was iron as they watched Virginia. The Cortalaza blade fell from her slack fingers, and she looked down at the tattoo of the chicken on her crepey skin. The animal came tumbling off her arm in the next moment, hitting the ground in a jumble of feathers. Virginia watched the struggling rooster with detached interest. Luigi, the leghorn who had been her companion for over a century, let out a feeble squawk.

Virginia plucked her deck from her pocket and tossed it to the ground. "Sorry, Luigi," she said, though she didn't sound sorry at all.

The tremors in the rooster's body finally shook it apart. Ernie watched with a sick feeling in the pit of her stomach as the creature disappeared, along with the cards. Virginia raised her head. "Thanks for the assist," she said to all of them. And then she vanished.

Ernie looked up at Gabe, whose face had gone pale. Minh stood just behind him, also looking stunned. But Kot was kneeling next to the carcass of the giant grasshopper, trying to scoop up an armful of its guts. The strain of his shoulders drew Ernie's focus, and she headed for him, thinking only to help her ally. But when she reached his side, she realized he was holding more than the carnage the Forger had left behind—he cradled Nuria's trembling body, naked and streaked with black but unmistakably alive.

"He separated her from the beast," Kot said in a hushed voice. "Look." He lifted her wrist and revealed a tiny green form taking shape on Nuria's pale arm.

As Ernie watched, the shape grew legs and a large black eye. She tore her gaze from the sight to see that the inside of the monster's carcass was studded with cards, as if they'd been lodged inside it the whole time. But as the new grasshopper took shape on Nuria's arm, the cards pulled themselves loose, fluttered to the ground, and began to slide toward their Dealer. "He granted the favor," Ernie said in awe.

"Not for me."

Ernie turned to see Tarlae standing a few feet away, her dress torn and her hair wild. In her hand, she held the Cortalaza, but the blade had melted and burned, leaving nothing but a hilt and a stump of metal. She tossed it over the edge of the mesa. "He did *nothing* for me," the Coconut Octopus Dealer said in a flat, dead voice. "And you . . ." She pointed a shaking finger at Ernie and then Gabe. "If you hadn't interfered, he could have helped me. Trey would be standing here right now."

"Tarlae," Gabe began, walking toward her.

"This is your fault," she screamed, and hit him with a strike that sent him skidding along the slickrock.

"Tarlae," Minh shouted, drawing his cards.

But the Coconut Octopus Dealer vanished.

"Damn," Minh muttered, shaking his head. He joined Ernie as she rushed over to Gabe's side again. They pressed Healing cards to Gabe's body, reviving him quickly. "I better go look for her," Minh said as they helped Gabe to his feet. "I don't think she should be alone, and I might be the only person she wouldn't try to kill on sight."

"Go, then," said Gabe. "And thank you."

"I don't know what the hell is going to happen now," said Minh, staring at the spot where the Forger had met his defeat.

Ernie shook her head. "None of us do." Virginia was the Forger now. Anything could happen, and she suspected it probably wouldn't be good. She gave Minh a hug and left him and Gabe to say their goodbyes while she returned to Kot's side. He'd helped Nuria to her feet, and she seemed a little steadier.

"How are you?" Ernie asked her.

Nuria's dark eyes were clear as she looked at Ernie, but her brow furrowed as she tried to speak. "Wuh-wuh-wuh," she began, and then growled in frustration.

Kot squeezed her. "She will need time."

"I see your deck is working," Ernie said. "Looks like Pol adjusted quickly."

267

Kot nodded, then held out his arm and released a glittering dragonfly, the size of a sparrow, that darted back and forth before settling on his shoulder. "We worked together," Kot said, smiling at the creature that gave him his power.

The dragonfly flitted over to land on Ernie's hand, making her gasp. "Well, hi there," she said.

"You have been a good ally," said Kot. "And we will remain so, I believe."

"Absolutely." She remembered the myths her mother had told her about dragonflies guarding and helping serpents. "I wonder if our decks have been allied for longer than either of us realize." She glanced down at her arm, where the dragonfly's feet danced only inches from Legs's rattle while the diamondback throbbed with a gentle warmth. She wondered whether the connection to the Dragonfly deck was one of the reasons Legs had chosen her in that fateful moment with Duncan, the moment that Ernie had grabbed his cards and set herself on this epic journey.

It wasn't over yet, and she had no idea what the future held. But as she looked at Gabe and Minh and Kot and Nuria, she knew she wasn't going to be alone as she faced it.

EPILOGUE

It had been eerily quiet for far too long, and Ernie had been on edge for days. The parking lot beer garden at Wedge had seemed like the perfect place to try to unwind, but the tension was inside her, keeping her on guard even while dozens of humans relaxed, oblivious, around her.

Ernie sipped her beer and listened to the lively bluegrass music with only half an ear. Next to her, Gabe seemed similarly lost in the haze of his own thoughts.

Both of them tensed when Virginia took a seat across from them. She was still dressed in that gauzy white gown she always wore, and her white hair was still a fluffy cloud around her head. But her eyes had changed. Now they were solid black circles, and the sight sent a chill down Ernie's spine, because the new Forger's gaze was focused on the man next to her.

"I've been expecting you," Gabe said calmly.

"Oh, stop spoiling my fun," Virginia replied.

He took out his deck. "I won't give it up without a fight, so I suggest we take this somewhere less populated."

Ernie's hand shot into her own pocket, alarm bells clanging in her head. But Virginia just chuckled. "Stop being a drama queen, Kestrel." Her spindly fingers slipped into her gown and came out with a glowing card, one with a kestrel on its back, carrying the world. "Here." She slid it across the table to him.

Gabe looked down at it. "My Wild," he said quietly. But he didn't take it. He seemed afraid to touch it.

Virginia clucked her tongue. "No strings attached. Now we're even."

His eyes met hers. "I didn't attack Andy to help you."

She smiled. "But help me you did, and I'd like to kick all of this off with a level playing field. It'll be more fun this way."

Her tone revived Ernie's dread. "What are you up to?"

Virginia's ebony eyes settled on her. "A wise man once said something about the arc of the moral universe."

Ernie's brow furrowed. "Martin Luther King Jr. He said it was long, but it bends toward justice."

The Forger grinned and stood up. "Let's see if he was right," she whispered. Then she vanished.

Gabe's hand closed over Ernie's as they both stared straight ahead.

"I don't know how to be ready for what she's going to do," Ernie admitted.

"If she comes at us, we'll figure out how to protect each other. We're not helpless. What happened to Andy proved that."

"She'll be ready for an attack."

"She's got a bigger game going than that, love."

Ernie knew he was right. She laced their fingers together and squeezed his hand. "Did you want to be the Forger?"

He laughed. "I wanted to keep Andy from destroying the people who matter most to me, and I was willing to do anything to stop it."

I love you. The thought was so powerful it made her eyes burn. So powerful she couldn't even say the words. All she knew was that she would do anything in her power to protect him.

But as they sat under the stars and listened to the music, as they held hands like ordinary humans, their grip on each other so easy to break, Ernie had a sinking feeling it might take more than her determination to meet the threat looming on the horizon.

She knew only one thing for certain, and that truth didn't come from her deck or her allies. It came from the very center of her: no matter what came, she would never give up and never surrender.

ACKNOWLEDGMENTS

Many thank-yous to the team at 47North, and in particular to Jason Kirk, Adrienne Procaccini, and Courtney Miller, for shepherding this book and this series. A special thank-you goes to Tegan Tigani, my developmental editor, for great phone calls, astute feedback, and one masterful Google Doc to keep us all on the same page—or, in this case, on the same card. Thank you also to Blake Morrow for shooting and designing the cover, Janice Lee for helping me keep all my time zones and idioms straight, Sara Addicott for making sure this manuscript stayed on the rails during its journey to bookdom, and Phyllis DeBlanche for zapping all the typos and giving poor Ernie a break from all that sprinting she was doing. Another thank-you goes to Kathleen Ortiz for advocating and organizing, and to my assistant, Jena Gregoire, for her amazing coordination, enthusiasm, and graciousness.

Thank you to my friends, especially Lydia Kang, Claire Legrand, Claudine Silverman, and Paul Block, for enriching my life and keeping me sane. Thank you to my family for tolerating and supporting me. And Peter, thank you for occasionally doing the thinking for both of us, especially when I'm on deadline.

A final note of gratitude to my fans: this is my twentieth novel, and I never would have made it here if not for you.

ABOUT THE AUTHOR

Photo © 2012 Rebecca Skinner

Sarah Fine is the author of more than twenty books and novellas for adults and teens. Her adult books include the Servants of Fate Series, The Reliquary Series, and *The Serpent* and *The Guardian* in The Immortal Dealers Series. She confesses to having both the music tastes of an adolescent boy and an adventurous spirit when it comes to food (especially if it's fried). Sarah has lived on the West Coast and in the Midwest, but she currently calls the East Coast home. To learn more about the author and her work, visit www.sarahfinebooks.com.